*Originally published as* Bleed: Ausgeblutet
*Translated by Stefanie Maucher*
*Voodoo Press, February 2016*



*Trepidatio books may be ordered through booksellers or by contacting:*

*Trepidatio Publishing, an imprint of JournalStone*

*www.trepidatio.com*



*ISBN: 978-1-945373-59-6 (sc)*
*ISBN: 978-1-945373-58-9 (ebook)*

*JournalStone rev. date: March 24, 2017*

*Library of Congress Control Number: 2017934032*

*Printed in the United States of America*
*2nd Edition*

*Cover Design: 99designs – Semnitz*
*Image: AdobeStock_122038160*
*Edited by: Jess Landry*

*For Paul and Donna*

## ACKNOWLEDGMENTS

I am indebted to Christopher Payne and Jess Landry of JournalStone for bringing this gruesome darling of mine back to life and making it a much better book. Much gratitude is also owed to filmmaker Paul von Stoetzel, who first expressed interest in *Bleed* when we met in Amberg, Germany, in the winter of 2013, and who never stopped hounding me about it until we became neighbors in Minneapolis, where he began work on the webseries adaptation. Without Paul's encouragement and enthusiasm, I doubt this book would ever have risen from the grave. Thanks, pal.

# B L E E D

# 1923

*Papa comes back at night. Three days he's been gone and she is beginning to see a glimmer of hope that he'd never come home. Everything would be just fine if he didn't. Agnes is old enough and in just a few more years she will be, too. Without Papa around the time will fly like a hawk. But he comes back in the moonlight—the darktime when Papa gets dark thoughts to do dark things.*

*She hears him come inside, the creaking hinges on the door and the groaning floorboards as he pounds loudly through the house. He grumbles and moans and sings a little ditty he makes up as he goes along.*

*Ah'ma teach 'at girl ev'rything Ah know, as soon as Ah finish this drink...Ah'ma open 'nother bottle and take a drink, as soon as Ah teach that girl...*

*The words come out wet and syrupy as though the liquor has filled him up too much and now it's bubbling out of him. He sounds maybe a little happy, but that's the worst time. He never does anything as bad as when he's feeling good. Anger only makes him sulk and drink and go to sleep. Feeling good makes him visit in the darktime, all reassuring whispers and scratchy, sandpapery hands.*

*Still singing and crashing around the house in the dark, he must be feeling good.*

*She shudders and pulls the quilt up to her chin. Her eyes bulge despite the blackness in the room. Beside her, Agnes does not stir. She's dead to the world, long inured to Papa's darktime fumblings and doubtlessly relieved that she is no longer the only one. In the hall he stumbles over some timber and tools, the supplies he's collected or stolen to build his attic. Wood scrapes against wood and an iron instrument clangs sonorously. Papa shouts and curses.*

*She holds her breath, listening. Maybe he'll grow too angry for what he came to do. Maybe he'll turn mad and drink some more, kick a hole in the wall and black out on the floor. Please God, please. Make Papa madder than he's ever been before. Make Papa forget all about darktime and Agnes and me.*

*She squeezes her eyes shut until they are replaced by small pink mounds of wrinkled skin, begging the Lord to intercede, but she expects nothing in response. God does not listen to her, never has. A thousand times she beseeched the almighty to strike the foul old lush dead, take him out of this world and out of their lives. Surely no loving and personal God would suffer a sinner like him to live. In her heart, she was sure she heard Him laugh at her request.*

*Suffer like Job, He jibed her. Suffer and be saved.*

*She does not want to suffer. Not anymore.*

*Ah'ma teach 'at girl…ev'rything…Ah'ma teach…*

*Oh no. Papa is not angry at all. He is happy as a pig in shit. Though Papa is both the pig and the shit.*

*Tears squeeze out of the corners of her eyes and she sinks further down under the quilt. She moans Agnes' name. The older girl fails to respond. Is she still asleep in spite of all this racket? Or is she deliberately ignoring the miserable, terrified child beside her? Agnes! Agnes! A hundred thousand darktime nightmares have turned out this way, with Papa on the prowl and Agnes frozen or dead and unable to help her. This is no nightmare, though. This is the real thing and it is darktime now and Papa's black sinister shadow is looming in the doorway, leering at her with tiny too-far-apart eyes that glint in the gray moonlight coming in through the window. She shuts her eyes and remembers Agnes telling her to play dead if she ever comes across a bear in the woods. Just play dead, just play dead, just like Papa was a grizzly come to gobble me up. She doesn't open them even when she hears the heavy steps stagger into the bedroom, compounded by the chilling jangle of Papa's belt buckle unfastening and clanging against his leg.*

*Gunna teach 'at girl…gunna teach her good…*

*Her spine sends a trembling shiver up to her shoulders. But her eyes remain closed. No sense in opening them up anyhow; it's dark as a pocket in here. She waits for him, for the bed to sink down on one side with a sickening squeal, for the coarse sandpaper hands to start their business.*

*She hears the springs squeal, but she feels nothing at all.*

*Agnes stirs. Moans softly. Papa lets out a gurgly wet chuckle, sounds like he's drowning in his own spit. Agnes! Oh, Agnes, poor Agnes!*

*Pulling into a tighter ball, her knees touching her chin, she trembles and cries but is careful to not make a sound. Papa might hear. He might change his mind. Got to let him take it out on Agnes, leave me be for one night just one night of peace please God just one night. Her brain reels. Guilt fills her up, sours her stomach and leaves a nasty taste on her tongue. It is not right to wish that kind of thing on her sister, not Agnes who takes care of her just fine when Papa's away, who'd be the best Mama she ever knew if only Papa would disappear and never come back again.*

*Huffing, snuffling. Papa grunts like a hog. Agnes sniffs.*

*She wants to scream. But she is quiet as a mouse when she slips out of bed and pads softly out of the bedroom, through the hall, into the kitchen. Even there she hears the horror in the bedroom.*

*Huff, huff, huff. Grunt, grunt, grunt.*

*The pig and the shit.*

*She climbs onto a chair, steps higher yet onto the table. She can reach the ironware from up here. Old and rusty, mostly. Mama's old Dutch oven, the one that belonged to great grandmammy, and the griddle and the pots and the big black skillet. That is the one she wants. She needs both hands to get it down from the sixteen penny nail in the wall and it's heavier than sin but she gets it and carries it carefully, quietly back down to the floor.*

*Clutching the cold iron to her chest, she pads back to the bedroom, frowning at the nauseating, soul-crushing noises she walks toward. But she needs the noise, needs it to find them. Him.*

*She follows it, rounding her own narrow bed until her hip bumps Agnes'. The thin, soiled mattress shakes and quivers. She feels the heel of Papa's boot brush her side. With a grunt of her own she heaves the massive skillet, hoists it over her head. It is only the work of a moment to send it crashing back down—its own weight does most of the labor. She expects it to ring out like a bell but there is only a dull crack as the heavy edge sinks into Papa's skull like it was nothing but pudding. He does not even cry out.*

*She lets the skillet drop out of her hands and it bangs loudly on the floor, cracking the wood. Agnes screams. She presses her body against her sister's and the tears flow. Agnes is splattered with Papa's blood and hard bits of bone.*

*Only family now. Only love. It is done.*

# SUMMER

# THE STAIN ON THE CEILING

## 1

The house was a fixer-upper, at least in Walt's eyes. It was a Gablefront house—a cottage, really, due to its single story—that the realtor claimed was built in 1930. There were ornamental brackets on almost all of the doors and windows, and a small crawlspace attic under the sharply angled roof. Upon seeing the house for the first time, Walt immediately fell in love with the double-hung sash windows and the clapboard siding. It was all so quaint and lovely, perfect for his needs. The realtor, a dowdy schoolmarm sort of woman, had not even tried to skirt the truth of the house's less than ideal condition. The walls needed patching, the moldy wallpaper had to be stripped, and all of the rotted baseboards were going to have to be replaced. Both bathrooms suffered from leaky toilet seals that had all but annihilated the subfloors, which needed to be ripped out and completely resurfaced. There was no carpeting in the house—another selling point for Walt—but the hardwood floors were terribly scratched with deep, dark grooves that would require refinishing.

And that was just the interior—the roof was another can of worms altogether.

Nonetheless, Walt was inspired by the work that lay ahead of him, and he got the house for a song. By the time the school year began in late August, he figured he would be well on his way to having the place right where he wanted it. By Christmas morning, when he finally got around to unburdening himself of the secrecy of the diamond ring in his sock drawer, Walt thought the house would be in perfect shape for a young couple with modest family ambitions.

Things were looking up.

Walt moved in on a Tuesday. The apartment in which he lived for the last three years had become crowded with his growing catalogue of belongings, but the square footage of the house far exceeded that of his former residence. Now he had space to spare and, as he looked at it, space to fill; quite a lot for a guy living alone. For the time being, he simply unloaded box after box from the truck he rented, stacking them against the walls of the dining room. With the exception of his meager furniture—a bed, a sofa, and a small antique writing desk—the entirety of his worldly possessions fit into that single room. He smiled at the hoard, imagining where everything would end up and what odds and ends he would need to pick up in order to fill the gaps.

In the meantime, he hopped into his aging hatchback and drove to the hardware store in town. In his head, he had a massive list of repairs and the supplies needed to make them, but he was far from overwhelmed by it. Rather, with every tube of caulk or foot of baseboard he set in the cart, he felt more and more like the real-life grown-up he never thought he would actually become. While he pushed the cart up one aisle and down the next, he conceived of every minute detail of his life for the next year or so. For some, he realized, this would be anathema. But for Walt, it was terrific. He knew he was going spend the remainder of the summer working on the house, begin his new career as a ninth grade English teacher in the fall, and with a little luck, complete his short story collection before the end of the calendar year. Then, on Christmas Eve, he would present the ring to Amanda (to which she would almost certainly say yes), and the spring would be taken up with plans for their eventual wedding. Walt could have danced to the register to pay for his overfilled cartful of supplies as he pushed them out to his hatchback in the parking lot, and then drove home, unaware of his own joyful humming along the way.

By dusk, he had already ripped out every inch of baseboard with his new crowbar. He replaced most of it before midnight, but he underestimated the amount needed. Another trip to the hardware store in the morning.

He located the box marked KITCHEN among the stacks in the dining room, unpacked his coffee maker for the morning, and then, finally wearing down, dragged himself to the bathroom to brush his teeth. Shuffling into the bedroom, he sighed at the unconstructed mess that was to be his bed. He meant to assemble the bed frame earlier, but he had not gotten around to it. He certainly wasn't about to fool around with it now—he was just going to have to sleep on an unraised mattress. No big deal.

He switched on the small rice paper lamp he had plugged in beside the bed. He figured on reading a little M. R. James until his eyelids grew heavy and then call it a day, though he imagined he'd never make it through a single paragraph. So he crawled beneath the sheets and fluffed the pillows and took in the musty smell of his new, old house. It was then that he first noticed it: in the hall, just beyond the bedroom door, there was a tiny brown stain on the ceiling.

The stain was barely visible in the dim light of the lamp,

and he couldn't make it out all that well. After a moment's hesitation—Christ, he was just so tired—Walt threw his legs over onto the floor and heaved himself up. He stumbled groggily to the bedroom door, leaned against the jamb, and squinted up at the mark on the ceiling. No bigger than his own fist, it was splotchy and the color of rust. Water damage, he concluded, due to the leaky roof. Another mental note for the pile, he thought, and headed directly back to the mattress on the floor.

By then he was definitely too tired to focus on reading. Walt switched the lamp off and was asleep in minutes.

## 2

The attic was small and stuffy, the hot, suffocating air ripe with the odor of mildew and mold. The pink insulation on the attic floor had gone almost white with age and it was spongy from the moisture let in by the holes. That was also going to have to go. Looking back up at the roof, he could detect no sign of flashing having been installed. No one had ever taken steps to waterproof the roof at all, from the looks of it. He pursed his lips and sighed. This one was beyond his ken as a home-improver. Walt was going to have to call in a contractor.

The roof had more holes than Walt bargained for. Most were tiny; scattered dots of morning light sneaking in from above. Hail damage was a distinct possibility, but he bet on nothing more than age and neglect as the culprit for the constellations of miniscule chinks in his castle's ramparts. A few of the holes, however, were startling sizeable, big enough for a child to crawl through. If there was a problem with nine-year-old cat burglars in the neighborhood, he was in trouble. Barring that, he was going to have to address the issue before the next rainfall.

In the meantime, he aimed his flashlight at the attic floor. He challenged his memory to recall the house's floor plan so that he could determine what was underneath each patch of moldy insulation and every supporting beam. He was standing directly over the guest bathroom by his reckoning, which put the hallway outside the master bedroom on the other side of the attic. Tentatively, he bent and stepped on the sideways beams until he traversed the unventilated space. On that side, most of the cottony insulation was missing, taken up and away by some previous owner and never replaced. He decided there was a good ten by ten area of naked rafters and warped board flooring in that part of the attic. There were a couple of pinkish rolls of insulation jammed into a nearby corner, but these too were damaged beyond usefulness by the moisture. Still another item for the shopping list that would not die.

Walt smiled and shrugged, perfectly happy in the role of the hardworking homeowner. The smile diminished, however, upon looking closer at the bare floor before him. This was indeed the part of the attic just above his bedroom and its adjacent hallway, but there was no water damage of any kind. He glanced up, and to his puzzlement discovered that the roof there was intact. Probably an old surface stain, he decided. An expense he didn't need.

Back in the kitchen, Walt plugged his phone into the jack on the wall and began flipping through the Yellow Pages in search of a roofer. He chose the first one with a kitschy ad (it featured a cartoon roofer with the crack of his ass peeking out of his pants) and arranged for an estimate the next day.

Feeling satisfied with his efforts, he poured a glass of ice water and ambled out to the front porch. He sat on the steps and enjoyed the clean, warm summer air.

The realtor had mentioned the nearest house to his new property was several acres away, far enough that he could not see it through all the intervening trees. Someday, the realtor had confided to him, people from all over the state would be moving here in droves, sucking up every square inch of this land for their respective retirement villas. A good deal of money was going to be made. He narrowed his eyes and peered into the dense woods beyond the edge of his property, trying to imagine old people in bright colored clothes laying down Astroturf on their backyards and yelling at the mailman. Someday, he mused, that would be him and Amanda. The thought elicited a chuckle.

When he got up from the steps to dump the remaining ice cubes in the grass, Walt heard a soft panoply of desperate mewling. He padded across his dry, overgrown lawn and gazed into the woods. There, on a sunlit patch of dead leaves and twigs, he saw a black cat on her side with five anxious kittens struggling at her teats. He brought his brows together and smiled awkwardly, wondering if these animals belonged to anyone or not. Had he been in the city he might have given a call to animal control, but in the sticks he couldn't imagine anyone much caring about a cat and her kittens. Clicking his tongue against the roof of his mouth, he walked back to the porch and went inside.

In the afternoon, he situated a step ladder directly beneath the ceiling stain and climbed up with a bleach-soaked scrub brush in his hand. He scrubbed at the spot until his arm started to feel sore, then he switched hands and scrubbed some more until that arm got sore, too. The bristles on the brush had turned dark brown, but the stain itself remained unchanged. He frowned at it and stepped back down to the floor. More serious measures would be necessary, but it was just going to have to wait. Walt needed to get ready for dinner with Amanda.

Walt and Amanda's first date, nearly three years ago, was at a small Cajun restaurant on Markham called Louisiana Joe's.

The place had since changed hands, and now a slightly fancier dining spot took its place. The new joint was called Maggie's, and that was where he met her just after sunset.

He had asked her to go ahead and get a table, but she was seated on the long divan in the waiting area when he arrived. Her curly brown hair was done up with only a few wild spirals cascading down the back of her neck and framing her freckled elfin face. She wore a dark blue dress Walt had never seen before; it looked elegant and it flowed down her small frame like a waterfall. He felt underdressed when he saw her, strangely self-conscious for a man nearly ready to propose. But Amanda did that to him—she made him feel like he didn't *deserve* her, like he'd won the lottery every day for almost three years straight. She smiled sweetly when he came into the restaurant. He returned the smile and accepted a peck on his cheek.

"It's changed a bit, hasn't it?" she said.

"A bit," Walt agreed.

"What do you suppose it'll be like in another three years?"

"Too rich for me, I'm sure."

"Don't be cheap, dear."

"You haven't seen the house yet. It's going to cost me a bundle before I'm done. Hope you like ramen."

"Love it."

"Then I do believe everything's going to be all right."

Amanda giggled, effectively ruining the playacting, but Walt didn't mind. On a list of things that made life worth living, her unique and infectious giggle was easily in the top five.

A college-aged kid in a starched white shirt collected a pair of menus and led them to a small, round table in the middle of the restaurant. They ordered mid-priced wine, white asparagus in sabayon sauce, and they each had filets de poisson. They ate and talked and laughed a little too loud, judging by the looks some of their fellow diners shot at them. When they finished eating, Walt paid the check and they walked hand in hand out to the parking lot where Amanda lit up a cigarette.

Walt frowned.

"Just give me until New Year's," she said between drags. "It's a psychological thing, I think. Quitting on New Year's, I mean."

"You said that last year, as I recall."

"And I may say it again next year, but you can't say I'm not trying."

Screwing up his mouth, he sighed through his nostrils. He hated that she smoked, but she always had and he felt more than a little uncomfortable trying to change her. All he really cared about was her health, but he also wanted to never smell that acerbic cigarette smell in his bed again. He loathed to ruin the mood of an otherwise terrific evening, so he let it go. Reading his mind, Amanda smiled and gave his hand a squeeze.

"Let's have a look at that house," she said.

"Oh, not yet," Walt protested. "It's a shambles, really. I want to get the place fixed up before you see it."

"You were a shambles the first time I saw you and that turned out all right."

"Funny."

"Come on. It's hot, and I just can't see sweating through the night for no good reason."

"You'd rather be sweating for a good reason," he smirked.

"You got that right, pal."

A pleasant shiver rocked his spine. He hadn't expected the evening to end like this, but now that events were turning that way, he had no intention of objecting. She planted a lingering kiss on his lips and said, "I'll follow you in my car."

Amanda wandered the house while Walt made coffee. He listened to her heels click-clacking on the hardwood floors. He liked the sound. He hoped to hear a great deal more of it.

"You installed these baseboards yourself?" she called out

from the dining room.

"Sure," Walt called back as the coffee maker started to drip. "I'm a regular Bob Vila."

Amanda laughed. "That so?"

"I am a man of many talents. I've even made coffee all by myself."

She click-clacked her way into the kitchen.

"I'm speechless," she said. "How did I ever get so lucky?"

"You must have been a saint in a previous life."

"I must have been twenty saints," she said, leaning in for a deep kiss. She gave a soft moan and said, "Make that a hundred."

"I hope it's paying off."

"In spades," she said.

Releasing himself with regret from her grip, he collected two mugs from the cupboard. As he did so, she reached into an open box on the counter and pulled out two dusty wine glasses stuffed with tissue paper.

"Got any wine?"

"I just made coffee."

She arched an eyebrow. He grinned boyishly, melting inside.

"Yeah," he said. "I've got a bottle of Brunello. Will that work?"

She pushed the glasses toward him and said, "Fill 'er up."

After he rinsed the glasses and poured the wine, they took their glasses and wandered to the dining room. There they sat among the piles of books, crammed together away from the new baseboards toward the center of the room, while Amanda sipped and Walt watched her adoringly.

"Have you read all of these?" she asked, grabbing *Martin Chuzzlewit* from the nearest stack.

"No, not all. My reading list is miles long. I buy them faster than I can read them."

"This one?"

"Sure. I've read all of Dickens. Until some mysterious, heretofore unknown manuscript appears, anyway."

"Any good?"

"My dear," Walt said, putting on a condescending, professorial tone. "There is no such beast as subpar Dickens."

She set the book down on the floor and turned her narrowed eyes back to the stack.

"Hmm," she said, searching.

She reached for another volume, settling on a dog-eared copy of *Tom Jones*, but tipped her glass, dumping its contents all over *Martin Chuzzlewit*.

"Uh-oh," Walt said as he leaned forward to take her wine.

"Oh, shit," she yelped, looking down at the fruits of her clumsiness.

"You've stained my Chuzzlewit."

"Oh, shit," she said again.

"And that's not even a euphemism."

"I can't believe it. Fuck, I'm such an idiot."

"Not at all," he assured her. He gently took the volume and held it up between forefinger and thumb. Red wine dripped from the leaves like blood from a wound.

"Oh, man," she moaned. "Good news is, your lady just so happens to own a bookstore."

"Don't worry about it…"

"Shut it. I'm ordering a brand spanking new copy first thing tomorrow. I'll even be sure to get some super academic notated edition, better than this poor mess."

"For God's sake, don't do that."

"Why not? I've got a distributor's discount."

"Print's too small."

"You're shitting me."

"Have you ever tried reading one of those things? You'd go cross-eyed!"

"All right, then I'll order a large print edition. And a magnifying glass."

"Such a dear girl," he said in a shaky, ancient voice.

"How about some butterscotch candy, too? Would grandpa like that?"

"I'd like some of your candy, my dear."

He tucked his lips over his teeth and smacked them noisily, a grotesque parody of an elderly letch.

"You dirty old man," she said, and began kissing his neck.

"Grandpa likes," he said.

"*Chuzzlewit* can wait."

"Yes," he agreed. "I suppose it can."

Together they rose and Walt went into the kitchen with Amanda close behind. He set the cups on the counter and let her lead him by the hand toward the bedroom.

They made love quickly and breathlessly. It lasted only ten minutes, but they climaxed simultaneously. Afterward, Walt and Amanda lay side by side on the unraised mattress, breathing hard and fast in harmonic union. When her breath began to slow down to a normal rhythm, she rolled onto her side and said, "Now, how about that coffee?"

He took his black, she added loads of milk and sugar. Cups in hand and dressed only in bathrobes—her dwarfed by one of Walt's—they retired to the front porch. They sipped at their coffee and Amanda chain-smoked, but Walt kept quiet about it. Instead, he waxed philosophic about the impressionable young minds he hoped to mold in the coming months, wondering out loud how many kids per year he might be able to turn onto Dickens or Conrad or even—fingers crossed—Herman Melville. In the long run, he hoped to include some of the macabre writers like Poe and Blackwood, but he had no intention of pressing his luck the first year in. The tight-assed parents in the PTA could get a little touchy about that sort of thing, so he aimed at ingratiating himself to them. Amanda absently commented that it sounded like a good plan.

They turned in a little after one in the morning. Walt slept six hours and might have slept a little longer had the racket in the hallway not woken him. He cracked open his bleary eyes and struggled to focus until he eventually made out the shape of Amanda standing on the stepstool.

"What're you doin'?" he slurred.

"Putting shellac on this stain. Ought to seal it up. Then you can paint over it."

"Oh," he said.

"But don't let it go. If there's a leaky pipe or something, this is only going to be a temporary solution."

"Right."

"I might put a stain sealer on it, too. So it doesn't show through the paint."

"That stuff smells awful."

"How do you think I like it up here? You're ten feet away from it."

"If you were a hundred saints," he said, sitting up, "then I was a thousand."

"There," she said as she descended the three steps back to the floor. "Give it a couple hours and then put on the sealant if you've got some. I'll paint it for you tonight, if you want. Got to go to work now, though."

"All right, but don't wear yourself out."

Amanda pulled her jacket over her shoulders and shot him a glance.

"Why? You got some strenuous activities planned?"

"Yeah—I need you to patch my roof, too."

She stuck out her tongue and blew a raspberry at him. He returned the gesture in kind before she click-clacked across the house and out the front door. Walt lay back on the mattress and grinned while he listened to her car rattle to life and drive away. And, a few minutes later, he was asleep again; dead to the world.

While he slept, ever so slightly, the stain grew.

# 3

He awoke to a rhythmic noise, persistent and loud. He scrunched up his face and glanced at his watch. It was noon. Planting his hands on the mattress, he hoisted himself up and listened closely. Drip, drip, drip. Rubbing the sleep out of his eyes with the balls of his fists, Walt peered into the hall and saw the source.

The stain on the ceiling had spread, and now it dripped down to the floor below, forming a small, reddish-brown puddle.

"Oh, for Christ's sake," he groaned.

Crawling out of bed, he stepped into a pair of gray sweatpants and staggered to the doorway to peer up at the spot on the ceiling. The shellac held, but the relentless stain had simply spread out around it, forming a rusty doughnut on the ceiling. Whatever the source of the leak, the shellac was not going to solve the problem. Walt let out a frustrated grunt and padded out into the hall, careful to avoid the puddle on the floor. His sleep-addled mind ran through a chronological list of duties, starting with making and drinking at least half a pot of coffee. After that, he admitted to himself, he would have to call a plumber.

So much for do it yourself.

The plumber—a bone-thin man of about sixty with hair in his ears—clambered up the ladder to the attic and called down for Walt to hand up his toolbox. Walt followed, curious to see what the old guy would find. After the floor was torn out and the paneling and ceiling joists were exposed, no obvious leaking was found. The plumber sat back on the rafters and scratched his head.

"Now that's odd," he said.

"What's odd about it?"

"No pipes here. None at all. Drywall's fine. Sturdy, intact.

Blocking's fine, too. Nothing on any side leaked at all. But looky here."

The plumber leaned over the hole in the attic floor, pointing his flashlight down at the paneling. In the center of the knotty wood panel, between the joists and the squared-off blocking beams, there was a faint brown spot.

"Ain't that about the strangest thing I ever saw," the old man said.

"What is it?"

"It's your stain, is what it is. 'Cept this is pushing through from the other side, instead of the other way 'round. Like if your house was upside-down."

"Upside-down?"

"Hell, I dunno," the plumber said. "All's I can tell you is maybe somebody's playing tricks on you. Having a bit of fun."

"Fun," Walt mumbled. "Sure."

"If I was you, I'd just clean up my ceiling, paint it over, and watch who I let in my house."

Walt smiled and thanked the old guy for his advice. He purposefully neglected to inform the plumber that the only person he had ever let in the house was Amanda. And that was after he first noticed the stain.

All the same, he slapped a twenty-dollar bill in the plumber's palm—despite the man's protest that he hadn't really done anything—and set to painting the rust-colored circle on the hallway ceiling. It took all of five minutes, and when it was done, Walt gazed up at the newly white area and smiled. He then retreated into his bedroom where he began undressing for a shower. Once he was completely naked, the doorbell jangled.

"Of course," he grumbled, pulling the sweatpants back up and reaching for his ratty old REO Speedwagon T-shirt.

Shuffling across the house, he bisected the shafts of sunlight that knifed in from the windows. At the door, he stared at the impatient-looking man on his front porch for a moment, and inwardly cursed himself for having forgotten all about the roofer.

"You been having a go at it yourself?" the roofer asked upon seeing the attic steps still pulled down to the floor.

"No, I just had a plumber in."

The roofer raised his eyebrows.

"It's a fixer-upper," Walt said.

"I'm gonna have a look. Might take a little while to assess your situation."

Walt nodded and informed the man that he was going to take a shower. The roofer set to roofing, and Walt vanished into the bathroom. He ran a near-scalding hot shower, stood under it until his skin turned red, and toweled off in the steam-filled room. No one had ever installed a ventilation fan in there, which would inevitably lead to mold or worse. Then again, he thought, he could always take a moment to wipe down the mirror and walls after a shower and save himself the time and cost. Slipping into his terrycloth bathrobe, he resolved to worry about it later. Much later. One thing at a time, he reminded himself.

He could hear the roofer moving around in the attic, stepping on creaking rafters and talking to himself. Walt glanced up at the ceiling then, and a gasp caught in his throat.

The stain had bled through both the shellac and the paint. It was bigger than ever, now spread out over an area of ceiling at least a foot in radius. And it was dripping all over Walt's bathrobe.

He dabbed at a thick red droplet on his should with the pad of his finger. Raising it to his nose, he inhaled. It was vaguely metallic; rusty, just as he suspected.

Walt said, "What the hell?"

The roofer stamped down the ladder steps from the attic, his tool belt clattering against his hips.

"Good news is I can do the job," he said before stepping off the ladder. "But it won't be cheap."

"Do it," Walt said as he wiped his finger on the front of his robe. "I can't stand the leaks anymore."

Amanda gazed up at the stain with equal measures of wonder and disgust. Walt had long since wiped both ceiling and floor with a dirty rag, but the stain went on dripping. Now there was a plastic bucket on the floor, directly beneath the stain, catching every drop.

"And there's no leaks?"

"Not up there, there isn't."

"Then what's between the drywall and the paneling?"

"Nothing. They're pressed right up against each other."

"Have you looked? I mean, have you actually pried them apart?"

"That would tear up the ceiling. And then I'd have to pay yet another contractor to fix something else."

"Yeah, but if it's between that and the stain that never dies..."

He let out a discontented breath and sagged his shoulders.

"This is why I rent," she said.

"Hand me that flashlight," Walt said as he started to climb the ladder. "It's in the tool bag."

"Are you going up there right now?"

"No time like the present."

"But it's pitch black up here!"

"It's driving me crazy. Seriously. Flashlight?"

Amanda crooked her mouth to one side and passed the flashlight up to him. A second later, he disappeared into the attic.

As soon as he was out of view, she began to feel the slow crawl of anxiety building inside her. On the one hand, she hoped Walt determined its cause right away, so that it would be over and done with and they could both move on to more imperative issues, like their future and what she hoped it might entail. But on the other hand, she could almost feel a desperate cry building up in her chest, bellowing out to insist he come back down right this instant. Instead, she just stood there, gazing up at the dark square in the ceiling into which he'd vanished, frozen with indecision. Why all the anxiety all of a sudden? Then, after a minute or two, there was creaking and scraping, following by a grunt and a loud crack.

"Walt? Are you okay?"

"Fine," he called down. "Just ruining my new house is all."

She furrowed her brow, unaware of the way she was anxiously bouncing on her heels. Another loud crack sounded from above, startling her. She jumped back, staring at the ceiling as a narrow fissure formed from one end of the dripping stain to the other. Flecks of paint and fiberglass drifted down between thick, red drops.

Then Walt screamed.

Amanda sucked in a lungful of air and scampered up the steps. Launching herself up onto the rafters, she peered through the darkness at the lone glow of Walt's flashlight across the attic from where she crouched.

"Walt? Walt!"

"I'm fine," he groaned. "I was just…Jesus, I feel dumb."

"What is it?"

"Don't come over here!" he yelled. "It's too dark, you might lose your footing and fall right through the ceiling."

"What made you cry out like that?"

"Some kind of animal. A rat, probably. I don't know how it got in between here, but man is it a mess."

Disregarding his concern for her safety, she reached a foot out in the darkness and felt her way from one rafter to the next. He grunted disapprovingly at her when she reached him, but shone the light on the spot in question all the same.

"Look."

On the flaky drywall was a sticky red mass of bloody flesh. Amanda gagged first at the sight of it, and then at its fetid odor. Strands of black hair were matted into the fleshy pulp, but not as though it had grown from the mass, and not quite just stuck to it, either. It resembled no living creature she'd ever seen.

"Whatever it is…was…it got crushed between the ceiling and the paneling up here. For the life of me I can't see how, but you can see it as well as me…"

"Jesus."

"I reckon it was a lot bigger than this, on account of all the blood that seeped through. Probably ants or cockroaches…"

"Stop," she said. "Just stop."

Fighting the vomit at the back of her throat, she scrabbled back over the rafters, found the opening in the floor, and hurried down the ladder. Walt just shook his head and whipped his T-shirt off, using it to scrape the bloody mess up with one side and give it a cursory wipe down with the other. He felt enormously relieved—not only had he finally pinpointed the origin of his stain trouble, he also managed to avoid doing too much damage to the ceiling. There was some, to be sure, but nothing he couldn't fix himself in the span of an afternoon. That much, he decided, could wait.

With his wadded up shirt in tow, heavy and squelchy with the pulp he'd scraped up into it, he descended the steps, pushed the folding ladder back up into the attic, and grinned triumphantly at Amanda.

"Aren't you proud of yourself," she said.

"I most definitely am," he beamed.

He strode off toward the back door to dump the wasted shirt in the outside garbage.

Halfway out the door, he turned back and shouted into the house, "This is why I own!"

Amanda went home that night. There was no argument, no fussing. She merely yawned and stretched like a cat before declaring how tired she was. Then she left. There had been no understanding between them that she would have stayed, implicit or otherwise, but Walt felt vaguely dejected about it all the same. It was not a particularly big house, but it was too big for just him. (Soon, he thought.) After the awkward experience in the attic, a terrible loneliness began weighing down on him. His logical side understood that everything was going to be okay, but this was not sufficiently communicated to his irrational, emotional side. And the more he thought about it, the more he obsessed over it, the emptier he felt inside.

He cleaned up the wet, gory mess on the ceiling one more time, tossed the rag into the bucket and left the bucket outside the back door. The roofer was supposed to return in the morning, so while he did his thing, Walt figured on finishing up the baseboards before turning his attention to the walls. While planning, he wandered into the kitchen to pour a glass of water from the tap. Halfway into the kitchen he observed a fat black cockroach skitter across the tiles and halt a few inches from his left foot. Walt sneered at the shiny insect. He then lifted his leg and crushed the cockroach under the ball of his foot, spattering the tiles with the insect's yellow guts.

He wiped the goo against the right leg of his sweatpants, and then shed the pants and his bathrobe on the hallway floor, and he went to bed.

Exhausted, his mind queerly frazzled, he forgot entirely about the water.

## 4

He awoke in a cold sweat. If he'd had a nightmare, he couldn't remember it. It was still pitch black in the house.

"Shit."

He glanced at his watch, which was supposed to glow in the dark, but it was far too dim for him to determine the positions of the hands. Walt resolved to get up and go into the kitchen to have a look at the digital clock on the stove when the knocker fell against the front door in a rapid, almost desperate pattern. He jumped, then grimaced. He couldn't have gotten more than a couple hours' sleep and now someone was pounding on his door in the middle of the night. Ignoring it for the moment, he continued into the kitchen; he still wanted to know the time so that he could throw it in the face of whoever was out there slamming the knocker as if their life depended on it.

Squinting through the hazy blur of his sleep deprived vision, he eventually saw that the clock read 7:25, which made no sense. At half past seven in the morning, in the middle of summer, it was never still dark. The clock had to be wrong. Either that, or it was almost seven-thirty at night. Which would mean…

The incessant pounding kept on.

"All right, all right!" Walt roared.

He stamped across the house, twisted the deadbolt and threw the door open to find his girlfriend standing on the porch.

"Amanda?"

"Were you asleep?"

"Of course I was asleep. It's barely past seven and I never get up until eight when I'm off. You know that."

"Walt, it's seven-thirty *PM.* Have you been asleep since last night?"

"I," he began, blinking. "Have I…?"

Scrunching up his face he pondered hard on that deceptively simple question. Had he been asleep for the better part of eighteen hours? It was possible, but he couldn't see why he would have. Still, he could not remember anything past going to bed after the adventure with that damned stain. And the cockroach; he remembered that, too. Now Walt hoped that he slept through an entire day. Otherwise, he'd lost time he should have remembered.

Amanda gently placed her hand on his chest and smiled weakly.

"Can I come in?"

"Sure," he said, almost too quietly to hear.

His throat hurt, scratchy and dry. He turned back for the kitchen, intent on getting a glass of water before anything else. Amanda followed him in and shut the door behind her.

"You don't sound one hundred percent," she said. "You don't look it, either."

He filled a glass from the tap and swallowed all of it without taking a breath. Exhaling loudly, he said, "I feel about twenty percent right now."

"Should I put some coffee on?"

Saying nothing, he concentrated only on refilling his glass. She nodded and got to work on the coffee maker, dumping grounds into a filter and waiting for him to wrap up with the faucet so she could fill the carafe. Once the machine got to gurgling and dripping into the pot, she leaned up against the counter and looked lovingly, and with noticeable concern, at Walt. He had streams of drool-infused water running down his chin and chest. His face was prickly with stubble and his hair was a tussled, greasy mess. She had never seen him in such a state, although probably only because they had not yet chosen to live together—an old-fashioned decision mostly belonging to Walt which she respected but found outdated. Once they did, she mused, she supposed they would see a lot of one another's down and dirty humanity. Still, he looked like hell—she couldn't deny that much—so she reached out to lay her hand on his forehead to see if he had a temperature. He jumped and moved back, spilling more water all over himself and the floor.

"I didn't mean to startle you," she said with a sheepish smile.

"It…it's okay," he stammered. "Maybe I'm a little under the weather. I'm going to lie down on the sofa."

"Sounds like a good idea."

Wiping off his face with the sleeve of his bathrobe, he stumbled out to the living room and collapsed onto the sofa. Within seconds, he was lightly snoring.

Amanda stayed and watched him sleep for a short while before rising to pace the house, her anxiety resurfacing at the quiet and the shadows.

An hour into Walt's second consecutive slumber, Amanda polished off the coffee she made and went into the dining room where his belongings remained packed up. One stray box on the floor was labeled BOOKS, and she decided to open that one up. Feeling a little bit like a kid at Christmas, she commenced taking the books out of the box one at a time, examining each of them closely and looking for one that might be good to read until Walt woke up again. She found Hawthorne and Cooper, Waugh and Dickens and the ubiquitous volumes of Melville. There were also dusty volumes of Wells and Verne in there, and a dozen paperback novels by Philip K. Dick. She found books on religion, books on atheism, and an art book filled with macabre erotica she would never have expected to find among her otherwise staid boyfriend's belongings. She wrinkled her nose at that one as she set it on the floor. Finally, near the bottom of the box, she extracted a thin volume of Lord Dunsany stories that promised weird tales of forgotten gods and elves and ghosts. Satisfied, she returned the rest of the books to the box and went back to chair by the couch upon which Walt deeply slept.

For a while, Amanda was content with silently reading and intermittently sipping her coffee. When the coffee had run its course, she got up to use the bathroom. Walt was still quietly snoring, having not moved a centimeter from his original position. She was worried for him, but she smiled and kissed him lightly on the forehead. He still didn't feel too hot, and she didn't think he was running a temperature. He slept on, and she padded off to the bathroom. She wondered how well he'd care for her when the tables turned and she was the one under the weather. *Men are such babies,* she thought, and smiled.

Groping blindly in the darkness, she eventually found a switch in the hallway and flipped it. The bright bulb in the fixture above her flared on, forcing her eyes to narrow to slits. As she became accustomed to the light, she gaped at the ceiling.

"God," she whispered.

Walt hadn't bothered to clean that horrible stain up at all. Worse, Amanda thought, she would be damned if it hadn't gotten bigger.

A lot bigger.

Walt slept through the rest of the night and woke up just before six in the morning. Discounting the few minutes of wakefulness at seven-thirty, he had managed to sleep almost twenty-nine hours straight. He was a firecracker, too. When Amanda awoke on the uncomfortable chair beside the sofa, it was to the sound of measured scratching; Walt had already removed most of the wallpaper in the house and was well on his way to repairing every hole, dent, crack and scratch. She rubbed her eyes and yawned loudly before shakily rising to her feet.

"How long you been up?" she mumbled.

"A few hours. Got a lot of work done."

"Well, that's good."

She yawned again and dipped a hand into her purse. Coming back with a crumpled pack of cigarettes, she awkwardly blew an unnoticed kiss to him and staggered out to the porch for a smoke. In front of the house, the back door of Walt's hatchback hung open, and she could see the piles of supplies inside. Shingles and lumber and baseboards, boxes of nails and can after can of white paint. She thought white was a bit unimaginative, but it was his house. He could paint it magenta if he liked, though a nice mint green would suit her fine.

She smoked the cigarette down to the filter, stubbed it out on the front lawn, and carried it back into the house to throw away. Her mouth felt fuzzy and tasted awful, so after she deposited the spent butt in the kitchen trash, she made a beeline for the bathroom.

There, she noticed the dripping stain on the ceiling, and the sticky puddle on the floor.

"Oh, Walt."

"What?" he called out from the dining room.

"You still haven't taken care of this nasty mess," she shouted back.

"What mess?"

"The...*blood.* On the ceiling."

"That? Of course I did. Cleaned that up last night. Or, no—the night before last. I keep forgetting I was in a coma there for a while." He let out a weak laugh.

"It's still here, Walt. And it's all over the floor."

Without waiting for a reply, she stepped over the noxious puddle and into the bathroom. That stain was getting to be a thorn in her paw. Who could just let something like that go? It was absolutely revolting, and worse still it was unsanitary. There was no telling what manner of vermin had gotten crushed to death up in the attic, nor what disgusting diseases it may have been carrying. She was tempted to clean it up herself, but some primordial maternal instinct kicked in that reproved her for it. No, she mustn't clean it up. If she did, what would Walt learn?

*Chrissake, Amanda, he's a grown-ass man.*

Besides, it was his house. He could crap on the floor if he felt like it. She just wouldn't want anything to do with him if he did. So what did she want with a guy who left animal blood all over the place? She sneered as she squeezed a dollop of toothpaste out onto Walt's toothbrush. The tube was neatly rolled up, squeezed from the bottom as he always did. He was a neat and conscientious guy. Or at least he always had been until now.

When she reemerged from the bathroom, she found him on all fours, cleaning up the floor with yet another dirty dishrag. He glanced up at her with wide, puppy-dog eyes and smiled like a kid caught stealing a cookie.

"I swear to God I thought I'd cleaned this up," he said.

"Maybe you dreamed it."

"I guess so. I'm sorry."

He sounded sincere, which was enough to make her feel downright terrible. Minutes ago she was reconsidering the welfare of their relationship, and over what? A misunderstanding, that was all. She felt like an utter bitch, and she told him so.

"Baloney," he said. "It's just crazy around here, is all. New house, new job coming up. It's all mine, but really, what's mine is yours. Right?"

"Right," she smiled. "Fucking A, that's right."

She guided him up by his armpits and planted a hard kiss on his mouth. Walt kissed her back with just as much force and substance, which went a long way toward making her feel better about the whole thing.

"What do you want for lunch?" he asked.

With the mess cleaned up and most of the visible interior repairs done, Walt and Amanda decided to call it a day. They showered together, made love, and ate turkey sandwiches on the floor of the dining room while they opened up boxes. The vast preponderance of Walt's belongings consisted of hundreds of books, for which he had more space than before, but not by much.

"I'm getting you bookshelves for Christmas," she remarked upon seeing the overwhelming number of volumes coming out of the boxes.

"Great," he said. "I'll need something like twenty of them."

He smiled furtively then, thinking about what he had already gotten for her: three princess-cut diamonds, one and half carats in total, set in a fourteen-carat white gold band. The ring cost more than three grand, and he was nowhere near paying it off, but he figured it would pay him back in spades. Amanda was worth it. She was worth more, even. Much, much more.

"What are you grinning about?"

He shook off the reverie and shot a coy look at her.

"Damn good turkey sandwich," he said.

In the late afternoon, his new dining room was no longer stacked to the ceiling with boxes—it was stacked to the ceiling with books. The rest of the boxes, no more than twelve in total, contained a few pots and pans, sundry knick-knacks he was happy to keep boxed up, and the record collection he never listened to. All of these could wait. They assembled the frame for the bed, smoothed out the bed sheets, and then collectively collapsed on top of it all with a united sigh. For a while, Walt remained still, listening to the rhythm of her soft breathing. Before he knew it, he was drifting toward that clumsy, watery place between sleep and consciousness.

Amanda shrieked.

Jolted, Walt shot up and searched for her. She was in the hallway, pressed up against the wall with her hands splayed out like claws.

"What happened?" he blurted.

"Goddamnit it's all over me!" she screamed.

Walt threw his legs over the side of the bed and hurried

over to her. He stopped just shy of the red, viscous puddle on the floor between them. His face twisted in disgust, and when he dragged his eyes from the mess on the floor up to Amanda, he saw that her white T-shirt was dotted with sanguine splotches. Worse, it had gotten in her hair and dripped down onto her cheek and chin. Dumbstruck, he looked from her to the floor, back to her, and then up at the ceiling. Sure enough, the stain had returned. There was no trace of the shellac or the paint they had slathered up there. There was only the nebulous reddish-brown patch on the ceiling, dripping down like a leaky faucet.

"What in hell?"

Amanda was trembling, her eyes wide and mouth hanging open.

"It's blood...Walt, it's *blood...*"

He seized her by the shoulders and guided her around the puddle into the bathroom. "Come on," he whispered, "come on."

"Blood," she repeated.

In the bathroom, he gently stripped her down, tugging her shirt up over her head. Once she was naked, he twisted the cold steel handle in the tub all the way to HOT and plugged the drain. Amanda lowered herself down onto the toilet seat, patiently but trembling slightly. While the water surged out of the faucet, he returned to the hallway and stared at the bloody mess on both ceiling and floor. He was absolutely certain that he removed every bit of the animal's remains from the attic, which left nothing to bleed out all over the place like this. Unless, he realized, something else had gone and died up there.

Frustrated and exhausted, Walt groaned. He waited for the tub to fill, and when it did he tested the water. It was hot, but not so much that Amanda would balk. He took her by the hand, led her to the tub, and she stepped in. Once she was sliding down into the bath, he kissed her on the top of the head, carefully avoiding the bloody spots in her hair.

"I'm going to look in the attic," he said.

"The attic? What for?"

"To see what the damn problem is now."

She pouted. But he went to the hall and yanked the dangling rope for the attic's ladder anyway. It jerked and shuttled out, clacking all the way down to the floor. A hot burst of musty air blasted him from above. He exhaled loudly and began the climb up.

He was already perched on the first pair of rafters outside of the opening when it occurred to him that he forgot the flashlight.

"Shit," he grumbled.

Walt paused, considering the necessity of climbing back down and searching for it. In the short time he had the house, he'd already spent an inordinate amount of time in the attic. He felt sure that he knew it backward and forward, even in the dark. It would be no problem getting over to the spot above the hallway; the only real concern left was what he found when he got there. But that wasn't much of an issue for him. All he expected to find was another dead animal, a rat or a pigeon. Maybe a bat. Whatever the case, he would not need the flashlight for that. In fact, it might even be better without one—he wouldn't have to see the poor, bloody thing in every awful, pathetic detail.

Walt set forth, carefully taking the rafters one at a time. Sweat began beading at his hairline, developing into fat, salty droplets that spilled down his face. The summer had been bad enough without spending so much time in an unventilated hotbox like the attic.

He knew he reached the spot when the insulation receded and the terrain under his feet turned to broken paneling. Pausing to catch his breath, he wiped his dripping face with his sleeve. The odor slammed his senses all at once. It was a warm, putrid smell, like bad hamburger meat left out in the sun. Whatever it was, it had to have been dead a long time to smell that bad.

Which, he realized, was impossible. Only a couple of days had passed since he cleaned up the last one, that unidentifiable mass of blood and sinew. For something else to crawl up there, die, and then rot enough to stink this badly would take a lot longer than two days or so. He buried his nose and mouth in the crook of his elbow and pondered his next move. Whatever it was he'd have to get rid of it, but he now understood this to be a temporary solution. There was a larger problem than he previously saw, likely some manner of infestation. A deep growl rumbled in the back of his throat.

This fucking house was getting to be more trouble than it was worth.

Amanda called up from below. It sounded like she was at the foot of the ladder. He ignored her. He had a more pressing concern at hand.

Bouncing on the balls of his feet, Walt reached out to the source of the fetid stench and sank his fingertips into something warm and wet. He gagged, fighting back the retching impulse triggered by the unanticipated contact. He wanted nothing more than to retract his hands, to get away from that awful odor, but instead he dug in deeper and tried to scoop up the soft, moist mass. It did not give. It seemed to be stuck to the panel. He pulled his hands back and frowned. A spackle knife would have been a welcomed tool just then, but he wasn't sure he even owned one. Something else for his goddamned home improvement list.

Grinding his jaws together he plunged his hands back into the mass, determined to dig it all up and get rid of it once and for all. This time, when Walt sank his fingers into the sticky substance, he felt it tighten around his digits. He let out a yelp and yanked his hands back again, but the mass on the panel would not relent. It held him tight, contracting like a baby boa until it hurt. Amanda called up again, yelling his name. She was a little closer now, probably climbing the ladder. In the moment he was distracted by her, the warm thing on the broken panel released him. Walt stumbled backwards and nearly fell between two rafters. He steadied himself in time, twisting into a spidery position to keep from falling through the ceiling.

In the soft yellow glow of the attic's opening, Amanda's head popped into view. Her shiny wet hair lay flat on her head, framing the pale face that searched the darkness for some sign of him.

"Don't come up here!" Walt shouted from across the shadows.

"Are you okay?"

"I'm fine," he answered quickly. "It's just dark. It's dangerous."

"Are you done yet?"

He wiggled his fingers and marveled at the hot, tingly sensation he felt. He then heard a slick, slithery noise beside him—the bloody lump on the panel, shifting and moving. The muscles in his back twinged.

"Yeah," he said. "I'm done for now."

He quickly scampered over the rafters to the ladder and almost knocked Amanda down in his rush to get back to the cooler floor below.

"What was it?" she breathlessly asked.

"Another dead animal. Rat, I guess."

She wrinkled her nose.

"I guess I've got a nest of them up there," he added.

"Nasty."

"I'll take care of it," he snarled.

With that, he stalked back into the bedroom, walking right through the puddle on the floor and leaving red footprints between the hall and the bed. His hands and feet tacky with blood, he stretched out on top of the sheets, heaved a sigh, and drifted off with a smile playing at the corners of his mouth.

## 5

Amanda slept on the couch, or at least tried to, in what little space it afforded such a typically restless sleeper. Though her mind attempted to rationalize Walt's increasing irritability, impatience, and nervousness to the pressures of a new home and a new job, somehow it didn't quite click. Now he'd gone to bed filthy with the gore and grue of the infested house practically all over him, and here she lay on his couch rather than with him. She'd have just gone home, but she was so tired. And so terribly worried about things she hadn't yet begun to understand. So Amanda tried like hell to get a little shut-eye.

But not five minutes after she closed her eyes she began to hear scratching and skittering coming from the ceiling. From the attic. It seemed to her that Walt was right—there were rats up there. And where there was one rat, there were fifty. She tried to block out the noise, but it was useless. Every time her mind let go and she started to drift off, she imagined the ceiling opening up and a torrent of screeching, clawing vermin pouring down on her.

With a heavy sigh, she sat up and switched on the lamp. She was exhausted but unable to sleep, a terrible dilemma she knew too well from years of persistent insomnia. Instead she merely sat there for some time, glassily staring at the wall and breathing the stale air that seemed as old as the house itself. The skittering continued unabated. She pinched her brow, fighting back the anxiety that was tightening in her chest. Things between her and Walt had been strained, to say the least. There had always been minor arguments and disagreements, bad moods and the inevitable apologies that followed. But ever since he bought this damn house...

A cockroach scrambled up the wall in front of her. Amanda narrowed her eyes at it, feeling an odd sort of hate for the insect, as though she was channeling all of the anger and disquiet of the last several days and firing it like a laser at the roach. It made it halfway up the wall, turned, and then scrambled horizontally across the length of the room. Launching herself to her feet, she gave chase. Even if she consciously recognized the absurdity of her sheer hatred for the insignificant bug, she aimed to kill it all the same.

At the end of the wall, a six-inch molding jutted out to separate the living room from the dining room. The cockroach crawled up and over it without slowing its pace and kept on across the dining room wall. Amanda scooped up one of her flats and hurried after it. Now the roach climbed up before turning away again, skirting the edge of the ceiling in a desperate escape. Amanda leapt up and smacked at it with her shoe, but she missed.

"Bastard!" she hissed.

She lost sight of it for a second, but the black blur in her peripheral vision sent her reeling back after it. The roach tried to climb down and under the molding toward the kitchen, teetered for a moment on two of its spiny legs, and then dropped to the floor with a quiet click. Amanda lunged for it, but the cockroach hit the ground running and skittered across the tiles toward the hallway beyond. The shoe slammed against a tile long after the roach had run off.

In the hall she flicked the switch on, bathing the white walls with a sickly yellow light. The cockroach quickened its pace, frantic to evade it, and climbed upward in a zigzag pattern toward the ceiling. Amanda shopped short of lunging again; between her and the roach on the wall lay the widening red puddle on the hallway floor. But her eyes remained fixed to the fast, revolting creature. Up it went, its six tiny legs clicking against the textured wall. It reached the corner where two walls and the ceiling met and momentarily paused as if it were reviewing its options. Then a thin crimson strand shot out from the spot on the ceiling, seized the cockroach, and pulled it back into the stain.

The insect struggled, wriggling spasmodically, but it could not break free. In an instant, the viscous blood enveloped the cockroach completely. Amanda heard a faint crunching sound, then nothing at all.

Only silence, apart from the thump of her own heart.

Dazed, she stared at the stain for several minutes while she tried to process what she had just seen. Contemplation, however, did her no good. She had no point of reference, no way to understand what just happened or how it was possible. If pressed, she could explain that a leaking blood stain reached out and ate a cockroach before her eyes. But that clearly made no sense at all.

"Honey?"

She jerked, startled. In the shadows of the bedroom, just beyond the scope of the hallway light, Walt stood naked.

"What is it, sweetheart?" he asked quietly.

Amanda froze, suddenly and inexplicably terrified of him.

"Come to bed," he said.

Walt took a step forward and she could see he was still sticky with the blood from the hallway. She gagged.

Before she could hear another word from him, Amanda was running for the front door in her bare feet.

The door slammed shut and, half a minute later, Amanda's car coughed to life outside. Walt shuffled over to the bedroom window, pulled back the curtain and peered out. All he could see were dim red tail-lights disappearing into the distance. For a moment, he almost believed he could feel the heat from those hazy red lights on his face. He wiped a slick swatch of sweat from his face with the palm of his hand and realized that it was only the house. As hot and humid as it was outside, the house acted like an incubator, making it that much worse inside. It was an old place, after all—nearly seventy years old, and with no central heat or air. He considered shopping around for a pair of window units in the morning, or maybe the day after that.

Then he went back to bed.

## 6

The phone kept ringing. Walt had no machine, so the irritating noise just went on and on. Still, he had no intention of answering it. It was probably just that roofer again, angry as hell that he showed up at the agreed upon time and found no one home. The truth was that Walt was asleep—deeply asleep—but now he didn't even want the roofer's services anymore. It hardly ever rained in the summer around there anyway. And even when it did, it was not as though a little water ever hurt anybody. Why did everything have to be so perfect, so damned structured?

On the other hand, it might also have been Amanda. Three days had come and gone since she went tearing out of the house in the middle of the night. He sat down on the edge of his bed and thought about three days without Amanda. If it was supposed to hurt or vex him, it didn't. All he had done was wake up to the obnoxious clatter she was making at that ungodly hour. It was her own mental unbalance that made her react so strangely. If she wanted to talk to him about it—which he thought had better include a sincere apology—she knew where he lived.

After thirteen rings, the house finally fell silent again. Silent apart from the wet sounds emanating from the hallway ceiling, at any rate.

It started the day after Amanda's bizarre departure. Walt was drifting in and out of sleep on the bed—he was just so damned tired these days—asleep enough to hazily dream but too awake to make any sense out of it. He tossed and turned and managed to kick the sheets off the bed, eventually snapping himself awake and calling it a draw. He did not see it at all, not at first, but he might have heard it. He certainly smelled it: that same rotten meat odor that permeated the attic. Stifling a retching gag as he had before, he slowly approached the doorway and peered up.

The stain had widened substantially. It was easily a foot and a half across now, and it was thick and gluey. The dripping appeared to have stopped so that the blood—or whatever it was—stayed in place. But it pulsed and undulated like ripples in a pond, and there were several wiry strands dangling down from it. He counted seven ropey fibers in all and judged them to be uniform in length, about six inches. They were the same rusty dark red as the stain itself, but with barely visible pink and white threads twisted throughout each one, kind of like muscle tissue.

He edged around it, careful not to pass directly beneath, until he was on the opposite end of the hall. From there he stared a while longer before withdrawing into the kitchen and retrieving a long pair of silver tongs from a drawer. When he returned to the end of the hall, he stretched his arm up at the strands until the tips of the tongs almost grazed them. The meaty strands pulled taut and shot at the tongs in unison, coiling around the rounded tips and wrenching them from Walt's grasp. He gasped and watched in horror as the bloody sinews mauled the tongs, turning them one way and then another before suddenly releasing them. They dropped to the floor with a loud clang. Walt jumped; he could hardly believe his own eyes. All he could think to say was, "Fuck."

The dripping tendrils in the ceiling seemed to quiver in response.

Despite his revulsion, Walt's curiosity consumed him. He found the rope hanging from the white square at the other side of the hall, yanked it hard, and hurried up the steps that clattered down to him.

The attic was an altogether different story.

Where the warm, spongy mass had been the night before, there was now a red, veiny lump the size of a football. Around the base of the lump, tiny splinters jutted out at various angles. He hadn't a clue what it was, but it was clear to him that it had successfully broken through the paneling.

Perhaps more disturbing were the sundry animal corpses scattered around the throbbing thing. They were the rats he'd suspected of infesting his attic, but these rats were eaten away, dissolved down to their bones.

It was no longer just a stain. It was a living entity.

And it was feeding.

## 7

Squashed up on one end of the couch with his knees touching his chin and a can of Stroh's in his left hand, Walt considered his options. His initial instinct, purely primordial and reactionary, was to try to kill it. He thought about poisoning it, cutting it, dropping a heavy weight on it and burning it. Then another proclivity hailing from deep in his genes kicked in: fear. What if he tried to kill it, but failed? How would the thing react? Gruesome visions of the pulsing red creature in the attic taunted his mind, images of the thing flying into a rage, growing, whipping those awful, dripping tendrils at him.

No, he decided he would not attempt to kill the thing in

his attic. At least not yet.

The next option that occurred to him was telling somebody. Not just anyone, but someone who could either identify the organism or at the very least take it to some laboratory far away from its present location. The university, or perhaps the government. Maybe, Walt wondered, he should just call 9-1-1. But that was no good, either. He had never placed much faith in the so-called authorities before, much less academia, and could see no reason to start now.

That left Walt right where he started, puzzled and scared. He sucked down the last of his beer and crumpled the can in his fist. He took a deep breath, held it, and belched. The squirming mass on the ceiling erupted into a series of nauseating wet noises, like a bucket full of worms crawling over one another. Walt shivered, stood up, and grabbed his keys from the kitchen counter.

Twenty miles or so northeast of Walt's house was a small bar called Tiny's. From door to door, one would have to travel down a twisting, two-lane country road for eight miles until it dunked down to the interstate, which went almost directly to the bar. Walt had never set foot in the place—in fact, he hadn't been inside a dive bar since his college days—but he'd passed by enough times that the place registered in his memory when he decided on a drink.

The sun was still out when he arrived, and there were scant customers inside. By the time business picked up and the jukebox started to swing, he was three sheets to the wind. He lost count of how many tall, frosty mugs of the house's cheapest tap he consumed up to that point, but it was sufficient to render him shit-faced. And, as men who are blotto have been doing since time immemorial, Walt was talking far too much, and much too loudly.

"Lost a woman, gained a lump a' meat," he slurred from his

seat by the men's room.

Most of Tiny's patrons, regulars and moonlighters, chose to ignore the mumbling inebriate in the corner. Nearly every bar had one, and the only real choice anyone ever had was to pay them no mind. For the giggling frat boys out on a bender, however, Walt was providing free entertainment they could not turn down. The shorter of the two was built like a fireplug and sported an outmoded blonde flattop. His much taller buddy, a reedy kid with a splotchy, acne-ridden face, kicked off the festivities when he slammed his mug down on Walt's table.

"What's this about your meat?" he chuckled.

"Big as my head," Walt explained without missing a beat. "Fucker eats rats."

"That so?" snickered the fireplug.

"Came with the house," he said, bursting into a gale of laughter.

Splotchy and the fireplug regarded one another with apprehensive looks. The latter rose up from his chair, stood beside by the former. Walt reached over and seized the tall one by his wrist and hissed, "Wanna see it?"

"No, man," the acne-faced kid nervously stammered. "It's cool."

"Maybe we can get it to eat a rat. You know, right in front of us, like that."

Walt's face split into a maniacal grin as the tall kid wrenched his wrist free and both frat boys made tracks for the door. His laughter chased them clear out to the parking lot. It also annoyed one of the stone-faced pool players nearby enough that the husky man toddled over to Walt, his beefy hands curled into fists.

"You want to knock it off?" the man roared.

Walt managed to swallow his laughter, wagging a forefinger at the angry man.

"I got a thing in my attic," Walt babbled, "that'd eat you up."

"That right? Well I got an automatic in my glove compartment that'd ventilate your fucking skull, so settle the fuck down."

Walt's eyes widened, his wagging finger went up to his lips. "Shhh," he hissed.

"Christ," the man grunted as he waddled back to the pool table.

The night dragged on in much the same way. Whenever anyone came within earshot, Walt tried to tell them about the thing in the attic. Those who did not simply dismiss him got either angry or a little scared. Eventually the husky, unshaven New Englander behind the bar came careening across the room to toss him out of the place. He was a bit rough about it—digging his knuckles into the small of Walt's back and employing some choice words—but Walt didn't particularly mind. He just ended up sitting on the concrete steps in front of Tiny's, staring at his own car in the parking lot and waiting until he was sober enough to drive.

After the better part of an hour had passed, he was still stewed. A little longer after that, the patrons started to stumble out of the bar and the red neon OPEN sign went off.

Walt stood up, swayed, and almost fell over. He steadied himself and staggered over to his car. Locating the correct key and getting it into the small, dark slot was a Herculean task, but he managed it and got into the driver's seat. In front of him the steering wheel throbbed, but he knew it was only his impaired vision.

"Goddamnit," he grumbled under his ripe, alcoholic breath. He was in no shape to drive.

He got back out of the car, locked the door, and started walking. It was six long blocks until he stumbled upon a dingy no-tell motel with a gravel strewn courtyard in the middle. *I'll sleep it off*, he told himself. *Just a couple of hours.*

The room cost forty dollars and there was a plastic baby

buggy parked in front of the door. He kicked the orange monstrosity out of the way as he fit the key in the lock. It was much easier this time around. He smiled and went into the room, where he was instantly assaulted with a haze of stale cigarette smoke, body odor, and alcohol. For a second, he thought he had gone into the wrong room, but when he switched on the light, he found it empty.

Walt shut the door and latched the guard chain. The room was nominally clean, but the smell was appalling. Still, he had to admit to himself that it beat that rancid meat odor permeating his own house. He lay down on top of the dusty comforter on the bed and was asleep in minutes.

Long serpentine strands slithered up the sides of the bed from underneath, probing Walt's body and leaving sticky pink trails everywhere they touched. His skin burned wherever they made contact with it, but before he could get away the tendrils were wrapping around his ankles, knees and wrists. Bound tightly, he bucked and writhed but it was to no avail. The throbbing entity under the bed had him and there was no escape.

He could hear the loud thumping, like a colossal heart that was pumping gallons of blood at an ungodly speed. Then it stopped all at once and the room was dead silent for several long seconds before the moaning started. It sounded like the deafening creak of a tipping long ship, but it was more plaintive than that, more *human*. Equal parts rage and sorrow echoed outward, splitting his eardrums as the monstrous moan grew louder and louder. When the dozen or so thinner strands sprang up and two of them found his ear canals, he was almost relieved. He could feel the warm, clammy strands push deeply into his head as more of them wiggled in front of him, pressing into his mouth and his nostrils. Seconds after the worm-like appendages pushed into his anus, Walt found that he could no longer breathe. What would have been a scream was stifled when the rancid tentacles began digging into his eyes.

He was already vomiting before he woke up. It was too late to staunch the heaving flow of it, so Walt was left to puke all over himself and the bed until it was done. His stomach ached and his throat felt like he swallowed a pinecone. The fresh memory of his nightmare lingered as strongly as the acrid taste in his mouth.

Bent over like Quasimodo, he lurched to the bathroom sink, tearing his shirt off along the way. There was no toothpaste, much less a toothbrush, so he rinsed his face and mouth with tepid water several times over. He rinsed the shirt, too, and rung it out over the tub before putting it back on. The comforter, he decided, was not his problem.

The good news was that he was stone cold sober now. He felt worse than he had in long, long time, but he would be able to drive home without endangering himself and others any more than usual.

He retraced the six blocks to Tiny's in a damp T-shirt, savoring the coolness of the faint, pre-morning breeze on his wet torso. He felt so good that he ran the air conditioning in his hatchback at full blast all the way back.

Upon reaching the winding country road leading back to his outlying house, a light rain started to spot the windshield. He fumbled for the lever to switch on the wipers, momentarily forgetting where it was. He found it, turned it down, and squinted through the smears left across the windshield by the worn wiper blades. His mind drifted to his ever-growing to do list, not adding *new wiper blades* to the throng, and he worried about the multitudinous holes in his roof now that it was raining. Walt managed to lose enough concentration on the world outside of his head that he only noticed the deer in the middle of the road when he was less than three yards shy of ramming it.

Jerking the steering wheel by way of reflex alone, Walt's hatchback skidded on the wet road and spun ninety degrees before slamming into a thick old growth oak.

Walt raised his head from the steering column. Blood ran down his forehead from a cut at his hairline. His eyes stung from it running into them. He sat back, wiping his face with his hands and moaning. When his vision cleared, he gazed through the windshield at the white steam rising through the rain from beneath the dented hood.

He pulled the door handle, kicked the door open, and stepped out into the warm, sprinkling rain. It pattered lightly and rhythmically on the leaves that hemmed the road, like the stain on his ceiling, dripping down on the floor. His stomach rolled at the thought.

Shaking it off, he crawled back into the car and shifted into reverse. He gently applied pressure to the accelerator and the engine growled, but the car refused to budge. Shifting back into park, Walt melted into the seat and glared out at the hazy columns of light extending from his headlights out into the wet, dark forest.

The car, he expected, was likely totaled. Two options occurred to him: he could sit in it until morning, or he could walk home. He chose option two, cutting the engine and locking the doors. No more than ten feet up the ink black backroad, the sky opened up and drenched him with hard, fast rain.

He smelled the sickening odor from the driveway; it hit him the moment he stepped onto the property. Combined with the persistent taste of vomit in his mouth and throat, it was nearly enough to knock Walt over. Once again shielding his face in the crook of his arm, Walt strode cautiously toward the house. The rain had abated somewhat, although it was still drizzling. His shoes squeaked on the porch steps.

He was digging into his pocket for the house keys when a silhouetted figure stood up on the porch and approached him. Walt gave a frightened shout, stumbled backward and fell on his rump.

"Christ, Walt," Amanda said. "What's the matter with you?"

He let out a long, labored breath and looked up at her.

"You scared the shit out of me."

"It's six in the morning. Where have you been?"

"Sleeping off a bender. That all right with you?"

He got back to his feet and rubbed his sore backside. His pants were as thoroughly soaked as the rest of him.

"Did you walk? From town?"

"No, just from where I crashed into a tree. About three miles back."

She gasped.

"You *crashed your car*? Goddamnit, Walt! You drove *drunk*!"

He sneered as he jammed the house key into the lock.

"No, I did not drive drunk. I slept if off, just like I said. There was a fucking deer in the road, I swerved and hit a tree. The goddamn car is totaled."

The front door creaked open and Walt fumbled for the foyer light. When it came on, he turned back to Amanda and pointed at the crusty crimson wound on his forehead.

"Thanks for your concern, by the way. I'm fine."

"Concern? You want to talk about concern? Three days I've been calling you. Three days, Walt! I've come by twice now. And not a word from you! Not one fucking word! What have I done, can you tell me that?"

He glared impassively at her.

"You're the one who ran screaming out of here."

"You didn't see it," she answered.

"See what, exactly?" Walt scrunched up his face and leaned against the doorjamb.

Her face paling, she dropped her chin to her chest and shuddered.

"That thing on your ceiling…"

"What thing? The stain?"

"It's not just a stain, Walt. I watched it…eat a bug. A cockroach, for Christ's sake."

Walt twisted his mouth into a crooked smile.

"Come on, now," he said.

"It's the truth! It reached out for it, swallowed it up. I saw it!"

She hugged herself tightly. Walt couldn't help himself. He erupted into a fit of wild laughter. Amanda was dumbstruck and more than a little humiliated.

"I'm sure you saw it, sweetheart," he said between snorting chuckles. "But it doesn't do that anymore. It's a lot bigger, now. It's moved on to *rats*."

Her mouth dropped open like a door on broken hinges. Walt went into the house, his laughter trailing after him as he vanished from her view.

Her eyes welled up as she turned the key in the ignition. She flipped on the headlights and the beams illuminated Walt's front porch. His front door was still open, but he was nowhere in sight. The tears spilled over and ran down her cheeks.

Her confusion was infuriating. Not only was she puzzled about Walt's bizarre behavior, she was puzzled by what, exactly, was upsetting her more: his heartless attitude toward her, or her revulsion at the thing growing in that house. Somehow, she was sure there was a connection between the two, the house and the rapid deterioration of her relationship with her boyfriend. In nearly three years she had never seen him like this; never before he moved into the Gable-front cottage at the edge of town. As she backed down the driveway and pulled out onto the road, she wondered if she was ever going to see him again.

Walt was still cackling when he seized a can of Stroh's from the refrigerator and cracked it open. The cold beer felt marvelous going down his throat, washing the acrid remnants of vomit away. He licked his lips and gulped some more. When the can was empty, he set it on the counter and headed for the john. He noticed that the front door remained open and saw Amanda's car dissolving into the darkness. He frowned. It occurred to him that he should care—about the door, at the very least, if not *her*—but for some reason he didn't. He shrugged and continued to the bathroom.

Inches from the bathroom door, something tickled the top of Walt's head. He stopped and looked up, having momentarily forgotten all about the thing on the ceiling.

One of its tendrils was probing his hairline, exploring the fresh, tender cut. He winced from the stinging pain and edged away from it. The stain was not much of a stain anymore. It looked much more like a massive slab of meat, as if someone affixed a thick raw steak to the ceiling. Walt curled his lips in disgust and hurried into the bathroom. He flipped the light switch and pulled his zipper down, and then he heard the loud, wet sucking noises emanating from the thing in the hallway.

He paused, unsure if he would even be able to urinate. Then he yanked the zipper back up and peered out and up at the organism above him.

With a frightened shout he fell back into the bathroom.

The thing was indeed making sucking sounds. It sucked with malformed lips, hidden amidst the wriggling tendrils. Sucked at its own sticky gore, at the air.

Changing. Becoming.

Growing there, a ghastly red face.

# 8

"You look awful," Nora said cheerfully.

She came around the counter and shoved her grinning face close to Amanda's. On her left hand crawled a black spider the size of a nickel. To Amanda's immense chagrin, creeping, crawling things were something of a passion for Nora. Amanda arched an eyebrow and sneered.

"Wow," Nora exclaimed. "You *really* look awful. What's up?"

"Rough night," Amanda croaked, ignoring the hairy spider that was now advancing up Nora's forearm. Her voice was coarse and quiet, the inevitable side effect of having cried all through the night.

"Walt?"

"Yeah," Amanda answered, noncommittally. Walt, sure—but also that thing, those tendrils…

The thing was, Nora had never laid eyes on Walt, and Amanda couldn't clearly put together why that should have been the case. She loved him, or at least she was pretty sure she did, and Nora was the best friend she had—it would only make sense the two of them would be acquainted, at the very least. Still, life was so much easier to manage with things, and people, neatly compartmentalized. And Walt was such a private and shy guy, far from prone to socializing and meeting new people. *Part of his subtle charm?* she wondered. *Or a red flag I've been ignoring?*

The bell over the door jangled and a customer came in; an older man with stark white hair and a moustache to match. Amanda smiled at him, but he ignored her and went directly for the computer books.

Amanda and Nora had opened the shop around the same time Amanda first began dating Walt, but they'd been close friends since college. It began life as a small bookstore they named In the Reads, but they now sold a host of useless accoutrements and knick-knacks just to keep up with the ample competition in town. Neither of them got rich, nor had they ever expected to. They got by, and that was enough.

"He didn't hit you, did he?" Nora said, leaning in conspiratorially.

"No! Of course not. Nothing like that."

"Another girl?"

"Not that I know of."

"Huh."

Nora looked stumped, as though physical abuse and infidelity were the only problems her mind could conceive. The white-haired man shuffled up to the register and slapped a thin paperback volume down on the counter. A collection of erotic fiction. *So much for computers*, Amanda thought as she smiled and rang him up. He paid in cash and left without a word. The women were alone again, and Nora still looked confused.

"Is it over?" she asked at length.

"I don't know. I hope not. But…"

Nora waited for her to finish, instead she just trailed off.

"But what?"

Amanda turned away from Nora, focusing on an endcap loaded up with novelty pens and playing cards with pictures of famous authors on the backs. But she did not see them; she saw the blood in Walt's house, reaching out and snatching the cockroach for a midnight snack. Only now it was more than just a roach. At least that was what Walt said.

*It's moved on to rats.*

He seemed so happy about it, like a proud parent. Amanda knitted her brow and returned her attention to Nora.

"Nothing," she said.

# 9

Walt got off the phone with the towing company and checked the clock on the stove. A quarter to two. Plenty of time.

*(Gurgling. Sucking.)*

*I got you. Everything's going to be all right.*

He flipped back through the phone book, moving from T (towing) back to P (pet stores and supplies). The tow truck was expected to pick up Walt's hatchback sometime between three and five, so if he called a taxi now there should be plenty of time to get to the nearest pet store and back before the battered vehicle arrived in his driveway. A cursory glance at the list of pet shop competitors informed him that Georgia's Pets on Mill Street would likely be the closest. He dog-eared the page and flipped back over to the T's (taxis).

Figuring it didn't matter which taxi service he used, he called the first one listed: AAA Cab Co. He stressed that he was in a bit of a hurry and that he would need the driver to wait to take him back home again.

The taxi arrived twenty-five minutes later. Walt considered himself fortunate that he did not get stuck with a chatty driver. The ride to Mill Street was blissfully quiet.

The girl in the pet shop was small and mousy-looking, with her curly black hair stuffed clumsily into a bun on top. She stared at Walt without expression when he came in, raising her eyebrows solicitously. He smiled and nodded, striding across the store and examining the sundry animals for sale.

The place smelled strongly of cedar chips and disinfectant. The front of the store was taken up by squawking birds and a dozen different types of rodents—rats, gerbils, hamsters, guinea pigs, and even a chinchilla. As Walt moved to the back of the store, the species turned largely reptilian, although there was a fair number of tarantulas and scorpions on the wall, as well. He looked around and sighed. No normal pets, just exotic ones. And there wasn't enough time to look at another shop. He crooked his mouth to one side and walked over to the shopgirl.

"How much for the guinea pigs?"

"Fifteen each."

He slid his wallet out of the back pocket of his jeans and peeked inside.

"I'll take three."

"All right," the girl said, starting to brighten up a bit. "What do you need for supplies? Not all of these cages come with water bottles…"

Walt reached out and touched her shoulder.

"I don't need all that extra stuff," he said. "Just the animals, okay?"

The girl's brow sank over her eyes.

"Get the hell out of my shop," she said.

Walt leaned back and grimaced at her.

"Excuse me?"

"You heard me. Piss off. I mean it."

"Do you normally chase paying customers out of your place of business, or just me?"

"Don't play dumb with me, prick. Anyone who wants to buy 'just the animals' and nothing to actually take care of them is up to no damn good. I've seen it before and it's heartbreaking. If you're not out of here in five seconds I'm calling the police."

"The police? For trying to buy some fucking *guinea pigs*?"

"Four seconds."

"This is outrageous."

"Three seconds."

"Go ahead and call them. I'm eager to hear what they say to you about this."

"Two seconds. I'm not messing around."

Walt's right hand curled into a tight fist. The girl flashed a smug grin at him.

"And that's one. Hang around and wait for them, if you like."

She marched over to the front counter, pulled a phone up from underneath it and began dialing.

"I've got a cab waiting," he said in a quiet rage.

He stalked out of the shop and got back into the running taxi. As the vehicle drove off, he could see the girl hanging the phone up and smiling triumphantly.

Walt seethed all the way back to the house.

The hatchback sat crooked in the driveway when the cab dropped him off. The front end of the car was caved in, a perfect fit for the big oak he slammed into. He shook his head at the ruins of his car, wondering what to do about it and how he was going to afford it. So much of his reserves had already been poured into the house, leaving scant cash for unforeseen events like a totaled car. He walked a circle around it, studying the damage and silently cursing himself for having had the accident in the first place. At least he could still live in a house with a hundred holes in the roof. And one very peculiar hole in the ceiling.

Walt turned toward the porch and took a few steps before a high-pitched mewling attracted his attention. He paused, turned around and narrowed his eyes at the tree line at the edge of his property. Although he couldn't see them from where he stood, he knew that the black cat was feeding her kittens in the woods again.

He slowly walked over to the trees.

The mouth twisted and puckered. It looked as though it was trying to speak, or maybe kiss. Walt hadn't noticed anything resembling teeth in it before, but he could now see small white nubs protruding at various angles beneath the sopping lips. Above the mouth, a chunk of pink cartilage jutted out of the sticky mass. The beginnings of a nose.

For a moment, he stared at it. Faces didn't form this way, layer by layer, from the inside out. But this one seemed to. He tilted his head to one side, studying it. Fascinated. Then a gnarled flap of bumpy flesh darted out from between the lips. Its tongue.

A cardboard box marked BOOKS sat at Walt's feet, its original content was now stacked neatly in the dining room. The box wiggled. A weak, quiet squeak emanated from within. He sneered at it, and then he regarded the deep crimson scratch on the back of his right hand. Mama had done that, enraged at the theft of her baby. Walt hadn't expected the cat to strike out like that, but the animal turned out to be feral. She had no trust for human beings and, as Walt clearly demonstrated, she had no reason to. Nonetheless, he managed to snatch the tiny kitten by the scruff of its neck and get away with no more than the one injury.

He opened the box and reached inside, seizing the crying kitten by the loose skin on the back of its neck. The tongue above him lashed about, dripping blood-infused saliva on Walt's face and shoulders.

"You're hungry," he said, not expecting it to hear or understand him. It had no ears, after all.

The mouth stretched open a little wider, cracking audibly. Walt lifted the kitten higher. A lump of red, veiny flesh wobbled in the mass, splitting apart to reveal a bloodshot eye. Walt gasped.

"Christ," he said, titling his head to get a better look at the solitary, roaming eye. The iris was a very pale blue. "Can you *see?*"

He waved the screeching cat back and forth beneath the eye, and the eye followed it intently. The mouth slavered, the tongue licked the lips with anticipation. When Walt lifted the struggling animal higher still, the wriggling strands shot at it and rapidly coiled around the kitten's neck and legs. One of the strands dug into the fresh scratch on his hand, too. Walt cried out in pain and jerked his hand free.

"Watch it!" he snarled.

If the creature on the ceiling understood him, it paid him no mind. It was far too occupied with the thrashing kitten in its grasp, pulling it close enough for that grotesque mouth to bite into its belly. The cat gave a chilling shriek as its abdomen was torn open by the gnawing teeth. Walt swallowed hard and looked away. Blood splashed on the floor behind him and he heard a loud crunch. When he looked back, the kitten was mangled.

The mouth greedily sucked at the fluids and viscera that seeped out of the split belly.

"Jesus Christ."

The eye revolved to stare at him while the blunt teeth tore into the remains of the kitten.

## 10

Amanda shivered as she stirred the can-shaped chunk of condensed soup into the milk that surrounded it. Her apartment felt cold. Cold and dark and strangely foreign. In the last few weeks, she'd spent little time in her own place. There was a time when Walt came over at least once a week, before the house. Before it. Mostly they went to his old place, or just out. She even joked with Nora that the one-bedroom walk-up served more as a storage unit for her stuff than anything else. After all, most nights she slept at Walt's. With Walt. But not tonight. Not the last few nights.

When the orange goop finally began to blend with the milk, she gave the concoction another whirl with the whisk before stealing away to the short hallway between the bathroom and bedroom. There was no light in the hall, so she had to turn on the bathroom light to illuminate the controls for the central heat and air. She almost always kept it off when she was not at home, and since her apartment was buried in the building with other units on top and both sides, it tended to get pretty chilly when the sun went down. She squinted in the dim light emanating from the bathroom, peering closely at the black and gray readout on the control unit. 62 degrees. Even the number gave her goosebumps. She flipped open the cover, played with the overly complicated network of buttons for several seconds, and finally convinced the damned thing to settle on a comfortable 71.

The soup on the stovetop had come to a boil during her two-minute absence.

"Shit," she grunted, seizing the pot by the handle. She quickly moved it to a cool burner, but it was too late. Her lunch-for-breakfast was ruined.

Her bottom lip quivering, she began to weep. Anyone would have thought she was nuts had they observed the spectacle; who breaks down over a ruined can of seventy-nine cent soup? But it was so much more than that. The soup was just the last straw, the one that broke her proverbial camel's back. And that camel was named Walt.

She dropped the pot in the sink with a resounding *clang*. Wiping her eyes, she weighed the pros and cons of giving him a call just to see how he was doing. Maybe, she thought, they would both end up apologizing and before long her blubbering would transform into relieved laughter. But even as she found herself dialing his number, she greatly doubted that would be the case.

The line whirred its soft ring once, twice, and then three times. Immediately after the fourth, she heard a click. Then silence.

"Walt?"

No response came from the other end. But she was nearly certain she could hear soft breathing coming through the receiver.

"Walt? Are you there?"

The breathing got louder, as though he knew he was caught and was not bothering to attempt silence any longer.

"I...I can hear you, Walt. Aren't you going to say anything?"

A short burst of air hit the line, a grunt forced through it. Like a mean little laugh. *Heh.*

The line went dead after that. She dropped the receiver and hung it back on the hook. She remained in the kitchen, staring at the wall with her arms hanging limp at her sides. She felt fairly certain that this was the end, that she had been unceremoniously dumped. As much as that pained her—and it pained her plenty—it was not the primary source of her hurt and confusion. It was the manner with which Walt did it, the coldness and total lack of kindness. That was not the same man with whom Amanda fell in love, the man who loved books and kids and got all giddy whenever he waxed poetic about their future together. Marriage had never come up explicitly, but there was always that knowing sparkle in his eyes when he slyly hinted at it. She didn't doubt that a proposal was just around the corner, at least not before he moved into that house.

That awful house. With that even more awful thing living in it. *Growing* in it.

Amanda shuddered, recalling the nightmarish sight of the puddle hungrily sucking up that cockroach and devouring it completely. At that point, the nasty thing was twice as big as it was when Walt first discovered it. There was no telling how much it had grown since then. Or what it hungered for now.

The back of her throat burned from the bile that worked up from her stomach. In her mind, she pictured shoving a flaming torch at the thing, burning it up and being done with it. Maybe then Walt might come back to the land of the living. Even if he still wanted to call it quits, he would at least return to being the same gentle Walt he had always been, before he moved into his new home in the boondocks.

"Yeah, sure," she muttered, shaking her head.

She couldn't exactly see herself bursting into the house like some comic book superheroine with a torch clutched in her fist, screaming, *Out of the way, Walt! It's that thing or me!*

It was stupid. She hung her head, jamming her chin into her breastbone.

She didn't know what to do.

The broad, open expanse of the field stretched from the end of Walt's property to a line of trees at least a quarter of a mile away. Broken wooden nubs protruded from the dry earth in intervals all around the expanse, rotting vestiges of what had once been a fence. Whoever owned the huge parcel of land now had let it go to seed; it was overgrown with tall yellow grass and thick tangles of weeds. In the week that passed since he brought the first box inside the house, Walt had yet to see a single living soul set foot there. In his mind, it was practically his.

Having slept most of the night—save for that irritating call from Amanda—he was fresh and ready to go when he set out in the first hour of sunlight. He wore his rarely used pair of beige hiking boots and carried a fire iron in his right hand. He would have preferred one of those litter pokers the convicts used on the interstate to collect all the garbage, but he had high hopes for the heavy metal instrument. A field like that was bound to be rife with all manners of creeping and crawling critters; snakes and moles and rabbits and such. Food for the hungry mouth on the ceiling.

He strode carefully into the field, his boots crushing the

deep growth underneath. Around him birds chirped and cackled. Something cut a rapid path through the grass several yards in front of him, too far away to do anything about it. Despite the early morning, it was already hot enough to break a sweat. The scent of his own perspiration fused with the strong, pungent odor of the rain-starved grass and the weeds that choked it. It smelled like summer, like camping. Walt smiled at the sensation as he moved further into the field.

When he was a quarter of the way across, it occurred to him that his plan of attack was not a particularly good one. No matter how quietly he tried to move, his boots still clomped and rustled through the undergrowth. No wild animal in the world was likely to miss his approach.

He stopped when he reached the middle of the field and slumped his shoulders. This simply wasn't going to work. At the very least, he was going to need to set some traps—something else he didn't know anything about. If he was serious about netting some game, he figured a gun might also be a good idea. Something with a small caliber, like a .22. But he didn't want to blow any of the little creatures to smithereens. Whatever he did, the damned fire poker was a ridiculous idea from the start. Hunting small game was not akin to sneaking up on a burglar. Walt blew a short burst of air through his nostrils and groaned. There had to be better options.

And, of course, he'd already ruined the pet shop in town for a resource. The hippie bitch who ran the place was likely to chase him out of there with a broom if he tried stepping foot in there again. He shouldn't have been so single-minded in his approach. He should have been aware of how it was going to look if he treated that little excursion like what it really was: grocery shopping. But then, hindsight was 20/20, for whatever the hell that was worth.

The creature—if one could accurately call it that—was clearly satisfied with the kitten. It fed on the poor thing for the better part of an hour before letting its decimated remains drop to the floor. It was a beneficial meal, too; in the day since that feast, the thing on the ceiling had grown appreciably. It covered more surface area, but more interesting was the small, knobby bulge beside its one probing eye. Soon enough, it was going to be blessed with three-dimensional vision. That would require sustained sustenance though, and Walt just didn't have the heart to steal another kitten from the black cat in the woods. The thought of it made his stomach flip.

In the interim, after Amanda's unwelcome phone call had wakened him, he attempted a different tack. By then the thing started to let out irritating screeching sounds, like a dying magpie or something. It was hungry again and, Walt presumed, demanding more meat. So he went back into the kitchen, opened up the refrigerator, and searched for something that would suffice. What he settled on was a half-pound of rump steak that he planned to grill in the next day or two. After extracting the cold, red slab from the fridge and peeling away the plastic, he brought it to the hallway and held it up with both hands like some ancient priest offering a sacrifice to its raging deity.

The tendrils went wild when the lone eyeball caught sight of the meat, wriggling and stretching out toward it. The mouth stretched open, and from within its dark pit came the probing tongue, dripping with saliva.

*Ahhhhhg*, it went.

Walt stepped back at the sound of the unexpected moan. His scalp tingled and the muscles in his back bunched. All the same, he maintained his supplicant pose, the meat held high in the air. The shiny red strands poked and prodded at the surface of the cool, marbled slab. They seemed uncertain, but the slavering mouth would not be denied. The strands dug into the meat and coiled around it, snatching it out of Walt's hands. They retracted, yanking the steak toward its mouth. The tongue slapped against the meat and licked it from one end to the other. Then the short, nubby teeth sank into the offering. Walt smiled nervously.

The mouth then snapped open and shrieked. It let go of the meat as though it was on fire, letting it fall to the dirty hardwood floor with a resounding smack. Walt jumped back and gaped. The mouth went on shrieking while the tendrils furiously writhed and snapped. Dead meat was never going to sate the ravenous creature on the ceiling.

Hence the fire poker and hiking boots. But that, too, was turning out to be a wash. Walt moaned with exasperation as he resolved to tread back through the brush and weeds to his own property. He slashed at the grass with the heavy iron poker along the way, imagining that it was a machete and he was some intrepid pulp magazine explorer in the humid jungles of deepest, darkest Africa.

The reverie came to an abrupt end at the sound of a high-pitched squeal. He actually hit something.

Stunned, he knelt down in the tall grass and parted the growth where the end of the poker last struck. There lay a small brown rabbit, hardly bigger than the kitten, moving in desperate, rapid circles on its side. Walt stared at the suffering creature, noting the blood in its fur and the awkward way its leg twisted and jutted backward.

"Huh," he said. "Must have broken it."

He grinned abashedly. In an odd sort of way, he felt pity for the rabbit. He hadn't meant to strike it, even if he had come into the field for that very purpose in the first place. Still, there was nothing else for it, now. A wild rabbit with a broken back leg was as good as dead, anyway.

He seized the shivering animal by the scruff of its neck,

just as he had seized the kitten before it. He raised it up until it was eye-level with him. Its mouth hung open and its glossy black eyes glared at him with horror.

"Lucky me," Walt said.

"If it were me," he said cheerfully, "it'd be Brunswick stew. Oh, with fresh cornbread, too. But for you, my friend…"

The red, dripping jaws clamped down on the rabbit's neck, sending a crimson spray splashing against the wall.

"…you can have it rare. A rare hare. Ha, ha."

He grinned broadly as the young rabbit ceased its struggling and the mouth sucked at its bloody tendons and the soft, juicy organs beneath them. As he watched it feed, the round knob beside the creature's eye split open, finally revealing the other one. He saw that both irises were the same pale blue.

He also realized that among the thing's many writhing tendrils, two of them had grown thicker. These two did not wriggle as much as the others, a disability caused by the development of bony joints in the middle. At the ends of the two jointed limbs were several knobby appendages, red and pudgy, like skinless baby fingers. They wiggled, trying to find purchase in the rabbit's blood-matted fur.

Walt stared and smiled with his mouth open.

"My God," he rasped. "Would you look at that?"

Ignoring his wonder entirely, the feasting creature paused in its gorging long enough to moan with pleasure.

## 11

"You look like you need a drink," Nora said, a little too loud.

An old, blue-haired woman in the cooking section shot her a nasty look. Nora smiled.

"It's ten-thirty in the morning," Amanda reminded her.

"Well, I didn't mean right now. Unless it's that bad. Sometimes you really do need a stiff drink first thing."

"I sincerely hope you're joking."

Nora laughed and nudged Amanda with her hip.

"Come off it—I went to college with you, remember? I've seen you chug two liters of PBR through a surgical tube, and in your matching red underwear, no less."

The blue-hair resumed her disapproving stare. Amanda turned white, the blood having drained out of her face.

"Keep it down, will you please?"

"You sure had a full dance card that night, I'll tell you."

"With shockingly little supervisory guidance from you, as I recall."

"Hey, my card didn't look too shabby, either. I swapped so much spit that night, a cheek swab would have driven the lab tech crazy."

Amanda wrinkled her nose.

"You're repulsive."

"I do try."

"Have you had a blood test lately?"

"Why, are you afraid of catching something?"

Amanda shot her a cool glance.

"You're fired."

"At last!" Nora said. "I can finally get some damn peace and quiet!"

The blue-hair snorted with discontent and shuffled out of the store. Amanda and Nora watched her go and then looked at one another.

"Think she was going to buy anything?" Amanda asked.

"I don't know. She looked pretty cheap to me."

"How do you think she gets that particular shade of blue, anyway?"

"A hundred and fifty years of trial and error, I guess."

Amanda erupted into laughter. Nora tittered as she picked

up a clipboard from under the cash register and prepared to log in that week's new arrivals.

"Okie dokie," she said, "let's see how many erotic vampire novels we've got today."

"Only three this time," Amanda called as Nora moved toward the back room. "I already checked."

As Nora vanished, Amanda heard a dramatic groan reverberate throughout the store. She shook her head, inwardly echoing the sentiment. A moment later, the phone beside the cash register rang.

"In the Reads, this is Amanda."

"You lied," Nora growled through the receiver. "There's four of 'em."

"One of those is a back order."

"Are you serious? That's a customer we don't need."

"We need *every* customer, you snob. Besides, how is that junk any worse than the porn you read with shirtless studs in kilts on the covers?"

"Because I *like* that junk."

"Of course. Is that all?"

"Still waiting on an answer about that drink."

Amanda rolled her eyes for no one's benefit but her own and sighed into the phone.

"When?"

"Tonight, natch. After work."

"Where?"

"Why not Tiny's?"

"What, that dive off the interstate? Are you out of your mind?"

"Kidding, 'Manda, kidding. Jeez, lighten up, would you?"

"Not going to Tiny's."

"I said I was kidding, didn't I?"

"Fine," Amanda said. She was losing patience with the constant joking. Often it could go on all day and she would just keep laughing along with it, but not right now. "Where, then?"

"La Jolla's?"

"Okay. La Jolla's."

"Excellent. Oh, and Amanda?"

"What?"

*"She arched her back when Sebastian sank his fangs into the soft, white flesh of her neck. 'Make me,' Rebecca moaned. 'Make me like you, my love.'"*

"Hanging up now."

The receiver cracked an echo across the store.

Feeling grateful that he only had the one, Walt dumped his telephone in the kitchen wastebasket immediately after unplugging it. His most recent phone bill went in right after it. He might have phoned the telephone company and cancelled the service, but that would have required time on the phone, speaking to some disembodied voice that couldn't give any more of a damn about him than he could about it. Besides, the damned thing had been ringing night and day. It couldn't possibly have always been Amanda. Surely she had neither the time nor the inclination to ring Walt thirty times a day. He presumed a small percentage of the calls had come from telemarketers, while others almost certainly originated from the school, or from his mortgage company, or from one of his egregiously disagreeable relatives. His spinster aunt, Janet, or his sister, Sarah. He didn't want to speak with any of them. He did not want to speak with anyone at all.

The only thing Walt wanted to do was build up enough courage to climb up into the attic to assess the state of things from that side of the ceiling.

The creature—which he had come to think of as his roommate—was getting testy with him. He tried to empathize; after all, he didn't know anybody who *didn't* get a little grouchy when their bellies were grumbling. But the roommate's belly (wherever *that* was) was always grumbling. Nothing sated it. When it finished with the rabbit, it let the teeth-scarred bones drop to the floor one by one before launching into that awful, ear-splitting screeching again. It wanted more. *Needed* more. Walt was not at all sure how to proceed.

On the one hand, he wondered how and why he should feel responsible for the thing's well-being. He hadn't put it there; he hadn't even invited it. It was Walt's house, he paid for it. Any other unanticipated visitor of another species would have been met with a stomping heel, a spray of poison or a call to the nearest exterminator. Conversely, he'd already begun to take care of his new roommate. It was a ball in motion, rolled down the infinite hill by his own hand and initiative. At this point, how could he possibly stop? That would be too much like taking in a stray dog and then suddenly refusing to feed it. Cruel. Inhumane, even. No, Walt *was* responsible for it now, whether he liked it or not. It was practically a binding agreement.

He started pacing, unconsciously wringing his hands like a worried mother. He crossed the length of the kitchen, doubled back and rounded the living room into the dining room. Then he returned and did it all over again, all the while thinking about his relationship with the roommate. At first, he labeled it symbiotic, but that was not exactly right. In symbiosis, both organisms stood to benefit mutually from the exchange, whereas Walt could determine no particular gain to be had. It wasn't truly parasitic, either; although the creature certainly seemed the parasite to him, he recognized that it had been his own choice to begin feeding the thing in the first place. In the end, Walt decided that his relationship with the roommate was rather more akin to a hermit crab and its shell—a relationship in which one of the parties is significantly helped while the other is neither helped nor harmed.

*Commensalism.* That was it.

Although pedantically naming the biological type of bond he shared with the thing on the ceiling did nothing with regard to allaying his fears and doubts, Walt felt better for having done so. Reenergized, he strode back to the hallway and peered up at the thing. It pulsed and wiggled, per usual. It searched the immediate area with its wide, blue eyes. And all but two of its tendrils seemed to be retracting into its main mass—all but the two that were beginning to look like arms.

"You're growing up," he said to it.

*Ahhhhhg,* it replied.

Walt curled his lip, caught between fascination and disgust. He then decided it was time to have a look in the attic.

La Jolla's was a sprawling bar and restaurant in the so-called warehouse district, just on the periphery of what passed for a downtown. It had no parking of its own, just perpetually unavailable street parking, so Amanda and Nora arrived in a taxi. They presented their respective drivers' licenses to the indifferent doorman, shuffled inside and worked through the crowd to the bar. Top 40 hits pounded from the speakers built into the walls and ceiling, rending conversation nearly impossible. Nora had to scream her choice of drink at the bartender.

*"Two Fuck Faces!"* she yelled as loud as she could.

Amanda blanched. Noting this, Nora gave her a wink and a coy smile. The multi-pierced bartender nodded and got to work. A few moments later, she presented two double shot glasses filled to the rims with dark liquid, a thin green straw floating in each of them. Nora slapped a credit card on the bar, told the girl to keep it open, and grabbed the drinks. Amanda took hers and followed as Nora cut through the dense throng of drunks and college kids.

When they reached the back patio, Amanda wobbled her head. The music was significantly quieter there, but her ears continued to throb from the ridiculous volume inside. Nora selected a well-weathered picnic table perpendicular to the surrounding green fence and sat down. Amanda followed suit.

"A third Wild Turkey, a third Jack, and a third dark rum," Nora said as she held up her glass. "Three fluid ounces of throat-burning, ass-kicking delight."

She took a sip, gasped and then let out a roar.

"Yow! Knock your socks off, sister."

Amanda glared suspicious at hers.

"No chaser?"

"Don't be such a pansy."

Amanda frowned and raised the glass to her lips. After her initial sip, her eyes bulged and began watering up.

"God in heaven!" she gasped.

"Good, huh?"

"Good? What the hell is your definition of good?"

"This," Nora replied.

She then dumped what remained in her shot glass down her throat. Amanda gawked.

"Good for what ails ya," Nora said. "So, what ails ya?"

"What do you mean?"

"What do you mean, what do I mean? I figure it's gotta be Walt, so what's up his ass? Or yours? What's the scoop?"

Amanda dug a crumpled pack of Benson & Hedges out of the front pocket of her jeans and lit one up. She drew long and hard at the filter, sucked the smoke deep into her lungs and then tilted her head back to blow it up into the air.

"I'm not altogether sure," she said at length.

"I knew it. What'd he do, stick it where it don't belong?"

"I'm not even going to ask what you mean by that. And no, he's just…"

"Just what?"

"Strange, I guess."

"He's always sounded strange to me."

"I'd have to start at the beginning."

"Then why don't you do that?"

"Because I didn't figure on an interrogation when you invited me out for drinks, that's why."

Nora arched an eyebrow and pursed her lips.

"Gimme one of those," she said as she seized Amanda's pack of cigarettes.

Nora lit the cigarette, but she only smoked superficially, drawing a little into her mouth before blowing it out again. A social smoker.

"It's too weird," Amanda said quietly between drags.

Nora furrowed her brow and then gently placed a hand over Amanda's.

"Tell me," Nora said.

Amanda puffed out her cheeks.

"He's got this new house, you know?"

"Sure, the Gablefront cottage. You told me."

"Right. Well. Just after he moved in, we find this dark stain on the ceiling, on the hallway ceiling. Maybe about so big." She made a ring with both hands, estimating the original size of the stain.

"Okay," Nora said. "Water damage?"

"That's what we thought. But he had a plumber out and everything, there was no leakage, not there anyway. It definitely wasn't a water stain, but it kept getting bigger. Getting worse.

"Eventually, it was dripping all over the floor. Thick, red gunk. Really nasty. And no matter where he looked, he couldn't find the source. He checked the attic, dug up the paneling and everything. It didn't come from anywhere. It was just there."

Amanda paused to suck down the last of her cigarette. She stubbed it out in the black plastic ashtray on the picnic table, then fished another one from the pack and lit it.

"Are you fixing to tell me you broke up over a leak?"

"We're not broken up. At least, I don't think we are."

"Okay," Nora said with a flourish of her hand. "Continue."

"Walt was getting sort of...I don't know, *distant*, I guess is the word. Daydreamy, kind of off in his own world. And the stain kept getting bigger. Bigger and more gross—and the worse it got, the less he seemed to care about it."

"You've never lived with a guy. I've got three brothers, babe. Their dog could shit on the living room rug and the bastards still need to be told to clean it up."

"Not Walt. He's a tidy guy, really. Everything has its place. Maybe he's even a little anal retentive. But that thing up there, he was definitely more interested in it than repulsed. Then, the last night I stayed with him, I saw it..."

Here she trailed off, bringing her brows into a tight knit and staring at the red glow at the tip of her cigarette.

"Saw it what? Spit it out."

"It ate a roach, Nora. It actually reached out and *ate* a roach. I don't know what that thing is, but it's alive."

"Nasty."

"This from a chick who plays with spiders."

"Spiders aren't nasty. But that is."

"It had, I don't know, tentacles, sort of. Thin, wiggly little things."

She shuddered. Nora screwed up her face and narrowed her eyes.

"Tubifex," she said plainly.

"What?"

"Hundred bucks says its tubifex. It's a worm. A while back, some city workers found something in the sewer over in North Carolina, pretty much exactly like what you're talking about. A huge, pulsing red mass just clinging to the walls of the sewer. Of course, everybody freaks out, calls it a monster. But it was just a worm colony."

"A worm colony?"

"Yup. Still kind of gross, but perfectly ordinary. Walt's got himself a pretty old house, I gather. Loads of mold, decaying wood, shit like that. Even without a leak those old houses tend to be pretty damp. I'll bet those little wormies are just snug as a bug in a rug in there."

"But it reached out and grabbed that cockroach, Nora."

"Worms, babe."

"Worms eat roaches?"

"Hell if I know. Maybe it only looked that way. Maybe the roach just got caught in the mass."

"Maybe," Amanda said uncertainly.

"Hundred bucks says it is. And here you're all heartsick over a bunch of dumb worms."

"You forgot about his attitude," Amanda reminded her.

"Did you—gee, I dunno—*talk* to him about that?"

"I screamed and ran out of the house after the thing with the roach."

Nora stared at her with wide eyes and an open mouth.

"You're an idiot."

"I'm an idiot."

"A colossal idiot."

"Huge."

Amanda's throat constricted, but she laughed in spite of it.

"Worms, you say."

"Probably a hundred thousand of 'em, yeah."

"I thought..."

"You thought it was a monster, and that it was *controlling Walt's mind!*"

Nora wiggled her fingers at Amanda and whistled the theme from *The Twilight Zone.* Amanda slapped at her.

"Oh, goddamnit," she croaked.

Nora smiled sweetly at her and stood up from the table.

"I'm going to go get another round. You can figure out how to fix this while I'm gone, all right?"

"Just no more Fuck Face for me."

"Two Gorilla Farts, coming up!" cried Nora as she marched back into the bar.

Amanda shook her head and crushed her half-smoked cigarette in the tray. *Worms*, she thought ruefully. *What have I done?*

For the time being, she had forgotten what Walt said about the rats.

The face was vaguely human, but not quite. *Humanoid.* It had eyes, part of a nose—a bony septum, at least. There was a mouth full of teeth that looked longer, closer together. And, of course, the tiny, stubby fingers that perpetually wiggled at the ends of its nascent arms. All of it still dripping, ever dripping, from its blood red surface.

The mouth had been rhythmically opening and closing for some time now. Initially, Walt assumed it was conveying its insatiable appetite, a fact for which he needed no reminding. Taken from another perspective, however, it also looked as though the creature was trying to speak. If he were a lip-reader, Walt might have determined the thing was attempting to say *ba, ba, ba.*

But that made no sense at all.

He dragged a stool from the kitchen to the hallway and silently observed his roommate for a while. He studied every minute detail of its skinless face and found that the longer he looked at it, the more human it appeared to become. He thought about its other end as well, the side that stuck out from the paneling in the attic. From that point of view, Walt discovered, the creature did not look human. Not remotely. There was only the gargantuan pod, run through with twisting, branching arteries and every bit as blood red as the face on the ceiling below.

Walt preferred the view from below. The constant movement of the mouth was somewhat disquieting, but he yearned to decode its silent message if one was to be found.

"I know you're hungry," he said apologetically. "I'm working on it. It's not as easy as it probably looks."

*Ba, ba, ba,* it mimed. It didn't pause while Walt spoke.

"Are you in pain?"

"*Ahhhhhhg,*" the mouth moaned, finally breaking the rhythm. Its tongue hung slack, unable to support the desperate need to communicate.

"What do you *need*?"

"*Buhwuhhhh,*" the creature replied. Thick strands of saliva dropped out of its mouth and splashed against Walt's pants. He didn't so much as flinch. He was far too preoccupied with uncovering the meaning behind the thing's plaintive groans.

"You'll never speak letting your tongue droop like that," he reprimanded it. "You've got it. Use it."

"*Bwuhhhhhhh.*"

Walt sighed heavily. He wondered which was going to require the most patience: his ninth graders in the fall, or the babbling entity in the ceiling.

"Bwub," he mimicked. Then, rising and grabbing the stool by its round, worn seat, he said, "Keep it up, then. You'll get there."

He dragged the stool back to the kitchen and decided to put some coffee on. *Let the old roomie ramble incoherently,* he thought. *I'll take my coffee on the porch and pore over some Coleridge.*

Indeed, the jabbering mouth went on with its gibberish, even as Walt shut the front door to block out the noise. After a few minutes of *Frost at Midnight*, the creature finally began to make noises that sounded like actual words. He was dimly aware of the thing's ongoing chatter, but only in its capacity as white noise. If he was unable to shut out meaningless prattle, after all, he would never make it as a schoolteacher.

Still, the incessant reminder of the creature's proximity

made it difficult for him to focus on the text in his hand. Every few lines, he found his mind wandering toward the troublesome question of keeping his new tenant in food. Sure, he could set any number of little traps out in the field behind his house, but even rabbits and moles were bound to catch on eventually. There had to be other pet shops in town, but how long would it take before they figured out what he was doing and put a call in to the ASPCA? And would that amount to a misdemeanor and a hefty fine, or a felony with a prison sentence? Were he to go to prison, there would be no one to feed the creature. *The roommate.*

He set the book down on the rocking chair and took his mug back into the house. Placing it on the kitchen counter beside the coffee maker, he pulled the carafe out and refilled the cup. He was about to turn toward the freezer for an ice cube to cool his coffee when the next utterance of the increasingly troublesome thing in the hall startled him, causing him to swing his hand and knock the mug off the counter. It sailed across the kitchen, spraying steaming black coffee across the linoleum before smashing into the floor and exploding into a thousand tiny ceramic shards. Walt gasped, gulping for air. His heart slammed in his chest and his face flushed.

Had he heard what he thought he'd heard?

He craned his neck and cautiously tiptoed over the warm, wet floor, careful not to step on any of the jagged shards in his bare feet. When he reached the archway between the kitchen and the hall, he gazed up at the ceiling.

The creature's eyes darted toward him, wide and shimmering. It parted its lips, licked them with the tip of its tongue and then groaned.

"*Bloooood,*" it said.

# 12

The sun sat at just the right angle to blast the porch with light and heat. It looked stark white, its edges blurry, wavering and indistinct. The sky in which it floated was the same hot white, and there were no clouds. The heat had burned them all up.

Walt sat still in the rocking chair, moving only to occasionally wipe the slick sweat from his forehead. The heat was getting to be unbearable, but he knew it was always worst at the end of the summer, right before the first cool of autumn finally swept in to relieve the suffering. He longed for a cold glass of water, but he lacked the initiative to get up and go get one. Besides, he promised himself he would not return to face *it* before he had a solution to their little problem.

He spent the morning back in the field behind his house, looking for critters to catch and bleed dry. Unfortunately for Walt, his luck from the previous trip did not hold. The rabbit was a boon, an unlikely fluke that was not to be repeated in the near future. Nevertheless, he strode through the tall, scratchy grass, scanning every square foot of the field and coming up completely empty. The only life he detected consisted of the black birds in the treetops and the stocky man in a red plaid shirt shambling through the reeds toward him.

The man raised a thick arm in greeting as he gradually drew nearer to Walt, who remained as still as a mannequin. When only a few yards stretched between them, Walt could make out the man's grizzled, deeply lined face and the shock of thick white hair that seemed to burst out of his scalp like fire.

"Hullo there!" the man shouted.

Walt nodded and gave a weak wave.

"Dudley," the man said breathlessly as he closed the gap. "Dudley Chapel." He shoved a flattened hand out. Reluctantly, Walt accepted the handshake.

"Walt Blackmore," he muttered.

"Reckon you bought the Shelton house back 'ere, am I right?"

Dudley released his hand and pointed. Walt followed the trajectory of Dudley's gnarled finger with his eyes. The older man was pointing at his new house.

"Shelton?"

"That's right. Darryl and Imelda Shelton lived in that house...oh, I'd say twenty years if a day. Well, Imelda, anyway—Darryl passed on some time back. She wasn't never the same after that, poor girl. 'Course, I been in mine for twice that long, but I'm just an old-timer."

"I see," Walt said in a half-whisper.

"Figure I'm your closest neighbor, on account of my place is three quarters of a mile up and over the hill, there." He turned his pointing finger in the opposite direction. Walt squinted. "You can't even see the hill from here, can you? Yep, and I'm the closest."

Walt said, "Huh."

"Seems I heard some rumblings about your place finally getting bought up, but I didn't come 'round to snoop. No sir, I'm just getting the blood moving. Don't do it near often enough. And I seen you in the field here, so I says to myself, I says, Dudley, you ought to go introduce yourself to that young man. So here I am!"

Walt fought to turn his genuine sneer into an entirely counterfeit smile.

"Glad you did, Mr. Chapel," he lied.

"Through them woods, over the hill; right at the bottom, that's my property. Used to be a working farm, but that was parceled up and sold off years ago. Big red house with white shutters, can't miss it."

Walt nodded some more and wondered when the annoying old man was going to go away.

"Any time you get the hankering to drop in," Dudley

continued, "I'm sure me and the missus would be just as happy as clams to have you in for a sit."

"I sure appreciate that, Mr. Chapel."

"And knock off that Mr. Chapel stuff, youngster! I'm Dudley, you hear?"

A huge grin spread across Dudley's face, exposing clean white dentures.

"I hear you, Dudley."

With that, the old man sauntered back in the direction from which he came, stopping only to yell back at Walt: "See you soon, Walt!"

Walt sincerely hoped that would not be the case.

Hours later, he remained empty-handed on the prey front and bereft of ideas. Dazed from the early afternoon heat, he drifted in and out of half-sleep in the chair on his porch, his mind wandering over the surface of the quandary but never quite landing on anything. He was nearly dreaming when a loud, high-pitched whine sounded in his left ear, snapping him awake. He wiggled his fingers in the ear, shooing the annoying insect away, but as soon as he returned his hand to his lap the bug returned, buzzing more frenetically than ever. Walt swatted with greater intensity and shook his head. The insect buzzed away. He let out a long, relieved breath and relaxed. But he was fully awake now. And the problem remained.

He pulled himself up and out of the chair, groaning and stretching. Somewhere in the far distance a dog barked. He wondered what time it was. Glancing at his wrist, he frowned at the white band of skin where his watch normally hung. He then narrowed his eyes at the mosquito further up on his forearm, frozen in place with its proboscis injected deep into his skin. With his other hand, he slapped the mosquito, squashing it. A tiny red streak dotted with crushed bits of black was all that remained on his skin. He tilted his head, avoiding the bright sunlight as he raised his arm for a closer inspection.

He wished he hadn't smashed the mosquito at all. A little blood was not so much to give, not to a creature that required it to survive.

Walt smiled. He went back inside.

The knife was sharp, but not exactly ideal. A carbon steel tourne knife, it had been part of a set Walt received as a Christmas gift from his sister, Sarah, some years back. To his recollection, he had never used it. He was not even sure he knew what a tourne knife was for.

Sharp as the blade was, he longed for something more appropriate. A scalpel would be the thing, but where did one get a scalpel? An art supply store, he supposed. He was relatively certain he had seen such instruments at the art shop in Madison, back in his college days when he decided to give painting a shot. But was it really worth the effort to drive clear into town for a blade that was probably no sharper than the one in his hand? Walt concluded that it was not. Then he began cutting.

The point of the knife made an indentation on his arm. The skin sank in, forming straight, thin wrinkles that arched down to the whitening nexus of the dimple. Walt applied a little more pressure and the skin broke. The indent welled up with dark blood more quickly than he expected. He pulled the knife away and watched the thick, round blob rapidly grow, burst and then trickle down his arm. He brought his brows together and wrinkled his nose. It really wasn't all that much. He was going to have to cut deeper.

Returning the point of the knife to the tiny wound, he pressed harder than before, digging a centimeter into the flesh. He winced at the burning sensation of his skin being cut apart. It was even worse when he began sawing at it, rhythmically moving the knife through the meat in a straight line toward his elbow. Now the wine-dark fluid really started to flow. He hurried, suppressing a scream and dropping the bloody knife on the counter, and he snatched up the transparent plastic bowl beside it. The blood ran down the deep canal he made with the tourne knife, welled up at the terminus of the wound, and then spilled out in fat droplets into the bowl. When the flow slowed to an infrequent trickle, Walt set the bowl on the counter and squeezed the injured forearm, forcing the blood out. The pain was sharp and intense; he hissed and whined throughout the procedure.

Behind him, in the hallway, a raspy voice moaned, "*Blood...*"

"I'm working on it, goddamnit," Walt groused.

The opening stopped giving, its dark red edges already drying, scabbing up. He ran the kitchen faucet and held his forearm under it, susurrating through his teeth at the agony of cold water on an open wound. When he couldn't take any more, he turned the water off and shifted his gaze to the bowl of blood on the counter. It didn't look like much. Surely his roommate got more sustenance from the kitten and the rabbit. He pursed his lips, picked up the bowl and examined it. The viscous liquid sloshed against the side, leaving a thick red trail.

"*Blood...*"

Walt grunted. The straws were in the utensil drawer; he found the box and extracted one. He dropped it into the bowl, carried it to the hallway. He looked up. The pale eyes stared at him, the mouth sucked at the air. Walt hoped it would be enough. With one hand—the one not attached to a freshly cut arm—he cupped the bowl and lifted it up. The straw shifted, rounding the edge before settling against the dark, bloody lips. The creature's mouth smacked at the straw, opening and shutting against its end as though it had no idea how such a thing might work. It gave a low, frustrated moan and then reached out with wobbling arms, curling its pudgy red fingers under the base of the bowl. Walt let go, startled and amazed by the new appearance of stubby little nails at the tips of the fingers.

The arms bent at the elbows, drawing the bowl close to the face. Its tongue darted out, flicked the straw away. It spun through the air, ejecting a couple of drops of Walt's hard-earned blood in the process. The creature then extended its shiny tongue as far as it would go and commenced lapping up the blood. Soft moans of satisfaction accompanied the sharp smacking sounds of the tongue licking up the warm, fresh fluid. When it finished and the bowl was virtually clean, it dropped the dish and let it tumble across the floor.

"*Goooood,*" it rasped.

Walt stared.

"Good," he whispered in reply.

"*More.*"

"More? I can't give you any more! That was my own blood, you know."

"*More!*" the thing hissed.

"I haven't *got* any more!"

The creature's eyes shimmered, its two black pits of a nose twitching. Thrusting its arms at Walt and snatching at him with its infant fingers, it roared.

"*Give...more! MoremoremoremoreMORE!*"

Walt quickly backed out of the hallway and into the kitchen. The tiny, misshapen hands continued grabbing at the air. The snarling, dripping mouth continued to shriek and roar.

"Christ," he gasped. "Oh Christ. Jesus."

He kept moving backward, too afraid to turn his back on the hallway despite his relative certainty that the thing was well-rooted to the ceiling. He felt something nudge his hip. He yelped and leaped to one side, knocking the stool that bumped him on its side with a noisy clatter. His eyes jumped from the stool to the hall. The creature was no longer visible from where he stood. But its dreadful, keening demands still filled the air.

"*MOREMOREMOREMOREMORE!*"

"Stop it!" Walt screamed, slamming his open hands over his ears.

*"MOREMOREMORE..."*

"Shut up! Shut the hell up!"

*"MOREMOREMORE! BLOOD! BLOOOOOD!"*

Walt screeched, partly with terror and partly with rage. He started this, he was the one who fed it first, allowed it to develop and grow and become this screaming horror. He recognized his responsibility, but for what? Was he responsible for maintaining its terrible existence, or for annihilating it before the situation spiraled wildly out of his control?

Sweat beaded his brow as he sank down to the cool linoleum floor, careful to keep his hands over his ears. He could still hear that thing's awful, incessant shrieking, but it was at least a little better this way. He could begin thinking. First he thought about the kitten, the repulsive and depraved death that innocent creature met at Walt's own choosing. The rabbit—being the central point of his next thought—was not as bad. People ate rabbits. But not kittens. That was purely reprehensible, and now he worried that the guilt would hound him for the rest of his days. It could have been worse, he realized, much worse. And should he decide to permit this hellish monster to live, he imagined it very definitely would. This was only going to escalate, growing bloodier and bloodier, until...

Walt felt a shudder work its way through his body, terminating in his ear canals. Slowly, he slid his hands down. The shrieking seemed to have quieted somewhat. That, or he was already growing accustomed to it.

*Well,* he thought, *not for long. If it's got a face, it's got a brain. And a brain is no match for a claw hammer.*

There was no question in Walt's mind that the creature felt pain. Nothing screeched like that unless it was in agony. But it didn't know the meaning of agony, not yet. Walt pulled himself up to his feet, curled his hands into tight fists, and went in search of his hammer.

## 13

Thin strips of light sliced through the blinds, several of them jabbing into Amanda's fluttering eyelids. She opened them, blinked repeatedly. Tiny motes of dust floated where the yellow-white slats cut through, but not in the shadows in between. She narrowed her eyes at them, enjoying the warmth but not the brightness. Rolling over on her side, she turned away and faced the digital alarm clock beside the bed. For a fraction of a second, she felt panicked; it was a quarter to ten, far too late in the morning to get to the shop on time. But she relaxed at the faint memory of Nora's promise to get the store running alone.

"Sleep in," she'd demanded last night. "Enjoy your coffee, read the paper, and call Walt when you feel up to it. Then call a goddamned exterminator. Those worms are pretty disgusting."

Amanda smiled, stretched, let out a quiet yawn. That Nora was a hell of a gal. Bat-shit crazy, but an incredibly loyal and valuable friend. While she gradually lifted herself up from the warmth and comfort of her bed, she considered options for demonstrating her gratitude. Her usual thank you gift was a book, but that was out. You don't give a book to someone who co-owns a bookstore. Flowers were normally appreciated, but Nora wasn't really the type for things that required perpetual attention. Amanda knitted her brow and shuffled to the bathroom. She peed, nearly falling asleep on the toilet.

Her mind felt sticky and sluggish. No decisions were going to be made until after the first cup of coffee, and maybe not until the second. She bobbed and weaved into the kitchen, like a punch-drunk zombie boxer, and set to getting the life-sustaining liquid brewing.

*Walt*, her sleep addled mind kept repeating. *Walt. Walt's worms. My apology.*

She only hoped it was going to be good enough.

The hammer didn't feel particularly heavy in Walt's hand. It was the very same hammer he'd used for the various repairs the old cottage required, and it was perfectly adequate for those needs. But now that he demanded a different job of the instrument—the job of bludgeoning a living being to death—it somehow felt slight, almost airy. As though he meant to kill a man with a feather.

But this was no man he aimed to kill. And, despite his apprehensions regarding the tool in his hand, it was most certainly no feather. *He* certainly wouldn't like to get smacked in the head with it. Which was just going to have to do.

For his own good. For Amanda. For them both.

Tightening his grip on the hammer's black rubber handle, he went to the hallway.

Her third cup of the morning—or, her first of the afternoon—went into her steel travel mug. With any luck, things would go well enough at Walt's that her fourth would be poured from his own stash of coffee. His tended to be a little fancier, anyway. Whole bean, dark roast. Stout stuff, but she liked it. Amanda swallowed a mouthful of her tepid store-brand brew and turned the key in the ignition. Then, with an anxious sigh, she began her journey to the boonies, to Walt's house.

## 14

The creature's face twisted up, its mouth curled into a savage sneer. Walt was not pleased to realize it was sort of nodding, a new development. It didn't matter, not really. Not in the long run.

The top of the stepstool was slick and shiny from the blood and slobber that rained down from the thing's snarling face and creepy little hands. Walt climbed up and raised the hammer, blunt end facing out. The creature growled, baring its dull, white teeth.

"I'm sorry," Walt said softly.

He reared back and swung the hammer. Its head crashed into the thing's brow, just above the left eye. Bone splintered, caved in. Blood sprayed Walt's face. It felt hot on his skin and tasted coppery on his lips.

The creature squealed, its eye sinking and drooping down. Walt yanked the hammer out of its head and sent it crashing back down, this time nailing the right temple.

"*Aaaauuuuggggghhh*," the creature bellowed.

So much for *more, more, more*. Its speech center was probably obliterated. A few more whacks ought to do it.

Walt ground his teeth together and slammed the hammer into the shiny red face again and again and again. With each impact, he groaned and the creature hollered and blood spurted all over the walls and ceiling and Walt himself. When he was done, there was nothing about the mass above that might remind an observer of anything even vaguely human. All that remained was a pulpy red mess, dripping with gory strings and jutting chunks of pink bone.

The creature, the *parasite*, was dead; Walt was certain of that. But his work was not yet done. There was still the matter of cleaning it all out, the ceiling and the attic, and then pulling up the paneling and knocking out the ruined plaster. He was going to rebuild it, paint it, make it good as new. And then try to forget all about the nightmare monster he had lived with the first few weeks in his new house.

After he climbed back down the stepstool, Walt examined

his front. He was splattered red from his chest and shoulders all the way down to his stomach. His arms were slick with the blood, and he knew his face had to be a sight as well. But there was no sense in cleaning up now, not before the grisly job of scraping the carcass off the ceiling and digging out the rest from the attic. That awful pod.

He frowned deeply. It would never have gotten this bad if he hadn't facilitated the process, exacerbated the problem. Unconsciously, he mopped his forehead with the back of his hand, effectively smearing blood with blood. He imagined he must look like Jack the Ripper, dripping with gore like he was. He gave a short laugh and resolved to at least wash his face before he progressed any further.

He had only just turned on the water in the bathroom sink when there came a pounding on the front door.

He jumped.

"No," he whispered. "Not now."

The knocking went on. His hands were shaking, the rest of him trembling almost as badly. Steam rose in white pillars from the sink; he tested the temperature with one finger and quickly withdrew it. The water was scalding. He turned down the hot knob and turned the cold knob up. Quickly he rinsed his face, checked it in the fogged mirror, and rinsed again. Leaving it to drip dry, he went out to the hall and paused.

There were only so many people among the list of possible visitors. For Walt, it broke down to Amanda, or not Amanda. If it was Amanda, then the blood that covered him was not necessarily the worst possible thing. She would be shocked, revolted even, but in the end he knew that she would be relieved. After all, it was the parasite that had been the problem all along.

On the other hand, it might be not Amanda. Someone else. In which case he could not possibly have cared less. Let them be offended, sickened, afraid. He couldn't please everybody all the time.

He steeled himself and strode toward the door. The pounding continued unabated.

"I'm coming!"

He drew the guard chain, unlatched it, and twisted the deadbolt before opening the door.

It was not Amanda.

Jarred from the bumpy drive down Highway 5, Amanda was relieved when Walt's nice, flat driveway came into view.

Her relief rapidly dissolved when the strange green SUV also floated into her field of vision. It was parked beside Walt's station wagon, its windows rolled halfway down, as if whoever was driving it did not expect to stay long enough to worry about it. Or, she considered, perhaps it meant that they *did* intend to spend a spell with Walt, and they were protecting their big green gas-guzzler from the stifling heat.

She pulled in behind the SUV, threw the stick into park, and then reconsidered. She had no idea what she was about to walk into, but the driver of the mystery car might require a quick escape. So she pulled back out, turned the wheel, and pulled in behind Walt's station wagon. From that position, she had a direct line of sight to his front door. It was standing wide open.

She narrowed her eyes, cut the engine. And she waited.

## 15

Tall and reedy, she looked like she might have been a rather pretty girl before a superfluous growth spurt stretched her past beauty and straight into awkwardness. Her straight brown hair probably went to her ass when she let it down, but she wore it in a conservative Protestant bun instead. Complementing that were her enormous eyeglasses and drab brown attire: a long-sleeved blouse buttoned to the neck and an ankle-length skirt. She was the picture of Victorian temperance.

She was also offended, sickened and afraid, just as Walt predicted.

"Muh—Mister, uh..." she stammered, her eyes wide and staring from behind the thick lenses.

"Ah," Walt said with a forced smile. "Miss Stuben, right?"

She nodded, very slightly, in agreement that she was. Margaret Stuben, as she was originally introduced to him, the vice-principal under Principal Byrne, the reigning honcho at Bowman High School and Walt's new boss. Whether or not Miss Stuben was his superior too, he wasn't entirely sure. But in any event, his blood-spattered state was unlikely to do well toward a good impression on the established higher-ups. As Miss Stuben's mouth gradually closed into a disapproving grimace, Walt's smile melted away. He recalled his first tour of the administrative offices at the school, Byrne guiding him past Stuben's office, where a simple brass crucifix was affixed to the wall above her desk. Hardly the norm for public schools, but he asked no questions and offered no remarks. He had the distinct impression that where Margaret Stuben was considered, ignorance was bliss.

"What's happened?" she asked.

She now wore an expression of bemusement. But the fear had not dissolved, not completely. By way of explanation, Walt lifted his right hand, using the hammer to point behind him. It came up so fast that Miss Stuben let out a frightened squeal and jumped back from what she momentarily thought might be an attack.

Walt gave a nervous chuckle.

"I had...a little problem. Please," he said gently, stepping aside. "Come in. I'll just change my shirt."

She cocked her head to one side, a quizzical look on her face not unlike that of a puzzled dog. But when he disappeared beyond the kitchen, she resumed her harsh look and went into the house, leaving the door open behind her. She was halfway across the kitchen when a car rumbled onto the concrete driveway outside, too far away for her to hear it.

"We've…uh…been trying to reach you by phone, Mister…uh…"

Stuben stepped cautiously over the linoleum tiles, her flats making quiet scratching sounds.

"Mister, uh… *Walter*?"

At the end of the kitchen where the white linoleum shared a border with the dark hardwood that floored most of the house, Stuben stopped and wrinkled her nose. There was a sickly-sweet metallic odor in the air. It was not pleasant. Prepared to investigate further, she took a few steps into the dark hall beyond when Walt popped out of the shadows, naked to the waist.

Miss Stuben yelped.

"Oh," he said. "Sorry, I was just, you know."

He held up a clean white T-shirt, smiled, and then put it on.

"I wasn't exactly expecting company," he said. "Come on, let's go in the kitchen. I've got iced tea, coffee. I can Irish it up for you if you like. It is summer, after all; no school tomorrow."

He placed his hands on Miss Stuben's shoulders to guide her back into the kitchen. She wriggled away from him, her mouth a straight line of stern censure.

"I can find the kitchen, thank you."

"Yeah, of course."

"And a glass of water will be just fine."

"Okay," Walt said. "Water, then."

He gestured toward the stool that was upended on the floor. With an arched eyebrow, Stuben bent over and righted it before sitting down. Walt poured two glasses from the tap and handed one to her.

"Nothing's gone wrong, I hope." Walt said.

"Wrong? Why, no. What do you mean?"

"I don't know. Like I didn't get the position after all, or something like that."

"Certainly not. It's only that we've called—well, *I've* called—for days. It just rings, so naturally..."

"You thought you'd drop by to make sure I still wanted the position."

Miss Stuben dropped her head a little, looking very much the child caught with her hand in the cookie jar. Walt laughed.

"No need to worry about anything like that," he assured her. "I've bought an old house is all. Wonky wiring. Nothing seems to work quite right, but rest assured—the phone company has been notified."

"Wiring," Miss Stuben dumbly repeated. "Well, of course."

"That's it."

"Then you can still be expected to attend the parent-teacher night? It's a week from Thursday, you know."

"I haven't forgotten," he lied. He had forgotten entirely. But watching the long-faced almost-beauty taking tiny sips from the edge of the water glass made him likely to say anything. She may have been a throwback prude and religious zealot, but he didn't think she was too terrible to look at.

"You'll be in attendance, then? It isn't exactly compulsory, but I should think being a new teacher and all..."

"Yes, of course I'll be there. Wouldn't miss it."

His thick attempt at charm did anything but disarm Miss Stuben. Instead, she seemed to retreat even further into herself, setting the glass on the counter and tightly crossing her arms over her small bosom.

"Fine," she said sharply. "In that case, would you please call the school the moment your phone line is working again? Mr. Byrne would like to know."

"As would you, I'm sure."

Miss Stuben rose and revolved her shoulders, as though

sitting on the stool had wreaked havoc on them.

"Thank you for the water, Mister Blackwell."

"*Blackmore.* Walter Blackmore. Call me Walt, though."

"Walt," she said with some unease.

With that, she turned toward the open door. Walt watched her as she strode toward it, forced to imagine the moving curves hidden beneath the awkward, draping folds of her conservative skirt. When the anguished moaning erupted behind him, his mind managed to ignore it completely, if only for a second. Miss Stuben, contrarily, spun around and stared.

"Are you all right?" she said.

"Hmm?"

"I, well...you—"

The moan went on, and despite her furrowed brow and glassy eyes, Stuben was gradually putting the pieces together. It was not Walt who had moaned.

"Who's back there? What's wrong with them?"

Walt's dreamy look sank into an aggravated frown. His right cheek twitched. He wasn't sure if he was terrified or enraged. He was both.

The thing, the monster in his house, was still alive. Worse, it proved to have tentacles of another kind; an invisible variety that wound their way into all other aspects of his life.

"It's nothing," he said.

"No," Miss Stuben insisted, striding back toward him. "There's somebody back there. I thought I smelled something. What's going on? What have you got going here, Mr. Blackmore?"

"Walt," he corrected her.

"I think I'd better have a look," she said plainly as she whisked right by him.

He stretched at her, seizing her by one arm and yanking her back like an impetuous child.

"Don't!" he shouted.

"Let go of me!"

Miss Stuben snapped her arm free of his grip and marched quickly into the hallway. Then she screamed.

# 16

Amanda stabbed a spent butt into the ashtray with one hand while she reached for the pack with the other. It would have been the third cigarette she smoked while waiting in Walt's driveway, but the scream that sliced through the house put a stop to that.

She jerked, dropping the unlit cigarette on the rubber mat under her feet. For a moment she couldn't remember if she had lit it or not; she folded over, fumbling for the smoke, only to find it cold. By then the scream had died out, but it still echoed in her head. Shrill noises like that always did when they stopped as abruptly as they began.

Yanking the door handle, Amanda threw her shoulder into the padded door, pushed it open and hurried to the front porch. Her feet clomped up the three wide steps, over the brief length of the porch and across the threshold. Now she heard panting—hard, strained breaths coming short and quick. And a sort of gurgling that reminded her of trying to talk to her sister underwater when they were kids.

She paused, her own breath hot and sharp in her chest. Her mind was spinning out, orbiting around what seemed like a hundred conflicting thoughts and feelings. She felt stupid for the pang of jealously she felt upon first seeing the strange SUV in the driveway. Even when the scream validated her fear that Walt had a woman inside—a woman Amanda did not know—she recognized that there was something altogether different from a dalliance going on inside. Something she supposed had to do with the house.

That, and the *worms.*

If indeed there were any worms. Because Nora was only speculating, after all. She had never even been in the house; she had never seen the grotesque thing.

She might not have any idea what she was talking about.

And, when the second scream erupted and was instantly cut short by a dull thump and a quick, sucking gasp, Amanda decided that Nora was full of shit.

She tried to convince herself that it was merely psychosomatic, or at the very least the result of shock. As far as Margaret knew, she suffered from no respiratory abnormalities, and so there was no practical reason she should not be able to breathe. Still, no matter how much she defied her present circumstances in a concentrated effort to remain calm, her lungs just wouldn't work. The air was stuck.

Her eyes bulged and she clawed at her throat in a desperate and pointless attempt to jumpstart her airway. Her head felt like it was contracting around her brain. The edges of her vision were starting to blur. And looming above her, his face as still and inexpressive as a corpse, was Mr. Blackmore, the new ninth grade English teacher. Dangling at his side from a half-clenched fist was that hammer, dripping red. For the time being, the horror and agony of the young man gone mad was all that existed in the entire world. Not even the pulsing, babbling nightmare on the ceiling could register in her fear-addled mind.

Now, while she tried like hell to remember if Mr. Blackmore had actually struck her or not, Margaret Stuben recalled the last cryptic thing he said to her.

"Don't you touch her," he'd snarled.

*Her? Her who?*

The one who was moaning, that was who. Someone in pain. Someone he wants so badly to keep secret he would…

what? Kill her?

The blurry periphery closed in, and all around it the world darkened to an impenetrable black. Another voice, another woman, somewhere else in the house. The suffering woman? Somebody else? Another lunatic?

"Hello?"

Margaret's eyes rolled back into her skull as the shadows washed over her.

Walt's head snapped to the left and he felt a strange jangle, like his brain followed the turn a little late. He tossed the hammer to the right without hesitation. It landed on the springy mattress in his bedroom without a sound. Dumb luck.

"Amanda?"

"Walt!" she cried. Her footsteps pounded across the foyer, through the living room and into the kitchen.

*No time to panic. Got to think.*

"Give me a hand!"

For the second time that day, he pulled off a bloody shirt and let it fall to the floor. He crouched down beside the prostrate form of Miss Stuben and hooked his hands into her armpits. Amanda appeared in the corner of his eye, rushing by the island counter. He heaved, jerking the tall woman hard and fast.

"The hell?"

"She's not breathing."

"Who is she?"

"Goddamnit she's not breathing!"

Walt dragged the woman into the stark overhead light of the kitchen and released her. Looking up at Amanda with wide, wild eyes he gasped, "Tell me you know CPR."

Amanda stood there in silence, staring and trembling.

"Amanda!" he shouted.

She remained frozen, stunned into inaction. He sneered and grunted at her. Then he leaned over Miss Stuben, pinched her nostrils shut, and expelled a long breath straight into her mouth. Having never taken any kind of emergency resuscitation training (although it was required within his first year of teaching), Walt could only imitate what he'd seen on television. He breathed into her lungs and pressed on her chest, on the bony part above her breasts. Amanda had begun to whimper, wringing her hands and saying, "Oh, oh, oh."

It didn't work. Miss Stuben neither breathed nor moved at all. For all Walt knew, she was already dead. Which would not be the most awful outcome imaginable, except that Amanda had come along to complicate everything so terribly. He tried one more round of breath and compression, and when that produced no results he laid a hard, open-handed slap across Miss Stuben's face.

Amanda gave a startled cry, but it worked—Stuben's eyes popped open and she wheezily gulped at the air.

"Oh my God," Amanda gasped.

Walt expelled a sigh of relief even as he acknowledged the fresh problem in front of him: if Miss Stuben could breathe, she could also talk. For now she was preoccupied with feeding oxygen to her bloodstream and rebooting her brain, but he did not expect it would take long before she got to blabbing.

"I'll call an ambulance," Amanda suggested, scanning the kitchen for the phone.

"Can't," he said. "Phone's dead."

"Oh shit, oh no," she mumbled.

"Calm down. She'll be fine. She just needs to rest."

"Who is she? What happened to her?"

"Will you calm down?"

"I just want to know what the hell is happening here, Walt!"

His face darkened as he rose to his feet, turning his glowering stare at her.

"Be quiet," he snarled. "Be quiet, be calm, or get out."

"Walt..."

Miss Stuben coughed.

"Geh," she weakly gurgled.

"Ma'am?" Amanda called to her. "Are you all right?"

"Geh," she repeated.

"You're walking on thin ice, Amanda," Walt warned her.

"Shut up!" she barked back. Then, to Miss Stuben: "Ma'am, do you need an ambulance?"

"Heh...help..."

"Help?"

"Help..."

"Jesus. Jesus, Walt. What is this?"

"You're not supposed to be here."

"What does that mean?"

"Help me," Miss Stuben croaked.

Amanda stormed past Walt, toward the woman on the floor, but he grabbed her by the elbow and pulled her back.

"Let go!" she roared.

"This is your last chance," he warned her.

Amanda drew her brows together and glared at him.

"Last chance? Last chance for what?"

Her eyes wandered back to the woman on the floor. Tears ran down either side of her face, pooling on the linoleum beneath her ears. A runner of snot hung from one nostril.

"What have you done?" Amanda whispered.

Walt groaned. That did it. Now it was too late.

"I didn't want this," he said by way of apology. Then he threw an undercut punch that collided with Amanda's chin and sent her crashing to the floor.

# 17

Nora sat on a rickety stool behind the counter in abject silence. No one other than her had set foot in the store since she opened it two hours earlier, which was bad enough in itself, but Amanda hadn't bothered to come in either. Though Nora had all but demanded her partner sleep in, by a quarter to noon there was still no sign of her. At 12:30, Nora rang her home phone, but she got the machine. At 1, she left a mildly concerned message. Now Nora was beginning to wonder whether her next message should be angry or worried.

This simply wasn't like her at all.

Although Nora and Amanda were equal partners in their faltering venture, Amanda had always been the driving force behind it. It was her idea, and she always played the part of boss-lady. That was fine by Nora. She got to be independent and do whatever she pleased, but inevitably there was someone to bear the brunt of the big calls and the bigger problems. They each had their roles, and life on the career front was exceptionally comfortable, if not terribly profitable.

Less comfortable was the fact that Amanda—a woman who had never called in once since In the Reads' grand opening—was nowhere to be found. And Nora did not fully realize just how worried she really was until the bell over the door jangled and her heart nearly leapt out of her mouth. For a fraction of an instant, she'd thought it was Amanda, merely running late. It wasn't. Instead, a short, chubby teenager snuck shyly in. With her neat, black bob and equally black T-shirt emblazoned with the words NAPALM DEATH, the girl wasn't one to melt into a crowd around those parts.

"Good morning, Alice," Nora said.

"Hi, Nora," the teenager said, her full mouth nearly forming a smile, but not quite.

"I daresay you've read every Anne Rice novel there is,"

Nora told her. "But we do have the new Poppy Z. Brite back there, if you're interested."

Alice nodded knowingly. She was one of the shop's few loyal customers, a sweet kid with a penchant for gruesome paperbacks. Without another word, she beelined to the back of the store and immediately began scanning the shelves in the horror section. Nora exhaled heavily.

*Where the hell are you, Amanda?*

They walked right into it. Both of them. Like flies stupidly setting down in the waiting maw of a Venus Flytrap. He was taking care of it, solving the problem. And in they walked, blind and hopeful, ignoring every creeping threat that lurked around them. Walt could hardly feel responsible. He was far from pleased about it, but there was no guilt. By God, he'd told Amanda to calm down. Now she was in the attic, her and that irascible Margaret Stuben. And she had no one to blame but herself.

Dragging the women up there had been no easy feat. He took Amanda first, still conscious but disabled by pain and tear-blurred eyes, and she kicked and fought all the way up. It was the work of an hour, all told, from the bottom of the pull-down ladder to hogtying her in the attic.

"It's only temporary," he explained. "I wouldn't leave you like this."

She screamed and hissed and spat. It broke Walt's heart to see her that way. He realized that their relationship had likely come to an end the minute Amanda went running out of the house that night (only days ago, but it felt like months), but this was another can of worms altogether.

"I hate you," she cried when he descended the steps again. "I hate your filthy goddamn guts!"

He gave a sigh and lowered himself down to the floor beside Miss Stuben—*Margaret*. No real need for formalities.

Not anymore.

She too was conscious, but in remarkably worse shape than Amanda. It was all a ridiculous misunderstanding, of course. The nosy woman had taken it upon herself to waltz back into the forbidden hallway and got an eyeful of the very quandary Walt had been working toward eradicating all morning. How was he to know that the damned thing was still alive? He'd certainly beaten it with the hammer enough to kill any ordinary creature, but then this monster was anything but ordinary. And oh, how she screamed. Like bloody murder, and like Walt had anything to do with it. By the time he caught on to what happened, those terrible red arms were stretching taut, reaching for her; a mouth full of chipped and broken teeth chomping at the air. Even half-dead and beaten to a bloody pulp, that thing was blood crazy.

Walt took up the hammer again, had it ready in half a second, and slammed Margaret out of the way with his shoulder, giving himself the room he needed to bash the creature's head one more time. Looking back on it now, he supposed he must have shouldered her right in the throat, although he couldn't see how that was possible. She was taller than Walt. But it was dark; perhaps she was stooped over for some reason. Whatever the precise order of events, she went down gasping and Walt swung but he missed, driving the head of the hammer straight into the wall.

After that, pandemonium.

"Christ," he said as he loosened Margaret's bun and ran his trembling, blood-stained fingers through her hair. "You two sure caused a clusterfuck in here today."

Margaret moaned sullenly.

"Well, then. Up we go."

Had Margaret been the first to go, she would have been easy. There was no fight in her at all. But the exertion of hauling Amanda up there took its toll, and now his every muscle and tendon burned under the weight of Margaret's limp body and the pumping strain of climbing the ladder. They were fit enough ladies, the both of them, but Walt was in no great shape and he knew it.

*Maybe I'll start working out*, he thought blithely at the top of the steps.

He forgot all about that once he had the women arranged at a safe distance from the pod. He secured Amanda with a length of frayed rope left in the attic by some previous tenant. He loosened and retied the cord, this time just around her wrists, which he held behind her back. She spat on his face when he was done, a whole mouthful of saliva she must have been working up for a while. He was a fairly good sport about it, though—he wiped his cheek with the back of his arm and smiled.

"Fair enough," he said. "But just the once, okay?"

"Bring me a cigarette," she gruffly demanded.

"Are you kidding?"

"No, I'm not. There's a pack in my car."

"Huh," he said, mostly to himself. "The cars."

"Never mind that. Just bring me the pack."

"You'll burn my house down."

"No I won't. You can watch me the whole time."

"You'll stink the place up. Besides, you know how I've been on your ass about that since, well, since we met, almost."

"I thought you were concerned about my health," she rasped.

"That, too."

"Sure."

He blew a snort of air through his nose, half laugh and half rebuff. The pod pulsed and a hollow gurgle bubbled out of it.

"What has that thing done to you, Walt?"

"I was killing it. Before she came, before you. I was killing the fucking thing. Well, too late for that now."

"Why is it too late?"

He didn't have to answer her. Because across the attic, below the throbbing, vein-streaked pod, came a pealing bellow that chilled Amanda's skin.

*"BLOOOOOOOOOOOOOOOOOOD!!!"*

Her mouth dropped open as if she were powerless to keep it closed. Tears welled up in her eyes and spilled down her cheeks. She croaked, trying to speak, but nothing more came out. Walt grinned knowingly.

"Everyone's got to eat," he said.

# FALL

## A NIGHT IN OCTOBER

### 1923

*The fire in Agnes' eyes is hot and angry. She does not know what to make of it. Only minutes ago she saved Agnes from a nasty thing, the worst bad thing. Saved her from ever having to go through it again. She should be hugging me and kissing me all over. Thank you, little sister, thank you!*

*But no. Agnes looks like a wild beast, a wolf about to tear its prey apart. Her eyes glimmer as though wet, tremble almost imperceptibly. The older girl is shaking with rage. Agnes closes two fists over her nightdress and drags her from the bedroom.*

*You are going up there, she says. Up into Papa's attic.*

*And you are never coming out.*

## 18

*"You have reached a number that has been disconnected or is no longer in service. Please check the number and try again."*

Sarah Blackmore-Hall dropped the receiver on the hook and frowned. This was a new development. Until now, the line had just rung and rung, countless times until she ultimately decided to give up. Now the line was dead and gone, cut off by the phone company. The question was, did he fail to pay his bill or did he intentionally kill the service?

Neither sounded very much like her little brother, despite how little she knew about the man. Sarah knitted her brow and glanced over to Mitch. He was engrossed in the morning paper, the sports section as usual. So long as he didn't actually bet on anything, she permitted him that much.

"Number's disconnected," she said.

"Hmm?" He didn't bother to look up from the sports page. Some hulking young kid in a numbered football jersey scowled on the front.

"I said Walt's number is disconnected."

"Huh," Mitch replied.

"Guess that means I'll have to go over there."

"Over where?"

"To Walt's. Are you even listening to me?"

Mitch smiled bitterly and laid the paper down on the kitchen table.

"I am."

"Momma's sick."

"I know she is."

"Don't you think Walt might like to know about it *before* she dies?"

"Nobody's dying, Sarah…"

"I'm sorry—what is your medical expertise again?"

He opened his mouth, about to reply, but thought better of it. Instead he picked the sports page back up and buried his face in it.

"I'm going to Walt's. Today."

"Mm-kay."

"It's a long drive. Won't be back until tomorrow at the earliest."

"See you then."

Sarah screwed her face up and glowered at the huge kid on the newspaper, the best substitute she had for her husband's hidden face.

"Fuck you, Mitch," she growled as she stomped out of the kitchen.

"Love you, too, sweetheart," Mitch said quietly.

He smiled; the Razorbacks had whooped A&M at the Southwest Classic. He would have bet on that.

Walt would have been staring out a window, but the room didn't have any. In fact, there were very few rooms anywhere in the building with a view of the outside world. One had the distinct feeling of being trapped in an underground shelter while the bombs dropped above. Nuclear fallout for a thousand years and entombed in this moldy, fluorescent lighted hell.

The school was built in the mid-Sixties, so he had to wonder whether the Bay of Pigs had something to do with its design. He vaguely recalled the panic on nearly every adult's face in those days, but of course it came to nothing. And this was Middle of Nowhere, USA. Nobody was going to blow them up. Nonetheless, the only windows he'd seen since beginning his first year as a teacher were in the offices and the hallways, the latter being small, frosted, and cross-hatched with ribbed iron rebar. Even light couldn't pass through. The classrooms were stark gray, no windows; the only light blared yellow from the humming fluorescents among the rotted ceiling panels. If it wasn't a bunker, it might as well have been a prison. They had uniformed security guards waving wands over the poor kids at the door every morning, not to mention regular surprise room and locker searches. It was a wonder any actual teaching got done.

His kids were quietly scribbling in the sixteen-page

bluebooks he'd passed out at the start of class. The month since the beginning of the school year was taken up by *Great Expectations*, a choice that elicited no dearth of moans and groans from the excitable fourteen-year-olds who faced him every day. Today, Walt waited for the bell to ring and then pointed to the question written on the blackboard: *Discuss the significance of the novel's title—what are Pip's great expectations?* He raised a single eyebrow at the school district sanctioned essay question once the students set to it. His own expectations were meager at best.

The bell sounded at the conclusion of the hour, and those students who remained awake groaned some more, having run out of time prior to completing their essays. Walt rounded the monolithic teacher's desk and leaned back on it.

"All right, pass them up."

Pages crinkled, paper shuffled. Soft murmurs gradually built to a crescendo of jabbering adolescent voices, every other word *like*. Walt ignored them, stacking the bluebooks, dreading to read them. As the last few students filed out of the room, he slumped in his chair and frowned at the cover on the top of the stack. The handwriting was barely legible; huge, looping letters intersected, invading one another's space. And that was just the kid's name. Walt grunted, looked up at the clock, and jumped at the portly girl obstructing his view of it.

"Oh. Hello, Alice."

"Hi, Mr. Blackmore."

"Is there a problem?"

"I didn't finish my essay."

"I doubt very many of you did. It's all right. I'll bear it in mind."

"Okay, Mr. Blackmore."

He tried to manage a smile, but his face refused to comply. So he dropped his gaze back to the unreadable garbage on the desk and waited for Alice to leave. Which she didn't.

"Mr. Blackmore?"

He ground his molars together.

"Yes, Alice?"

"What do you think happened to Miss Stuben?"

"How should I know, Alice?"

"I didn't think you actually *knew*. I was just wondering what you *thought*."

"Well, I'm a teacher, not a policeman. It's not for me to speculate."

The girl squeezed her eyebrows together into an upturned point and let her eyes roam the drab room.

"I guess everybody figures she's dead."

He cranked his mouth up to one side and inhaled deeply.

"Well," he mumbled, "let's hope not."

"She is. I know she is. She'd have turned up by now, someplace. Even if she just ran off with some guy. My sister did that, see? She just disappeared one night and my mom, she cried for two weeks. A policeman told my dad she was probably dead, but then she ran outta money and called from Tennessee."

"There you go. Your sister was fine."

"Not really. The guy beat the shit outta her."

"Alice..."

"Sorry."

"I wouldn't worry so much. You should be focusing on your studies, getting good marks. Making friends and having sleepovers, things like that."

Alice grinned sheepishly.

"You don't know very much about teenage girls, do you, Mr. Blackmore?"

He leaned back in his chair, studying Alice's grinning face with a quizzical look.

"I'm fat," she said frankly. "I haven't got any friends."

Walt wanted to scream. This was getting out of control. He signed on to bore teenagers about Dickens and Shakespeare and (God willing) Chaucer, not to listen to their whiny perspectives on how the world was constantly turning against them. But he didn't scream. He folded his arms on top of the desk and said, "You're not *fat*, Alice." (She was.) "And besides, no one is exempt from friendships."

"I was right. You're hopeless with girls."

"Haven't you got anything for third period?" he asked impatiently.

"Study hall. In the *cafeteria*, for God's sakes."

"Then you'd better get going." He pointed at the clock on the wall. "You're already late."

Awkwardly, Alice turned to one side. She looked at the clock.

"Right," she said softly. And then, as she passed into the dirty, ill-lit hallway, she whispered, "Farewell, monotonous acquaintances of my childhood..."

With that, she was gone. He smirked. At least one kid had managed to read the damn book after all. Still, he could not have been more relieved at her departure. All those stupid questions, as though he was not bombarded with them enough on topics that actually mattered. *What happened to Miss Stuben? Was she dead?* Christ, no she's not dead, he would've liked to shout at her. What use would she be then?

Realizing that he was sneering, he flattened his mouth and returned his eyes to the indecipherable mess on the desk. He turned the cover over and grimaced at the first page of the booklet. It was still chicken scratch, but he could make out the solitary sentence the student had managed to write in the course of an hour: *Pips a fagot.*

Marking the inside cover with a thick red F, Walt moved on to the next bluebook.

# 19

She awoke to the terrifyingly familiar odor of musty wool and fiberglass, the attic's copious insulation. Together with the nauseating coppery smell of the pod, it never let Amanda forget where she was. Not for one second.

She blinked, taking in the dim, dusty place where she'd been for the last few weeks. A narrow streak of sunlight filtered in through the broken slats of a vent where the roof made an inverted V. The light was soft and white, but everything else was bathed in brown shadows. She could hardly tell that the wispy layers of insulation were at all pink.

Reaching down to her ankle, she slipped her forefinger between the scabby skin and the cool steel shackle. The shackle was U-shaped with a thick pin through the stems, a lot like a halyard shackle but big enough to fit around her thin ankle. Walt had banged the clevis down on either side of the pin with the same bloody hammer that started the whole nightmarish ordeal. Margaret had one just like it.

They were both tethered to one of the attic's support beams. Five feet of steel cable connected the shackles to the posts, allowing them barely enough room to use the bedpan Walt provided without any sense of privacy. Not that the women required any privacy from one another. Margaret rarely ever spoke, but Amanda understood that a bond had developed between them all the same. They were sisters-in-arms, fellow sufferers in the same hellish agony. The only person in the world who could possibly comprehend Amanda's plight was Margaret, and vice versa. Accordingly, she made up her mind before the end of the first week that she would not leave that house without her. If she got out of there—no matter what might happen—Margaret was coming too. She would rather die than leave Margaret alone to deal with that monster. Either of them, the creature or Walt.

Where the skin around her ankle wasn't scabbed, it was pink and raw. An inveterately violent sleeper, she had yet to train herself to remain still at night, or whenever she slept, to prevent this kind of damage. Naturally Walt showed up with a bottle of peroxide or some Neosporin every few days, and applied it as gently and caringly as he could.

Good old Walt. He was going to get his. Eventually. Somehow.

Margaret stirred. Sometimes it was difficult for Amanda to determine her level of consciousness. She spent about half the time floating somewhere in between sleep and wakefulness, the other half dead asleep. There were only brief windows wherein the shell-shocked woman was entirely cognizant of her surroundings and situation, and even then she didn't usually feel much like talking. Walt and his monster had really done a number on her. She had the same worn down raw spots and crimson-black scabs on her shackled ankle, but that was the least of her worries.

She was the one with all the cuts.

At first, he cut her every day. Not always the same time of day, but at some point between dawn and midnight, Walt climbed up the attic stairs with an art scalpel (a #16 according to its package), a plastic bowl and a first aid kit. As soon as the stairs shuttered down, Margaret would begin whimpering. She knew the pain was about to come, and she knew how weak she was going to be after Walt took her blood.

He started with her arms, making two-inch incisions that covered the top of her left forearm, then her right, and then he moved on to the undersides. Two weeks went by like that, cutting and squeezing and draining the blood into that little bowl. After a while, Margaret's arms were a mess, covered with a dense network of furrowed scabs and leaking wounds. So Walt moved on to her legs. By that time he had ceased bothering to dress her again when he was done; he just kept her in her bra and panties. And, of course, the various bandages that mummified her arms, legs and, eventually, her torso as well; all of which started out white, but now the gauze and her undergarments were stained red and brown. Margaret was in bad shape.

And she was getting weaker all the time. He was taking too much.

Amanda demanded—and later begged—that he split the bloodletting between them. Even after he'd diminished the regularity of the cutting to every other day, and then every few days, Margaret was fading away.

"Cut *me*, you bastard," Amanda cried. Later, it devolved into, "Walt, *please*. I've got plenty you can have. Give her a break."

But he wasn't having any of that.

"I'm not cutting you."

"Why not?"

"Because I love you."

Amanda cried when he said that. Not because she believed him, and certainly not because she felt the same way. She wept because there was no denying it anymore. Walt was crazy. Certifiably bugfuck nuts.

Margaret lifted her head, cracking her eyelids open to narrow, watery slits. Her shoulders lurched and she tried to hoist herself up on one elbow. It didn't work, so she lay back down.

"Good morning, Margaret."

That had started as an attempt at dark humor. Amanda would say *good morning* and Margaret, when she answered at all, would say *oh, sure* or *nice day for it*, something like that. One morning she just cried. Now Amanda meant it as a beacon of hope, as though by wishing her fellow captive a good morning and actually meaning it, there might really be a *good* morning on the horizon.

Today, Margaret only moaned.

As if by way of response, the pod gurgled. Amanda felt a shudder that terminated somewhere in the back of her throat. It just hung there, threatening to trigger her gag reflex and force her to vomit.

She remembered when she first saw it, in the summer. It looked like a gigantic rotten egg then; so red it seemed black in the shadows. Repulsive, like century eggs, a Chinese delicacy she'd encountered in San Francisco, all putrid brown jelly on the outside and dark green bilge in the center. Since it had grown, however, the pod had taken on the appearance of an immense amniotic sac, translucent when the sunlight shone on it and filled with burbling black fluid.

Within the sac, floating in the dark liquid, was something else. Stalks, like marsh reeds, wriggling inside. Sometimes they poked the walls of the sac, forming a veiny, fleshy tent. But they did not do that anymore. Now the two thick stalks only moved back and forth, kicking like legs.

They probably *were* legs. It only made sense. Walt's horrid new friend was growing, and all with the help of Margaret's blood. Even he likely did not know where it was going to lead, what it would eventually become, or how much more of Margaret it was going to take.

"I thought it was worms," Amanda said quietly. *Funny,* she thought. *I haven't told her that yet.*

"W…worms?" Margaret murmured.

"Fucking Nora," Amanda cryptically replied.

Why hadn't she come looking for her? Perhaps she had, and Amanda was unaware. But she could always hear Walt down there, lumbering around, talking to himself, talking to *it.* Surely she would have heard any visitors. Nora, the police, anybody at all. Anything other than *blood, blood, more blood!*

She glanced over at Margaret. Her eyes were closed, her chest rising and falling in the rhythm of sleep. In that way, she was fortunate; the blood-loss weakness permitted her a sort of escape unknown to Amanda. How odd, how awful, she realized, to dream of that kind of mindlessness. Yet still, she envied Margaret for it.

Soon, Walt would return. Yank the stairs down, climb on up. It had been a few days since he last cut into Margaret, she was probably about due. There was never going to be enough. Not until Margaret was dead. And perhaps not even then.

Perhaps he'd bring food. Amanda couldn't quite tell how long it had been since he last brought something—peanut butter sandwiches on stale white bread. Fucking prison food, for what were they but prisoners?

Amanda wrapped her arms around her bent knees and dropped her face between them.

"I hate you, Walt," she muttered between choking sobs.

## 20

Dry brown seed pods crunched under Sarah's feet as she walked the length of the parking lot from the convenience store to her car. The store was hedged in by tall Sweetgum trees, their green five-pointed leaves having died and fallen, leaving only the multitude of their spiky pods behind. She recalled their omnipresence back home, when she and Walt were small kids, making slingshots out of dry branches and rubber bands and firing the thorny projectiles at one another in the backyard. Walt called them monkey balls. Sarah preferred bommyknockers. They smelled sweet and fragrant in the spring, when they were green and fresh. Now, as an adult, they were nothing more than a minor annoyance, exploding with almost every step she took but otherwise entirely insignificant.

She carried a paper cup of gas station coffee, which was

bitter with a weird aftertaste like pencil shavings. She didn't mind, as long as it did its job and kept her alert for what remained of her drive to Walt's middle-of-nowhere burg. Once she slid back into the driver's seat she took a sip and burned her upper lip. It was going to have to wait. Maybe it would be cool enough by the time she hit Mount Pleasant. Setting the cup in the cup holder ahead of the gear stick, she snatched the map from the passenger seat and unfolded it to her current position. As far as she could tell there were still a good two hundred and fifty miles to go. If she stayed on course and didn't stop more than once or twice, she might make it before dark.

She returned the map to the empty seat, started the car and stretched the seatbelt across her torso. The radio was worthless out there and she hadn't brought any tapes. It was going to be a long, quiet drive. Just Sarah and the hum of the engine and her own morbid thoughts.

*Momma's dying and Walt doesn't even care.*

Her mouth curled up into a sneer as she backed up into the street.

*He'll start caring when the will's read.*

She turned the wheel, got herself in line with the crumbly road.

*I don't even know why I'm doing this. Who the hell moves away to a* smaller *town, anyway?*

She'd kept up enough through family to keep tabs on her brother, but even that was more than she wanted to do with him. Sarah hit the gas and sped west, to a place she'd never been and never wanted to go.

## 21

Walt shut the door of the rental car the insurance set him up with, saw that it hadn't closed all the way and bumped it with his rump. He glanced at the house, its angled roof pointing up. Alone in all the world but for the naked branches of a thousand trees silhouetted against the gray, featureless sky. A single black grackle flapped overhead, its oily wings silent against the cold autumn air.

Walt sighed and it came out in a white puff. He was not really alone in there. But for all the seething hate that seeped out of the attic he might as well have been. Even the insatiate beast, still hanging, dripping from the hallway ceiling, showed him nothing approaching affection, much less appreciation. Perhaps still bitter about the business with the hammer. But hadn't he more than made up for that by now? Surely he'd harvested ten gallons or more from that insufferable Stuben woman. (*Was she dead? Hell no, she's not dead.*) Still, all it did was moan and demand more, more, more.

Most of the time, he ended up angry with himself, wondering why he bothered. Just destroy the thing and be done with it.

But, on occasion, he marveled at how fast it healed from the hammer attack, and how increasingly human it looked. The arms filled out, lithe and muscular. The fingers no longer stubby, grotesque little knobs, but thin and long. And those piercing, startling eyes.

In a strange sort of way, she was almost beautiful.

*It. It* was beautiful. Briefcase in tow, he traversed the gravel path to the porch, climbed the steps, jammed the key into the lock. Inside, all was blissfully silent. No whimpering, screaming, or moaning. He smiled and gently shut the door behind him. If this kept up, he might even get to finish grading those awful essays. Maybe get some reading in.

"*Guhhhh!*"

He shook his head, the soft smile melting into a grimace. He didn't think he was going to get off that easy. It was just waking up, he could tell. And it always woke up hungry, like a newborn baby screaming its fucking head off.

He wished it really *would* scream its head off.

"*Gahhh! Wah... Wah.... WALT!*"

"Yeah..."

"*WALT!!*"

He let the briefcase drop to the floor. One corner struck the hardwood and chipped it, leaving a whitish, triangular indent.

"Shit," he hissed.

"*WALT! WAAALT!*"

"I heard you! I'm coming! For Christ's sake!"

Walt groaned, an animal growl deep in his throat. The container in the refrigerator still had a little blood left in it, but he knew it was getting low. He doubted there was enough to quiet the creature, much less satisfy it.

He was going to have to bleed her. Tonight.

"Goddamnit."

Jerking his head to one side, he heard his neck crack. It felt good. He jerked it the other way, but it failed to crack that time. The last of the evening's luxuries.

"*Bloodbloodbloodbloodblood*," the thing jabbered from the hallway.

Walt crossed the kitchen, opened the fridge and extracted the plastic container. Only the shallowest bit of Margaret's thick, dark blood remained. He took it with him to the hallway and flipped on the bathroom light.

"*Bloodbloodbloodbloodblood...*"

"I've got it, I've got it."

"*Waaalt...*"

"I'm here. I've got it."

He popped the lid off and looked into the creature's eyes. Its face was so much clearer now, so much more human. It still had no skin, but its head was full and round, replete with an aquiline nose and a slender, angular chin. It smiled broadly and genuinely when their eyes met, flashing two rows of straight, white teeth.

"*Waaalt,*" it said through clenched jaws.

"You look terribly like a hungry old dog," he said.

"*Not niiice.*"

"Only quoting. Dickens said it, not me."

"*Dickens not niiice.*"

"It's been said. Here." He held up the plastic container and it accepted it with bloody hands. "I know it's not much."

"*More.*"

"I'll get you more."

"*Maaaargaret.*"

"Yes, that's right."

"*Give me Maaaargaret.*"

"I mean to. But I've got to bleed her first."

"*Blood cow,*" it said with a creaky laugh.

Walt's face clouded. Only rarely did it advance an attempt at humor, but it was always chilling when it happened. The measured, throaty laughing did nothing to allay the unpleasantness of it. While he recoiled, backing away into the kitchen, the creature shoved its dripping face into the bowl, lapping the blood up from within.

He was readying his instruments when the bowl hit the floor and skidded off into the dining room.

"*Bring her,*" it said.

"Working on it," Walt impatiently replied.

"*NO!*" it bellowed.

He raised his eyebrows and turned to look at it.

"What do you want?" he shouted back.

"*HER!*"

"I told you, I'm working on it!"

"*NO MORE BLOOD! FLESH! MEAT! MEEEEEAT!*"

Craning its neck to face him directly, the thing resumed its clenched-teeth grin. Its eyes bulged wide and its nostrils flared. Walt leaned back on the island counter, afraid that his knees might give out at any moment.

"Oh my God," he rasped. *What have I done?*

It didn't take long for its head to heal from the blows of Walt's hammer, and as soon as the teeth grew back it started to talk. Nonsense words to begin with—baby talk. Then, the same as before: *blood* and *more*. When it was sated, it was silent. That was not often.

As its features developed and the head separated from the stringy red mass on the ceiling, the creature's voice softened and its vocabulary improved. It learned Walt's name and called to him frequently. It made macabre jokes and grinned like Mr. Sardonicus from that old William Castle movie. Or Hugo's Gwynplaine from *The Man Who Laughs*.

*Never had apparition more frightful grinned in nightmare*, he thought grimly.

The time had come for Walt to start asking questions.

"What are you?" It was the most basic question, the question from which all future determinations would be based, he supposed.

"*I am me.*"

"And what is that?"

"*Hungry.*"

Always it spoke in circles, avoiding answering any question in a direct manner. Always it came back to the matter of blood.

"Where did you come from?"

"*Here.*"

Never an answer.

"What is your name?"

"*No name.*"

"You haven't got one?"

"*Give me.*"

"Give you what? A name?"

"*Yesss.*"

And so Walt began thinking of the smiling monstrosity in his house as Gwynplaine.

"Margaret. Margaret, wake up, dear."

She cracked her eyes open, peered through the sleep gunk and saw only indistinct colors mixing together in the vague shape of a face. But she knew who it was.

"You've got to take this," he said.

A cool glass touched her limp hand. Cool and dripping with condensation.

"What's—"

"It's medicine. Good for you."

"Don't drink that, Margaret!" Amanda shouted from someplace near. She sounded as though she was in a tunnel. But everything usually did anymore.

"Shut up, it's just water."

"Don't drink it. Don't."

He gently brushed her cheek with his fingers.

"Here, sit up," he said. "It's only sleeping pills."

"You woke me up for sleeping pills?"

"You weren't sleeping, just dozing in and out. You're not very well."

"Hmm."

"It's okay. I just want to help you rest. Get better."

Margaret propped herself up on an elbow, but it buckled and she crashed back down on the panel. He reached down and lifted her up, giving a little grunt. He leaned her up against the support beam he had chained her to. Then he took her hand, uncurled the fingers and laid a handful of pills on her palm.

"Pills?"

"They're hers. Amanda's. They're safe. You're only going to

sleep for a while. A nice, long sleep—wouldn't that be nice?"

"Hmm."

"If it's mine, you can't take more than two," Amanda called out from her tunnel. "Much more than that is really dangerous, Margaret. He's probably trying to kill you."

"Oh, for Christ's sakes, will you be quiet? Why would I kill her now? It's been five weeks! I'm trying to *help* her!"

"You're a liar!" Amanda squealed. "A liar and a murderer and a piece of dog shit!"

"I've never lied to either of you, nor have I killed anyone." He turned in Amanda's direction. "You're still here, aren't you? Jesus, I haven't even bled *you*. You should be thanking me."

"Thanking you? Thanking *you*?"

"Yeah, all right. Maybe not. But please, be quiet."

Margaret swayed a little, feeling the weight of the pills in her palm and trying to guess at how many were there. Eight? Twelve? She couldn't tell. The shouting match he was having with Amanda was too distracting.

"It's okay, Margaret."

He returned to face her. "Ignore it, she's just upset. Take your medicine."

Without giving the issue another thought she popped the entire handful into her mouth. He quickly pressed the wet glass in her hand, helped her raise it to her lips. She drank greedily, gulping the clean, cool water and letting it wash the pills down her throat.

"There you go," he cooed. "That's a good girl."

"Margaret, no!" Amanda cried.

"S'okay," Margaret answered her after a satisfied gasp. "M'gunna sleep now."

"That's right," he said, stroking the back of her head. It felt nice.

"Sleep now," she murmured again.

She closed her eyes and felt the floor go soft, breaking

apart into gentle waves that rolled beneath her. Floating on top of them, she let them rock her to sleep. As consciousness evaded her, Margaret tried to remember who he was, this nice man who took such good care of her.

## 22

First she saw the blue sign on the roadside: GAS FOOD LODGING. Under the headers *gas* and *food* appeared the same name: BERT'S CAFÉ. *Lodging* was curiously vacant. The sign was stippled with buckshot.

Sarah hated the country.

She noted the exit number and, when the off-ramp loomed on the horizon, flipped on her turn signal. It was time to refuel both the car and herself.

The building stood alone and looked abandoned. From the shape and color of the structure, it was obvious to Sarah that it had once been a fast food joint. In front of the dingy restaurant, a cracked and greasy parking lot stretched out to the service road. Two ancient fuel pumps were erected in the middle of it, the kind with the scrolling numbers. She pulled up to the closer of the two and jammed the nozzle into her gas tank. While the numbers slowly rolled off with an irritating series of clicks, she gazed at the field surrounding the property. It was nothing more than patches of brown and yellow glass that was occasionally interrupted by a copse of stubby, diseased hickories. Their naked branches clawed at the gray sky and looked like veins. Far beyond that stood a reddish-brown farmhouse, its roof caved in.

The pump sputtered and clicked for the last time. Sarah tapped the nozzle and returned it to the pump. The gas smelled astringent in the cool October air.

After moving the car to a parking space directly in front

of the restaurant, Sarah went inside. Country music squawked tinnily from a pair of banged up speakers suspended from the ceiling. With the exception of the few green silk faunas placed strategically throughout the dining area, everything in the place was either brown, yellow or orange. Cracked plastic booths, aging Formica tabletops, and even the once-white walls subscribed to the motif.

Sarah scowled.

A hefty middle-aged woman in a wrinkled waitress uniform (yellow and brown, of course) looked up from the table she was wiping down.

"Take a seat," she drawled. "Any one you want."

"I got some gas," Sarah said.

"I'll put it on your ticket," the waitress said, sounding annoyed.

Sarah strode past her and quickly located the cleanest looking booth, which was not particularly clean. She scooted into it anyway, nudging her purse between the wall and her hip. A greasy laminated menu was propped up against the adjacent window that looked out over the dead field. She picked it up and frowned when her thumb slid across its oily surface.

"What'll you have?"

Sarah glanced up at the waitress, who had her ticket book open and ready. She did not smile; her face was like granite. *Aren't service people supposed to be polite?*

"Coffee," Sarah said. "Aaaand....the club, I suppose."

"Coffee and a club," the waitress mumbled as she waddled off. She didn't bother to write it down.

Sarah guessed that when you're the only game for miles and miles, you can afford to be undiplomatic.

Placing the menu back on the window, she wiped her greasy fingertips on her skirt and scanned the grimy environment. An older guy with a bushy white mustache and a mesh trucker's cap sipped coffee at a table by the restrooms. He was reading a dog-eared paperback Western. *Blood River*. Sarah blew a puff of air through her nostrils. *Funny*, she thought. *Doesn't* look *literate*.

The song changed—another warbling country tune—as the trucker closed his book and stood up from his chair. He dropped a few crumpled bills on the table and moseyed on out.

Now Sarah was alone. It felt eerie to her. She didn't think she'd ever been all by herself in a restaurant before.

Momentarily the surly waitress came around with a mug of coffee. She set it on the table without a word and wandered back to the kitchen. No sugar, no creamer. Sarah sighed. She started sipping at it anyway.

She was in mid-sip when a steel serving basket clanged against the tabletop in front of her. Sarah jumped, spilling a dollop of hot coffee on her blouse. She gaped at the basket; it was full of sugar packets and little plastic cups of creamer. Then she glanced up at the stubble-faced man who put it there.

He was short and stocky, with pale gray eyes and a greasy brown pompadour. When her eyes met his, he smiled, displaying crooked, yellow teeth. Smoker's teeth. She could smell the nicotine all over him. He was like a living ashtray.

"Here you are," he boomed. "Service with a smile."

Raising one eyebrow, Sarah said, "Thanks."

"Don't mention it."

She expected him to go away then, back to wherever he came from. Instead, he slid into the booth across the table from her. Sarah rolled her eyes.

"I'm married," she said sternly.

"That a fact? A great institution, or so I've heard tell. Never got hitched myself. Always on the move, don't make for a good marriage."

"That's very interesting, but if you don't mind…?"

The man lifted his brow, waiting for Sarah to complete her request. She sighed again.

"Don't mind what?" he asked.

"Are you serious?"

"Not usually. Got me a great sense a humor. I got 'em laughin' all the time."

Astonished with his audacity, she shook her head at him. This guy just couldn't buy a clue.

"Look," she growled. "I don't particularly feel like making any new friends today, all right?"

"Aw, that's too bad." Once more, he flashed his tar-stained grin at her.

"Which means I'd rather be alone."

"You mean to tell me a pretty lady like you ain't waiting on somebody to join her? Now that's a damn crime."

"That's right," she barked before the gravity of the man's question hit her.

Was he just fishing to find out if she was traveling alone?

And did she just walk right into his little trap?

Shit.

"What a shame," the man went on. "Good thing I came along then, ain't it?"

"I sure wouldn't say that."

"No?"

"Hell no."

"How come?" He pouted dramatically.

"Because I know an asshole creep when I see one, and you just so happen to be an asshole creep."

In an instant, the man's playful face contracted into a savage glower. Icy needles danced up Sarah's spine. He took in a deep breath, like he was about to lay into her. *Here?*

The kitchen door swung open and the waitress came waddling out with a brown plastic tray balanced on one hand. Atop the tray was a single plate, and on the plate was Sarah's club sandwich.

She didn't suppose anybody in the history of the world had ever been so happy to see a roadside lunch.

"Club," the waitress said as she transferred the plate from the tray to the table.

Sarah looked up at her helplessly, her eyes wide and pleading. The waitress twisted her mouth up and turned to face the man.

"King, you buggin' this lady?"

"Who's bugged?" King pleaded. "We're just talking."

"He's talking," Sarah cut in. "I'm bugged."

"Crissakes, King. Leave her be. You're such a dumb shit sometimes."

For a second King looked genuinely offended. But then he held up his hands, palms out, and a smile spread across his hairy face.

"Just being friendly, ladies. No harm done."

With that, he scooted out of the booth, flattened out his flannel shirt, and crossed the dining area to another table where he sat down. Sarah let out a breath she hadn't realized she'd been holding in.

"He don't mean nothing," the waitress assured her as she ripped off the ticket and dropped it on the table. "King's a piece of work—he's an asshole—but he don't mean nothing."

"Thanks for rescuing me," Sarah said softly.

The waitress smiled for the first time since Sarah came in. "No charge," she said.

After that, the waitress tottered out the front door, extracting a pack of cigarettes from her apron pocket along the way. Sarah watched her go. Then she looked over at King. He was looking back at her. And still grinning. Sarah sneered at him and turned back to her lunch.

And while she ate, King stared at her.

Five or six miles further down the road, Sarah gave up on trying to find a tolerable radio station and turned it off. The sandwich felt good in her belly but the coffee was making her a little jittery. She wished she had a good book on tape, something to calm her mind.

She was nervous and upset from the incident at Bert's Café, still angry with her brother, and tired of being on the road. And now, looking up at the rearview mirror and seeing a pickup truck barreling down on her with its high beams on, she felt scared, as well.

*King. What a ridiculous name.*

*The ridiculous name of the guy who is going to rape me and murder me.*

She blasted past a stop sign without so much as slowing down. The red octagon only registered in her peripheral vision in the instant before she passed it. There was a sharp intake of breath that accompanied the quickening of her heartbeat. Out there, in the middle of nowhere, a cop would count himself fortunate for the opportunity to pull over some city woman just passing through; anything to interrupt the monotony of small town police work. She considered whether or not it would be a boon to get pulled over with the truck catching up to her. She was undecided. For all Sarah knew, King *was* a cop. Or was in with them. Fishing buddies or some dumb hick shit like that. Out there in the middle of damn nowhere, where no one was really accountable for anything they did, anything could happen.

Sarah swallowed hard and glanced up at the rearview mirror again. There was no truck; only vacant road stretching on forever behind her. It probably hadn't been King at all. Just some redneck kids out for a thrill ride. Never even noticed her.

And luckily for her, the transgression with the stop sign went unseen. After five minutes passed without the alarming presence of flashing bubblegum lights or threatening high beams in her rearview mirror, her breathing and heartbeat began slowing to relatively normal rates.

*Only fifty miles left*, she reminded herself. Less than an

hour before she expected to be pulling into Walt's driveway (if he had one). It was about time to start preparing what she was going to say to him, and how she was going to say it.

*You were never around so you shouldn't get a dime from her.*

Sounded fair enough to Sarah, but hardly the right foot to start out on. Besides, Walt wouldn't even know that his mother was ill, much less on death's doorstep. He *should* have known, he *should* have been aware of all pertinent goings-on in his own family, but he had long ago made his choices and stuck to them. Walt was never the black sheep by nature, but by self-design. Sarah found that disgraceful, and it was the subject of many an argument between her and Momma. She loved her boy, as mothers are wont to do, and so she consistently failed to see what a perpetual prick he was. She would always cry a little when Walt missed Mother's Day or went three years in a row failing to remember her birthday, but she always forgave him. Not that the bastard ever apologized. The forgiveness was implicit.

Now that she was on a roll recalling every sordid detail of her unpleasant experiences with her brother, she tried to remember exactly how long it had been since the last time they spoke. She decided it had been thirteen months, on the phone. She hadn't actually seen him in more than four years. Over the course of Walt's twenty-some years, they'd never gotten along. And not getting along very often amounted to violence and anger. He would never expect so serious an enemy to darken his doorstep unannounced.

He was in for a surprise.

## 23

Even with the strip of duct tape firmly affixed over her mouth, Amanda managed to scream. She watched with bulging eyes as Walt dragged Margaret's inanimate body across the attic floor and down the stairs.

Walt's skin felt hot, too tight. Amanda knew the house was miles from the nearest neighbor, and so her carrying on could accomplish nothing apart from annoying him. He was on the verge of scampering back up to the attic where he would threaten her with the same fate should she continue making such a scene. But Gwynplaine could not wait.

"*Hurry*," it rasped. "*Quick, Walt. Quick.*"

Its mouth hung open, its fingers wiggling with eager anticipation.

"She's here," he said.

"*Meat, Walt. Quick—the meat!*"

He blanched. He never expected to do much more than bring Margaret to Gwynplaine.

"I—I can't," he stammered.

"*You must. I'll die.*"

"It's murder!"

"*No! It is meat! Only meat!*"

"But what if I'm found out? What if I'm caught?"

"*You won't be*," it said matter-of-factly.

"You don't know that!"

"*I will protect you. Always.*"

Once again, its mouth spread into a ghastly grin, the origin of its apt name. It was a sardonic grin, appropriately. Ricus sardonicus. The Hippocratic smile.

"Sure you will," he replied.

"*Please.*"

He looked at Margaret, stared at her open mouth and sleeping eyes. She already looked dead.

"*Pleeeeeease*," Gwynplaine begged.

Walt slowly filled his lungs and held it for a moment before letting it out just as gradually.

"What do you need me to do?"

Gwynplaine sneered wickedly.

"*Butcher it.*"

Amanda blew hard through her nostrils, ejecting thick ropes of mucus onto the floor in front of her. It was no good; she could hardly breathe at all. Knowing it would infuriate Walt when he saw it, she reached up and tore the tape from her mouth anyway. Her skin prickled and stung.

If there was anything to keep her from snapping completely, it was the knowledge that Margaret never woke up. Amanda waited for a bone chilling shriek of agony, but it never came. She heard the wet, crunching noises of a body being ripped apart, just below her at the bottom of the attic stairs. Walt would murmur (*oh God oh Jesus*) and that unnatural monster would cruelly respond (*yes oh yesss give me a taste Walt put it to my lips the meat*). All the while, whack after sickening whack, Margaret came apart and Walt fed her to the creature, piece by piece.

Amanda had nothing apart from sheer willpower to prevent herself from vomiting. Instead she cried. It was something real, it was necessary and natural, and she could focus completely on that and nothing else.

Still the nauseating *thump* of some cutting implement meeting flesh and bone, splitting it and separating it from the whole, went on. Still the monster moaned in ecstasy while Walt whined and muttered. He was in a sort of agony, but Amanda could not reconcile that with the cruel, heartless Walt who stole Margaret's blood all those weeks and kept them both captive in the attic. Nor could she reconcile the Walt who lived in the cottage on the outskirts of town with the man she had dated for the preceding three years. That Walt was a gentle man who never raised his voice or grew especially angry, much less resorted to any sort of violence. He was eccentric, to be sure, but in an endearing, and even sexy, way. The quiet, introspective bookworm whose mind was apt to wander over any number of esoteric literary subjects, regardless if he was talking to her or just idly rambling. The man she loved more than anybody else in her history.

*Thump. Thump. Thump.*

"Oh my God," she heard him moan.

Somehow, she couldn't make herself believe that this was entirely his fault. It was that thing, that monster growing in the attic, through paneling and past the hallway ceiling below. The thing Walt had started called *Gwynplaine*, whatever that meant. Its name, she supposed. As if it deserved one.

She was not exactly inclined to believe in anything like mind control, despite the desperate fears she'd expressed to Nora. But then Nora was wrong, it wasn't worms at all. It really *was* a monster. And if Amanda could believe in monsters, then the door stood wide open. Maybe it was a ghost returning from the Great Beyond, or an alien life form from millions of light-years away. Maybe it was a demon from Hell.

But then, Amanda didn't believe in hell. Not even now.

She couldn't afford to.

*Thump. Thump.*

Something went splat. Walt groaned plaintively. He sounded as though he might be crying. Which was met with throaty laughter from the monster. From Gwynplaine.

"*Give it to me!*" came the gravely, androgynous voice.

Amanda shuddered.

This was it. Margaret was dead; there was no question about it. Now she had only herself to consider.

She had to find a way out.

The rug Walt laid down in the hall did little to prevent the spatter he'd hoped to control. Blood coated the walls, dripping down in thick crimson rivulets from the broad splotches that spotted the hallway. He, too, was covered in gore; he now wished he'd had a smock and some goggles before he began the impossibly repugnant work of dismembering a living human being. His shoulders ached from the strain of chopping with the cleaver. It was made for splitting bones, though certainly not of the human variety. Nevertheless, it did the job. Margaret was reduced to shiny red slabs of meat, all but the organs, hands, feet and head. Her abominable, still staring head.

Walt reached over, suppressing a gag, and pressed her eyelids shut with the tips of his fingers. Something warm splattered against the back of his neck and he flinched, drawing back and looking up.

It was only Gwynplaine. A very messy eater, that thing. Like a fussy baby. It was drooling blood all over the place as it rent Margaret's raw flesh apart with its teeth.

Walt scooted backward, crab-like, toward the kitchen.

Gwynplaine growled, its mouth full of dripping, blood-raw meat.

"*Thtay*," it said. *Stay.*

Walt's face screwed up into a horrified sort of pout. He could barely stand looking at it anymore, at least for the time being. It held the huge slab with both hands and sucked the warm fluid from it. This was the sizeable chunk Walt carved from Margaret's left thigh. Gwynplaine had already eaten the right one.

"I can't," he complained.

"*Not...done...yet*," it said between slurps and nibbles.

He slid up the wall, not trusting his knees to support him on the way to standing. Almost involuntarily, he looked at the repulsive mound of butchered human flesh on the area rug beneath him. He immediately squeezed his eyes shut and muttered, "Oh, God."

"*No God.*" Gwynplaine said. "*Only meat. Now. I must grow.*"

Walt turned his head away. Away from the grisly sight of

what he had done, away from the smell of human gore in his nose and the taste in his mouth. He retched, unable to hold it back any longer. He sprinted through the kitchen toward the double sink. He made it, but barely.

Gwynplaine laughed uproariously while Walt vomited.

The chilling laughter, however, was abruptly cut short by the loud bang in the attic, like something very heavy had been dropped from a great height. A bowling ball or a barbell. Neither of which Walt owned.

It was Amanda.

Spitting a mouthful of chunky saliva into the sink, he wiped his mouth with the back of his hand and made his way back to the attic stairs.

## 24

Holding the shackle steady with one hand, Amanda pried at the clevis in the pin with the other. The tips of her fingers turned white as she dug them into the bent piece of metal, but it was to no avail. It didn't budge. Still she kept at it, digging at it in what she knew was a futile attempt to free herself. Her forefinger slipped, but she held tight. This turned out to be a poor choice—her fingernail caught the end of the clevis when the finger continued to slide, ripping half of the nail off completely.

She yelped as her cuticle welled with blood. It hurt like hell, a hot and stinging pain, but she wasn't about to give up. She popped the bleeding finger into her mouth and sucked at it while maneuvering her ankle around in the shackle. There just wasn't any way out of it.

Keeping the seeping finger in her mouth, she struggled upward to a standing position. Her knees almost buckled and her head felt light. She gave the steel cord a yank, pulled it taut. A few tiny splinters broke away from the support beam where it chafed.

She gave another, harder yank. And then another. More splinters came off. She could still hear Walt crying and arguing with the creature, but she did her best to ignore it. Instead she focused her attention on the beam. One more yank, good and hard, and then she'd try scraping the cord back and forth to whittle the wood away. She hoped the roof didn't cave in if she was successful. At least, not on top of her.

Amanda took two steps closer to the beam to provide a length of slack. Then she kicked her leg away from it.

She heard the snap first; a crack, like a stalk of celery pulled apart. Then she felt the burning agony in her ankle. She went down, crashed against the beams and landed face first in pink insulation. Something off to her left smashed against the paneling. Something tall and black. A candlestick, maybe. She let out a pained whine.

When she bent at the waist and craned her neck, she could see what became of the ankle. The foot was perpendicular with the leg, jutting out to the right at a ninety-degree angle. The bones had snapped right in half, fibula and tibia both.

She tried to scream, but nothing came out.

And then came the pounding footsteps below.

Walt was coming to investigate.

He swept up the cleaver on his way, failing to register how sticky the handle was. Everything was sticky that way now. Margaret's blood was everywhere. So much of it, it would never come out. Walt would have to burn the house to the ground to get rid of that much blood.

Skidding over a broad slick on the hardwood floor, he regained his traction on the area rug, leaping over a glistening mound of human meat. He rounded the drop-down steps to their front and scrambled up. Above and behind him, Gwynplaine hissed and tittered.

Popping up through the attic door like a prairie dog, he narrowed his eyes. He scanned the gray shadows, waiting for his eyes to adjust to the darkness, looking for Amanda. His heart thudded in his chest. He climbed all the way up and crouched, ready for anything, the bloody cleaver gleaming in his hand.

He saw her, finally, sprawled out over the beams. She was surrounded by a cushion of fiberglass insulation., her face twisted miserably. Walt paced cautiously closer.

Baring his teeth he hissed when he saw the ankle, twisted so badly it had to be broken. Already it was turning dark purple at the joint. Her foot was bent at an impossible angle.

"Shit," he said.

"Help me," Amanda whispered.

"What did you do?"

"It hurts!"

"Jesus, Amanda…"

She braced herself with her palms and hoisted her torso up so that she could look at Walt.

"Help me, goddamnit!"

He hemmed and hawed, made an O with his mouth, and then scurried to her side.

"What can I do?"

"Get the shackle off!"

Walt frowned.

"I can't do that, sweetheart."

*Sweetheart*. She could not believe that.

"Why the hell not? Just take it off!"

"You'll run away."

"On this?" She jabbed a finger toward her mangled ankle.

He raised his eyebrows and nodded. It couldn't be denied—she wasn't going to run anywhere.

"Hold on," he said, displaying his palms. "I've got to get some pliers."

"Hurry!"

"I will! I'll be right back."

She moaned in pain and let herself sink back down to the floor. Walt danced over the beams and insulated panels toward the door in the floor. He disappeared in seconds. Amanda groaned, squeezed her eyes shut and then opened them again. White sparks flickered in front of her face for a minute, and then gradually dissolved. When her vision was clear again, she found herself staring at a curious object, something she could not have even wished for in her wildest fantasy.

A wooden-handled meat cleaver, covered in blood, sat inches from her face.

# 25

The pliers had to be somewhere, only Walt was not sure exactly where that might be. Despite the fact that he'd moved into the house months ago, he never got around to unpacking everything. Just the essentials. Loads of knick-knacks, the unnecessary flotsam and jetsam accumulated over the course of a man's life, remained stored in taped cardboard boxes. Many of these boxes were still stacked in the dining room, whereas others had been shoved into closets. Any one of them could contain his pliers. There was no telling which.

He found himself standing with knees bent and arms akimbo, whipping his head left and right, wondering where to begin looking. *Tool kit, tool kit…where's the tool kit?* He had his hammer, the selfsame hammer with which he pummeled Gwynplaine and locked the clevis in place on Amanda's shackle. That must have come from the tool kit. So where was the rest?

He squeezed his eyes shut and tried to picture the kit in his mind. He remembered where the hammer fit into it, right on top, but he had no recollection of unpacking it. Perhaps the hammer had already been unpacked. Perhaps it had never been in the red toolbox at all.

"*Waaaalt,*" Gwynplaine called from the hallway, all sing-songy and creepily seductive. "*I'm...not...done.*"

"Just a minute," he called back. "I've got to think."

Needle-nose pliers, with red rubber handles. Walt knew he had them.

But where?

Why couldn't he remember?

Pinching the bridge of his nose between forefinger and thumb, he strained to place it, certain that he must have taken it out, used it. All those repairs. The baseboards and the roof, and...

The roof.

The *attic.*

"Fuck," Walt said.

It was the quickest of motions. Her arm shot out, her fingers curled around the wood handle. It was tacky with blood. She then retracted the arm, sliding the cleaver beneath her, between her breasts.

And she waited.

Walt sped back through the kitchen and into the hallway. He leapt over Margaret's grisly remains and landed on the attic stairs' penultimate step. Gwynplaine gnarled.

"*Leave her!*"

Walt ignored the creature. Of course it would want him to let Amanda suffer. Suffering was all it knew. It thrived on the agony of others, Walt's included. He had been willing to facilitate its ghastly needs thus far, but allowing harm to come to Amanda was too much. Regardless of the torment he'd put her through in the past several weeks, he still loved her. And the woman he loved was presently languishing in excruciating pain.

He bounded up the steps and hopped up into the attic. Amanda lay on her stomach, her contorted ankle darker than before. She was motionless. Walt let out a gasp.

"Amanda?"

No response came. He paused, conflicted between rushing to find the tool kit and checking on Amanda. He made a quick scan in the dim gray light of the attic and, not seeing the toolbox, decided on the latter. He scrabbled over to her side, crouching down and gently setting a hand on the back of her hot, damp neck.

"Sweetheart? Are you—?"

*Okay? Alive?* He didn't have the opportunity to decide which adjective to employ. In that instant, Amanda turned on her side and unleashed a banshee scream. Walt's eyes popped and he started to back away, the hand on her neck flying up and away from her. He only caught the quicksilver gleam of the cleaver when it was already slicing through his index finger. When the middle finger joined it on the floor and the blood started spurting out of the two ragged stumps, he shrieked.

Amanda lurched forward on her stomach and swung the cleaver again. Walt dropped onto his back, narrowly missing the blade as it passed a half inch from his neck. Before she could swipe at him again, he quickly skittered backward, putting as much distance between himself and Amanda as possible.

"I'll kill you!" she screamed. "I'm gonna kill you!"

"Jesus!" he wailed. He planted his hands behind him for support, and then screamed. Pain shot up his arm, filled his shoulder and neck and head.

He fell back and slammed his head against a support

beam, the one Margaret had been chained to.

There was an audible thump, and then he was silent and still.

Amanda growled, swinging the cleaver. Walt didn't react. She threw her arm back over her head and hurled the blade at him. It only clanged against the beam and landed in his lap.

"Oh, shit," she whimpered.

In the span of a second, her rage turned to despair. She might have killed Walt after all, but with him out of reach and no means to get the shackle off, there was no hope for escape anymore.

She pounded her fist against one of the beams underneath her and burst into tears.

"You rotten son of a bitch," she sobbed. "You can't even die right."

# 26

Gravel sprayed out from beneath the skidding tires when Sarah hit the brakes. She'd gone too far down Highway 5 and missed the turn-off. It would have been nice if the web mapping site mentioned how obscured it was—there was nothing but trees out there and she never even saw the street she was supposed to turn left onto. It was downright primeval.

Jerking the stick into reverse, she backed up to the opposite side of the road heading southbound. She slammed it into drive and was about to hit the accelerator when she saw the possum in the middle of the lane in front of her. It was a fat, mangy creature with splotches of yellowish white fur and beady, too-far-apart eyes that shimmered in the glow of the headlights.

"Ugly cuss," she said.

She revved the engine, hoping to scare the possum off. But

it didn't budge. She revved it again, and this time the animal bunched up its back and growled, baring its fangs.

"I don't have time for this."

The sun was on the verge of setting, a phenomenon that seemed to come quicker in the dark of the old growth forest. Plus, she'd already gotten herself mixed up once, and that was with light. There were no streetlights out there, no houses or apartment buildings, or even a mobile home. Once it got dark, it was going to be dark.

Sarah tapped the pedal, lurching the car forward a couple of feet. The possum backed up, but remained in the road. Twice more they repeated the dance, and still it refused to get out of the way. It just snarled and growled.

*Probably rabid*, Sarah thought. *A mad possum. Ought to be put out of its misery.*

"But not by me," she said aloud. It was nasty, the possum, but she couldn't bring herself to harm it.

Instead, she turned the wheel and slowly pulled over to the left lane. The animal stayed where it was, watching her as she rolled past it. When she was clear, she sped up and took the hidden road on the right. She was now less than a mile from Walt's front door.

The brakes screeched as the truck came to an abrupt halt. He thought it was a dog at first, and he wasn't about to run down some poor pooch. But now he could see it was only a damn possum. The disgusting thing wasn't anything more than a giant rat.

He punched it. His truck sped from zero at six feet away from the possum to forty-five on top of it. With a soul-rending squeal and a loud pop, the mammal split apart beneath the weight of his right front tire.

King grinned as his truck sped down the road, leaving a thin red smear in its wake.

"Now where are you, girl?" he whispered to himself.

The porch was dark when she got there. She might have passed right by it had she not recognized Walt's old station wagon, the same one he'd had for years. It had the same snobby bumper sticker Sarah had noted the last time she saw it: READ THE BOOK—IT'S BETTER.

Classic Walt. Always the smug pedant.

She pulled in behind the station wagon, parked and stepped out onto the driveway. She could only barely make out the shape of the house in the gray moonlight. There wasn't a single light on inside.

Taking each step with blind caution, she crossed the front yard to the porch, slowly ascended the steps and found the front door. Here she paused, glanced around, and her eyes settled upon the ruined front end of Walt's car. *What the hell?* She felt around for a doorbell but found none. Accordingly, she knocked.

Then there was silence. Somewhere in the dense trees beyond the yard an owl hooted. She waited a couple minutes more, then knocked again. Nothing. Not even footsteps or breathing from the other side of the door. She checked her watch, but she couldn't even see its face. At any rate, she knew it was not quite nine o'clock. Too early to be sleeping, but it was possible that Walt was out.

One last time, Sarah rapped her knuckles on the door. She expected no result and got none. Nobody was home.

She recognized the outline of a rocking chair in front of the darkened bay window and walked over to it. She sat with a deep sigh, allowing the impetus of her weight in the chair to gently rock her. Her eyes slid shut, not that it much mattered. It was just as dark either way.

Her mind floated over her options. She could wait for him, but there was no telling when he would return. She could find a motel and come back in the morning, but the nearest hint of human civilization was at least fifteen miles back the way she came. That seemed somehow regressive. Sarah decided to wait.

And while she waited, she drifted to sleep.

## 27

Somewhere in the void was a hollow pounding. It sounded like it might be underwater, but Walt didn't think he was submerged. If he was, he wouldn't be able to breathe. Or sleep.

He danced over the notion of investigating the noise.

Seeing where it was. What it was. If it really was subaqueous.

Like in the ocean.

But he could not sleep in the ocean.

So he ignored it.

## 28

Fixing her teeth on the beam beneath her face, Amanda bit down as hard as she could. She had a miniscule glimmer of hope that the ankle would eventually go numb and the pain would stop. It didn't. It hurt more now than it had since she broke it. Walt was no help, of course. He was still blacked out four yards away. There was nothing else to do but to bite and bear it.

That was what she had been doing for half an hour when she heard someone knock on the front door. The sound was faint, little more than a distant tapping from where she lay in the attic, but she recognized it for what it was. Someone was there. Someone who might save her.

*The police? Nora?* Anyone would do. Amanda unhinged

her jaw and pulled her teeth out of the bitter-tasting wood. She did not realize how deeply her teeth had sunken in. Ropes of drool slavered out of her mouth, which she wiped on her shoulder. She listened.

For a while there was nothing more. But then the knocking resumed.

Sucking in a long, deep breath, she filled her lungs beyond capacity. She was preparing to scream louder and longer than she'd ever screamed before.

*"Don't. Scream."*

The air in Amanda's lungs pushed out of her mouth in a quiet sputter. Her heart was slamming and her breath came in short, sibilant bursts.

It was the monster.

The thing Walt called *Gwynplaine.*

Whatever the hell that meant.

The two words, spoken in a calm and glottal manner, terrified her enough to keep silent. All she could hear for several minutes thereafter was her own hissing breath. Then the knocking returned, louder and more insistent than before. Her shoulders jumped, pulling at her body and raking her destroyed ankle against the sail shackle. She let out a shout of pain.

"*Quiet!*" the monster growled.

Silence drifted back down on the attic like a coat of dust. The minutes passed. Five, ten, fifteen. She didn't know how long it went on, but it seemed like forever to her. A whole night.

Then the scraping started.

A sandpapery, scratching sound, coming from the far end of the attic. The end where the creature was. She peered into the darkness; she couldn't see a thing, not even in the weak, ashen moonlight that snuck past the broken slats in the air vent. But the noise went on; scraping, scratching, *cracking*.

The paneling, the spot where the stain first showed up when Walt moved in. That's where it was. The stain had grown into a nightmare, and now the nightmare was breaking free.

"Please," Amanda whimpered.

She was not at all sure what she meant. All she knew was that she was afraid. And she didn't want to be hurt anymore.

"Please."

Wood splintered, snapping apart in a rapid series of loud pops. The creature moaned. Amanda could not determine if it was from pleasure or pain. Maybe both.

*Ahhhhhh*, it went.

A soft, raspy chuckle erupted from that corner.

"Oh, please."

She started to cry. She didn't want to, but it couldn't be helped. As the tears filled her eyes and blurred what little vision she had, one last splitting crack filled the air. It was followed by a strained grunt and a pair of hollow thumps.

It was crawling near.

# 29

Sarah awoke to a warm, damp hand closing over her mouth. She tried to gasp, but ended up sucking at the sweaty skin of the calloused palm on her face. When she smelled the stale cigarette breath steaming out of the mouth at her ear, she knew exactly what was happening. And it terrified her.

"Hello there, pretty lady," King hissed. "Almost lost you. But here we are, right?"

Sarah shivered. She had been right about that truck the first time. It hadn't been any redneck kids. It was King all along.

And now it was too late.

"How come you're sleeping on the porch? 'Cause this ain't

your house? Sounds about right. You thought you was free and clear, but ain't nobody home. Poor lady. Lucky King."

He gave a phlegmy chortle. His breath was unbearable, filtered only by the stale reek of his hand so close to her nose.

Sarah murmured, unable to make herself heard.

"What's that?" King asked.

She murmured again.

"Can't hear you. Trouble is, I take my hand away and you scream your goddamn head off, don't ya? Then where'd we be? That's no way to start this romance."

Warm tears oozed out of her eyes and ran down to his fingers. Strange as it seemed to her, she kept thinking about Walt. Specifically, that this was entirely his fault. If he hadn't gotten his phone line disconnected, if he hadn't always been such a contemptible bastard, none of this would have ever happened.

She wouldn't have driven out here so suddenly.

And she would never have met King.

*Fuck you, Walt. I hate you even more than I hate this piece of shit creep.*

"So I reckon you'd better tell me, and tell me straight. Is there anybody in that house right now?"

She shook her head, at least as much as she was able to with King holding her so tightly.

"You sure about that? 'Cause if you're wrong, it's gunna be bad, pretty lady. *Real* bad."

He pressed his thin lips against her ear canal.

"For you," he whispered.

She nodded to indicate that she understood. She was ninety-nine percent certain that Walt was not at home. But even on that off chance, that one percent that he might be in there, she felt comfortable with her response.

Because maybe King would just kill that rotten bastard and put him out of everybody's misery.

"All right, then," he said happily. "Let's us go on in, now."

# 30

Naturally, the door was locked. There was a time when people way out in the boonies never locked their doors, but the collective anxiety of home invasions had reached its black tendrils even this far. It was not, however, a problem for King. All he had to do was deliver a threesome of powerful, full-bodied kicks and it split apart from the jamb. Then only a nudge was needed to push it in, and ingress was secured.

"Easy," he said.

With his hand still gripped so tightly around Sarah's arm that the skin was turning paper white, King dragged her into the foyer and bumped the door back into place.

The house was dead quiet and pitch black.

"Find the light switch," King instructed by way of a harsh whisper.

"I've never been here before."

"I didn't ask you that, pretty lady. Find it."

Sarah tried to move away from his grasp, but he held firm. She yanked on her arm, but he kept her where she was.

"Do you want me to find it or not?"

"You make a break for it, and I'll make a break of you."

Sarah sneered in the darkness. Dangerous and stupid—a remarkably loathsome combination.

King released her arm and she cautiously wandered close to the wall, feeling for the switch. She found it quickly and flipped it up. A porch light came on outside; it provided enough light through the window for Sarah to see the panel now. There was another switch, which she also flipped. A light fixture dangling from the ceiling came on, illuminating the foyer. King stared up at it like he'd never seen a light bulb before. Then he turned his gaze on Sarah and flashed one his toothy grins.

"Good," he said. "We'll find the bedroom in a minute.

First let's see if we can scare us up some hooch."

She trembled. The son of a bitch wanted to get tight before he ravaged her. The situation just kept getting worse. She could see no reason why he wouldn't slash her throat once he was done. Seemed like the bastard's style.

"Come on. Hurry up."

This time King left her bruised arm alone and seized her by the other one. Then he dragged her into the kitchen.

The area was shrouded in shadows, but the light from the foyer kept enough of the darkness at bay for him to make his way to the refrigerator with Sarah in tow. He opened it up, spilling a sickly yellow glow out onto the linoleum. After a brief inventory, he grunted.

"Shit. No beer."

"I don't think he's much of a beer drinker," Sarah offered.

"Who?"

"Walt."

"And who the hell is Walt?"

"My brother," she said bitterly.

"You don't say."

King shut the fridge and, letting go of her arm, started rifling through the cabinets.

"So this shit-bird is your brother, but you never been in his house before."

"We're not close."

"That so? How come—he fiddle with your clam when you was little or something?"

Sarah huffed.

"You're repulsive."

That elicited a hearty laugh from King.

"Do my best, pretty lady. Do my best."

Moving from one mostly empty cabinet to the next, he finished up his search by slamming the cabinet door as hard as possible.

"Goddamnit!" he shouted.

"No liquor either, I take it."

"This shitheel brother of yours a Baptist or something?"

"Not that I know of."

"Fuck, man. This is shit. Be okay if I had some blow on me, *something*. But *this* is shit."

King saddled up to Sarah, rubbing his chin.

"Best hope that fella don't come home tonight. I'll break his neck just for that."

An acidic laugh escaped Sarah's lips.

"Be my guest," she groaned.

"Hell," King said. "I just don't like it without a buzz at least."

Sarah was about to ask, *Don't like what?* But she knew. Her throat tightened up as she curled her hands into fists.

"Let's not, then, and say we did," she said through clenched teeth.

King burst into a peal of raucous laughter.

"Nice try, woman."

Seizing her roughly by the shoulders, he pulled her toward him and smashed his lips against hers. Sarah moaned and wriggled, but she couldn't overpower him. When he slipped his tongue between her lips, she considered biting it off. It would be easy; just suck it in, clamp down and don't let go. But then what? Would a severed tongue stop him from tearing her apart?

Sarah did not bite. But when she tasted the sour, nicotine moisture on King's tongue, she did gag. Her throat lurched and a wet, hollow gurgle bubbled up from it. King snapped his head back and landed a hard slap across her face.

"You wanna puke in my mouth? Is that it?"

"I'm sorry..."

"Don't piss me off, pretty lady. I mean it."

"I know you do."

"You'd best think about what makes King happy. 'Cause you try something I don't like, you ain't gunna be such a pretty lady anymore. Get it?"

"Yeah."

"I said *get it*?"

"I get it."

King smiled thinly.

"Good, baby. Good."

He kissed her once, softly, and then yanked her by the wrist as he went deeper into the darkness.

"Let's find us that bed."

"Oh, God," she sobbed.

The hell into which she stumbled could not get any more real. All she wanted to do was shove Walt's selfishness in his face for once, turn around and return to her perfectly ordinary, boring life. Mitch and the house and the stupid neighborhood association. The most intense experience she wanted to have was bullying Maude Kruppa into cutting down that rotten pear tree in her front yard. It was a goddamned eyesore.

But this.

King pulled her across the kitchen and into the tar-black hall behind it. Sarah sucked in a deep breath and lashed out with her free hand, raking her nails across King's face. He screeched.

"Bitch!"

He brought both hands to his face, an instinctual reaction. It bought her enough time to break into a sprint back through the kitchen, toward the light of the foyer. She was almost to the door when a shrill scream sounded from above.

Sarah skidded to a stop.

*What the hell was that?*

She wondered if the house had an attic. It had to. There was no second story, and that scream definitely came from above. Someone else King was abusing? But he could not have been in the house before she got there—he had to follow her to see where she was going. Still, she had been asleep for a bit, although she had no idea for how long.

All of this passed through Sarah's mind in a fraction of a second. King would have already come to his senses by then and come running after her. Now she faced a tough choice: get clear of King and this damned house, or stick around to check on whomever was screaming in the attic.

No contest.

Sarah threw the door open and leapt out onto the porch.

Before her feet hit the ground, King wrapped a beefy arm around her waist and wrenched her back inside. He slammed the door shut with his free hand and dragged her back into the shadows.

"No!" she shrieked.

"Feisty is good," King said with anger in his voice. "But now you've gone and stepped over the line."

Sarah bucked and squirmed, but King's thick, hairy arm might as well have been an iron girder. He was breathing hard, grunting. She was beginning to feel faint.

"I'm a man of my word, pretty lady. When you and me are done with what we come for, I'm gunna slash your fucking face to ribbons."

Sarah whimpered.

The light from the foyer abandoned her as they descended deeper into the house, past the kitchen into the ink black hallway. A cruel chortle escaped King's lips. He was enjoying himself.

*But didn't he hear that scream?*

*Of course he did. He's got more irons in the fire than just me.*

She closed her eyes and held her breath. Not quite resigning herself to her fate, but accepting that it was inevitable. Inwardly, she cursed Walt.

Everything was his fault. Always was.

Completely immersed in the dark, she felt the world tilt and turn. She figured she was just passing out until King emitted a startled squawk and they tumbled over one another. Sarah hit the floor, landing hard on her ass, and King crashed down on top of her a quarter of a second later. Pain shot up her spine, tingling in her shoulders. She planted a hand on the floor to steady herself, hoping to crawl out from beneath King's dead weight. Her fingers sank into something warm and wet.

"What..."

King growled and rolled off of her. She heard a moist splat.

"The fuck is this?" he grunted.

Taking immediate advantage of the distraction she scooted backward, over the soft lumps and sticky wetness that covered the floor. A sour odor filled the air; excrement, but with a tangy metallic smell floating over it. Wrinkling her nose, Sarah kept skidding over the mess until her back hit a wall. What had Walt done here? Some kind of major septic leak, she guessed. More of an explosion than a leak, though.

*This is revolting.*

She tried to shimmy up the wall, but her clothes and hands were so sticky from the nasty stuff all over the floor that she just slid back down. A second attempt concluded with the same results.

Another shriek erupted from above. Following it was a guttural yell. Something clattered in front of her.

King shouted, "Shit!"

Sarah flipped over onto her hands and knees and scrambled for the kitchen. She could hear King slam into something and skid across the slick floor. His boots squealed. Once she was out of the morass of the hallway, she was able to spring back up to her feet. This time there would be no hesitation. She bolted for the door.

Sarah was on the front porch before she realized that she

was coated in blood. Her blouse and skirt were dark with it, and her bare arms and hands were red and dripping.

"Oh my God," she mewled.

Footsteps pounded heavily behind her. She gasped and rushed down the porch and across the front yard.

"You're dead!" King bellowed close behind. "DEAD!"

Then a chilling howl filled the night air.

King bleated, "...the hell?"

He yelled. Something slammed, hard.

Against her better judgment, Sarah stopped where Walt's yard met the road and turned back toward the house. The door stood open and the bright foyer shone out. King lay on his stomach in the doorway. Crouched on top of him, someone—*something*—flailed their arms, raking at his back and neck. It howled and shrieked and cackled madly. Sarah shuddered, frozen with fear and bafflement.

In the light of the porch and foyer, she could see that it was bright red.

*A full body suit? No, that lunatic is just covered in blood, like me.*

King blubbered and shouted under the maniac, struggling to crawl away but making no progress. In seconds his shirt was shredded and the attacker was clawing at his exposed skin. Laughing. Grinning like a villainous clown.

Even at that distance, Sarah could see its brilliant white teeth gleaming in the porch light. By the time it thrust its face into King's back, gnashing at the flesh with its teeth, it dawned on Sarah that it wasn't merely covered in blood.

It had no skin.

Red and white tendons stretched where cheeks should have been. Bunched cords of muscles twisted and retracted with every move it made. The slippery crown of its exposed head glistened in the light, dripping fluid on all sides.

The creature snapped its head back, throwing viscous ropes of blood and saliva from its mouth. Its bright, wide eyes turned on Sarah and it resumed its horrific smile.

Sarah pivoted to face the road, planning to break into a run.

Instead, all of the light in the world was snuffed out as she crashed into the dewy grass behind her.

## 31

Amanda couldn't determine if Walt was still breathing or not. It didn't seem to matter that much, whichever the case. She would still be in agony and facing a grim future, such as it was.

When the monster's face was illuminated by a weak shaft of moonlight in the attic, Amanda knew that she was about to die. The wicked smile told her that much. The bloodied, skinless abomination was free now, no longer dependent on Walt to butcher its meat and feed it. It could take care of that nasty business all on its own. And it was bearing down on its next meal—Amanda.

She winced, shut her eyes, and screamed. The creature laughed at her, chattering its teeth with loud, quick clicks. It moved slowly, stiffly. Not yet accustomed to its legs.

She knew now those awful stalks in the pod were limbs.

Then it passed out of the light and back into the darkness. Amanda could only hear its approach from then on out. Gluey, squishing steps on the beams and panels, drawing ever nearer.

But the steps abruptly stopped at the ruckus that erupted at the bottom of the attic stairs. Thumping, clattering, squeaking of shoes and gasps and shouts.

The monster tittered. *Hee hee hee.*

Amanda screamed again.

And then it was gone, down the ladder. Out of the attic and out of sight. Whoever was down there—no one else was left, who could it be?—provided a sufficient enough distraction to prolong Amanda's life. But for how long?

She waited and listened. Pounding steps, a pair of them. Huffing and snuffling. A man's voice hollering threats.

*You're DEAD!*

The creature howled. The man shrieked with pain and horror.

Food for the abomination.

*Poor son of a bitch,* Amanda thought.

For a long time after that, there was nothing. Not one sound drifted up into the attic from below. She started to theorize.

*Perhaps it killed the guy, ate its fill and took off for parts unknown. Maybe it's gone, really gone. All that's left is getting the hell out of here.*

She wasn't sure that she really believed any of that. But it certainly sounded nice.

"Walt," she called. "Walt, can you hear me?"

He didn't stir.

"Walt, you've got to wake up. Wake up, Walt."

"Hnm?"

"Walt?"

"Wuh."

Amanda let out a long sigh. She realized that it did make a difference, after all. If Walt died then and there, she could never escape. As much as she hated to admit it, she needed his help.

"Where are the pliers, babe?"

"Pli-uh...?"

"Focus, babe. The pliers. Where are the pliers?"

"Gwen...plaine..." he mumbled.

"Snap out of it, Walt. We've got to work fast."

"Where is she?"

"Who?"

"Gwyn. Plaine."

"Fuck." *He's totally out of it. Probably concussed.*

She stretched her arms out on either side and felt around in the darkness for something, anything, to pick up and throw at him. She came up empty.

"Now what am I going to do?" she asked no one.

At least an hour later, Amanda heard shuffling from inside the house. It came back. If indeed it ever left. She'd expected as much.

It moved around noisily, snuffling and groaning. Something got knocked over. Then, when it sounded like it was directly underneath her at the foot of the attic steps, the slurping began. The creature was feeding.

Amanda wanted to cry, but she was all cried out.

The creature was still loudly slurping and gulping when exhaustion finally overtook her. She dropped into a deep, restless sleep.

## 32

"Walt."

The voice sounded muffled, like it was coming through a brick wall.

"Waaaalt."

He heard it, though. But he felt incapable of responding in any way. He was too tired and in too much pain. His head was throbbing, his muscles sore and stiff. Whoever it was, Walt just wanted them to go away and let him sleep.

Fingers gently brushed his cheek. The fingertips were tacky and coarse. Warm breath spread over his face. It smelled of old pennies.

"Gwynplaine," he whispered as he opened his eyes.

The bare, glistening musculature of Gwynplaine's broadly

smiling face loomed over him. He could hear the slick noises of the sinews moving against one another as the smile broadened. And it wasn't in the hall any longer. It was looming over his bed.

"You're free."

"Yessss."

"How?"

"It was time."

"Wow."

He tried to hoist himself up but his elbows faltered and he slumped back against the pillow.

"Oof. I feel awful."

"Amanda hurt you," Gwynplaine spat.

Walt narrowed his eyes and, remembering, looked at his hand. It was well wrapped in bloodstained bandages.

"You?"

"Yessss."

"Thanks."

"Hurtssss."

"Yes, it does."

It continued to grin, in spite of his admission of pain. Or perhaps because of it. Somehow that seemed more likely to him.

"Amanda," he said after a long silence. "Is she…?"

"Attic," Gwynplaine rasped. "Sleeping."

He exhaled and faintly smiled. He was terrified that he was going to hear otherwise, that Gwynplaine killed her and ate her flesh hot and raw. Then he considered his mangled hand again. She'd sliced right through it with his own cleaver. Lopped the fingers right off. That was not something Walt supposed a man could grow accustomed to.

"You sleep now," it said.

Walt was not one to argue. He watched with drowsy eyes as the bizarre being strode slowly out of the room. Naked for want of clothes or skin, and leaving shiny red footprints in its wake. More astounding than that, however, were the two heavy crimson sacks swinging from its chest as it shambled off. Dark red nubs protruded from the center of each of them.

Breasts.

Walt stared. Gwynplaine was a woman, after all.

The woman across from Sarah whimpered in her sleep. One look at her gnarled black ankle told the story. It was swollen to the size of a cantaloupe and the darkness spread all the way down to her toes. There was no way she was going to be able to save the foot, much less most of the leg.

Of course, that was assuming the poor woman ever got out of there. As things stood, the prognosis was not good. Sarah had come to before the break of dawn, confused, afraid, and more than a little nauseated. She was immersed in near total darkness, all but the small square of yellowish light that partially illuminated the woman chained to the nearest support beam. Immediately, Sarah had leapt up to try and help her, realizing right away that this had to have been the woman whose screams she'd heard. She must be in the attic. But when she rose up and lurched forward, a cold grip yanked her back and down to the hard crossbeams on the attic floor. She, too, was chained.

By Walt? Or by that loathsome thing that attacked—*killed?*—King? Sarah much preferred marking that part down as a shock-induced hallucination, but deep in her heart she knew that was not true. She saw it, all right. In all its nightmarish, blood-encrusted horror.

Now, hours after sunrise and still chained to a sturdy oak post, Sarah languished across from an insensate woman she did not know. She also didn't know how either of them got there, nor what was to become of them.

And then there was the appalling mess on the other side of the attic.

Illumined by the light leaking in from the holes in the roof, huge, membranous flaps of tissue, splayed out around a hole in the floor. It looked like someone crawled up through the hole and lost their skin on the way. The amount of rusty fluid drying all around it was suggestive of blood, anyway. Sarah shuddered to imagine what it was and how it got that way.

It was clear enough that it had something to do with the creature that killed King. Where it came from, perhaps. Maybe, she considered, it *hatched* there.

*What the hell was Walt up to?*

Growing monsters in the attic? Summoning demons from Hell? At this point, nearly anything seemed possible to her. Her own imminent death at the hands of that creature somehow seemed the most possible of all.

She scrunched up her face, fighting back the tears that were threatening a deluge. Instead she changed her focus to the injured woman with whom she was sharing her unenviable accommodations.

"Hey. Hey, lady. Can you hear me?"

The woman did not move or make a sound.

"Lady. *Pssst.*"

Nothing.

"My name is Sarah. Sarah Hall. Well, Sarah Blackmore-Hall, if you want to be anal about it, but I'm not feeling so great about the old family name just now. I guess you know tons more about what's going on here than I do, but I'd stake everything I've got that my worthless piece of crap brother is behind it. Do you know him? Name's Walt. If you do, I'm sorry for you." She sighed. "But I guess if you're here, you know him all right. Unless you were kidnapped or something. He didn't just snatch you, did he?"

The woman mumbled something incoherent. Sarah's face brightened. *She's awake!*

"What was that?"

"Mm's grrfrin."

"Sorry, I didn't catch that..."

The woman turned her head without moving anything else, just rolling it over like a bowling ball until they were facing one another. Sarah narrowed her eyes, taking in the stranger's features. She was quite pretty, despite how ragged she looked.

"I'm his girlfriend," the woman said quietly.

"No shit."

"Was. Two, three years. I don't...I don't know what...what happ—"

With that, the woman broke down. She softly cried for several minutes, making no attempt to disguise her grief. Sarah didn't know the woman's full story, but she could guess at most of it. It was obvious enough: after a couple years of romantic bliss with the world's biggest creep, good old Walt finally came clean and showed his true colors. Truer colors than he'd probably ever shown anyone, replete with torture, kidnapping, probably murder, and a bit of horrific voodoo madness. And now here she was, whoever she was...

"What's your name?"

"Amanda."

"My college roommate was named Amanda."

"Yeah?"

"But she was awful. Just awful."

"Oh."

"I can tell you're not, though. I didn't mean..."

"S'okay. No hard feelings."

Amanda immediately followed that with an agonized squeal. Sarah instinctively lunged forward to help her, only to pull the steel rope taut, hurting her own ankle in the process.

"Ow!"

"Careful. You don't want to end up like me."

"Did he do that? Walt, I mean?

"No. That was my own fault, really. I was trying to figure a way out, fell head over ass and snapped it in two."

"Oh my God…"

"Got him pretty good, though."

"Walt?"

"You bet."

"What'd you do?"

"Sliced a few fingers off with his cleaver. He won't forget that. Even if he kills me, he won't ever forget that I got him back for it."

"Jesus," Sarah moaned.

Amanda screwed up her face, quiet in her patent anguish.

"Did you…see it? The monster, I mean?"

Sarah grimaced. Somewhere in the back of her mind she'd hoped she imagined it, or that it was only a person and she misjudged what she saw. Amanda's matter-of-fact question put that to rest. There was a monster. And it was roaming free.

"I guess I did."

"It didn't attack you?"

"I saw it kill a guy, I think."

"Oh, no…"

"It's okay. I mean, it's not okay, but he wasn't with me. He was just some inbred redneck who followed me here. He was going to…well, you know. Probably kill me when he was done."

Amanda gave a sour laugh.

"Well, what do you know? I guess the devil does favors sometimes."

Sarah trembled. They were both silent for several minutes thereafter. It was Sarah who eventually broke the silence.

"Amanda?"

"Yeah?"

"What is it?"

"The monster?"

"Yeah."

"I suppose only Walt could tell you that. Or maybe he

couldn't, I don't know. All I know is I had a perfectly sweet and gentle guy until he moved into this goddamn haunted house."

"Haunted?"

"Not literally. I don't think. See, there was this stain on the ceiling..."

Amanda told the story to Sarah, as much as she knew. For her part, Sarah listened quietly and intently, her face constantly betraying her horror and near disbelief. Indeed, had she not seen the glistening, blood-coated thing with her own eyes—much less the stomach-churning charnel house it had made of the hallway below—Sarah could never have believed something so outlandish, so nightmarish. It was fodder for paperback horror novels with lurid, gory covers, but nothing that could ever actually transpire in the real world.

Except that it could. And it did.

At the conclusion of Amanda's terrible tale, Sarah buried her face in her hands and wept.

"Poor Margaret," she sobbed. She never knew the woman, never would, but she grieved all the same. No one deserved a fate that awful, not even Walt. "How could this happen, Amanda? How?"

"I can't tell you, darling. I suppose this house has got some pretty nasty secrets."

"I'm so sorry."

"Sorry? For what?"

"I'm just so sorry you ever had to meet my brother."

Sarah's eyes spilled over again. Amanda's did, as well.

"Yeah," she said. "Me too."

## 33

"What is your name?"

She laughed. Walt had been glaring at her for a half hour now. He remained in bed, recuperating, while she—the *creature*—perched on the high back chair in the corner with her knees up to her chin. Watching him.

"Gwynplaine."

"But that's just the name I gave you."

"Good enough."

"Haven't you got one of your own? I mean, you came into the world able to speak, grew into an—an adult, I guess."

"Yesss," she hissed. "I am nearly done."

*Nearly done*, Walt thought. *Like a roast in the broiler.*

He gazed at her face, studied the fine strands of her exposed muscles and tendons, her omnipresent rictus grin. It was an eerily knowing face. It betrayed knowledge and experience Walt was not sure he wanted to be privy to.

"You were around before all this, weren't you? In some weird way?"

She smiled thinly and nodded once.

"What were you called then?"

"Does not matter. That is past. Now I am Gwynplaine."

"Gwynplaine was a man," Walt protested, his mind involuntarily turning up the grotesque image of Conrad Veidt in the role of the perpetually grinning freak.

And then, her grin faded; a rarity. She moved her jaws back and forth, deep in thought.

"Gwyn," she decided.

"Like Gwendolyn."

"Gwyn is good. Only Gwyn. I am Gwyn."

"All right. You're Gwyn, then."

In spite of himself, he smiled.

He slept for most of what remained of the day, waking only when he turned in his sleep and jammed the fresh stumps where his fingers used to be. In those instances, Walt snapped awake with a shout; Gwyn was at his side each time in seconds, hissing comforting words in his ear as she ran her sticky fingers through his sweaty hair. After everything that happened in the night, from the chaos in the attic to the astonishing development in Gwyn's case, it never occurred to him that he failed to show up at school that day.

It did occur to the administrative staff in Principal Byrne's office. They were forced to scramble for a substitute at the last minute, an inconvenience brought about by the unusual call the secretary received from a gravel-voiced woman at half past seven that morning.

"Missssster Blackmore is sick. Very sick. He comessss back next week."

And with that, the sibilant voice was rendered silent by the click of the disconnecting line.

Walt's phone, and his phone book, were then returned to their hiding places, the only evidence of their use the claret smudges staining both.

## 34

Three days after Amanda's ankle was broken, the infection became apparent. The entire joint swelled to bursting. It went from red to bronze, and from bronze it turned a sickly black-green. Enormous blisters speckled the area from the middle of her foot to the center of her shin, which reeked of putrescence when they broke and started to leak.

There were dreams, nightmares, though too fragmented to make any sense of them. Nothing worse than the life she now led, such as it was, and eventually indistinguishable from her waking hours. Everything was foggy, indistinct. Painful.

*Was this the cost of love?* she wondered, vaguely. *Was there love without trust? Was there love when the hate felt stronger?*

One *chose* love, she'd once concluded, long before Walt. No one helplessly fell—the helplessness came later. Amanda chose wrong, and now her helplessness was acute, her destiny complete. Had she selected a monster in a charming mask to love, or had the monster only gradually come to replace that man? Her memories were too slippery, her recall failing. She tried in vain to search her brain for evidence, red flags she'd missed, as though it could make any difference now. Weird little flashes of anger, shifts in mood, dark omens portending this atrocious outcome. Perhaps, she thought, that monster was in every man, just waiting to be properly germinated before springing to life, overtaking him and everything around him. No amount of kind gestures, heart-melting smiles, or soft touches could counter something like that.

*Christ*, she thought before slipping into a black-out sleep, *even Hitler loved dogs.*

On the afternoon of the fourth day, she dry-heaved for hours. Not long after sunset, she collapsed into a coma.

Sarah remained awake throughout the night, weeping loudly and calling Amanda's name. Screaming it.

By dawn on the fifth day after the injury, Amanda was dead.

Sarah decided it must have been gangrene. Walt had not done a thing about it. He had not come up into the attic at all since Sarah woke up there. But she could hear him down below. Talking to *it*.

She made up her mind then and there. If Walt did not kill his sister first, she was going to kill him.

# WINTER
# ALICE

## 1923

*Dragging the frantic child up the ladder that goes to Papa's attic is no simple feat for Agnes. The girl spits and shrieks like a cat, pumps her legs and throws blind punches behind her. None of them find home. Agnes is much too strong.*

*She climbs the rungs with one hand and pulls the girl by the hair with the other. The child thinks her scalp will tear away from her skull as though she was being mutilated by some Indian warrior.*

*But it holds all the way up. All the way up to Papa's half-finished attic.*

*Open air and fresh cut pine beams, rusty old tools Papa got second-hand from the five and dime scattered here and there. The roof is a yawning maw of incomplete crosshatched boards and though the waning dawn moon can see every indignity and every atrocity, it does nothing but gape and gawp.*

*Agnes hurls the child over an upended sawhorse. She lands hard on her hip and cries out in pain, cries out with puzzled horror, why Agnes why? Her older sister's eyes glint in the fading moonlight; glowing silver they seem to reflect her innermost badness, the core of her being that the girl never knew was there.*

*Papa was mine, Agnes shrieks, he was mine and you took him away. Mine, mine, mine.*

## 35

When Walt was fourteen years old, his father and stepmother's house burned to the ground. He was aware of that piece of history now as he roamed its inexplicably pristine rooms fifteen years later, but somehow it seemed insignificant to him. The house was never quite home to him, but there were hundreds of memories here all the same. The bookshelves in the study that reached to the ceiling. The fireplace in the master bedroom with an extra opening in the master bath. The kidney-shaped swimming pool out back and the naughty games Walt had played in it with Cheryl Atkinson when his folks were away on vacation. There were probably a hundred things he could seek out as he floated from room to room, slowly remembering, but for some reason all he wanted to do was find his old bowling ball.

Sure enough, the oily smelling leather bag was right where he'd left it the last time Walt was in the house, on the top shelf of his upstairs bedroom. He was a hell of a bowler in those days, top of the youth league and better than most adults he ever played against. He took excellent care of that ball and recalled how, of all the things he'd lost in the blaze, it was that ball he most regretted losing. But here it was now, just above him on that high shelf. He reached up and pulled the heavy blue bag down. The shelf was not as high as he remembered it. Of course, he was taller now.

Setting the bowling bag on the unmade bed, Walt trembled with anticipation. It was just a bowling ball, in no way particularly superior to any other ball he'd ever used, but it was this one with which he'd won so many tournaments. It was this one that had miraculously been returned to him. Or was it the other way around? Perhaps it was he who had been returned to the ball. To the house. It didn't matter. He licked his lips and unzipped the bag. The metal teeth spread apart and he dropped both hands into the musky darkness inside. His fingers pressed hard against the firm surface of the ball. He hefted it up and out of the bag.

And then he yelled with fright and revulsion. He was not holding a bowling ball at all, but rather the gray, severed head of his own father.

He let go of the head and let it fall back into the bag. It thumped against the bottom. Walt shivered and quickly backed away from it, scrabbling backwards to the closet. His momentum was halted when his back hit the slatted closet door. The door slammed into the shelf. A half dozen more decapitated heads rolled off the shelf, raining terror down on him. He screamed. Then he realized he was awake.

The dream lingered in his mind as if trying to break out of his brain and into reality. He recognized the difference between nightmares and the waking world, but he found himself worrying about what he was going to do with all those damn heads nonetheless.

*There are no heads, stupid*, he chastised himself. *Get up and shake it off.*

He did. Flinging the sheets back, he sat up on the edge of the bed and forced his eyes wide open. He sucked the cool night air in through his nose and then blew it out of his mouth. The heads began to dissolve along with his sleepiness.

He stood up, stretched, and fumbled around in the dark bedroom in search of a shirt. The floor yielded only underwear and socks. The top of the dresser was clear of all clothing save for his sweatpants, which he snatched and stepped into. Carefully, Walt searched the bed. He found no shirt.

He didn't find Gwyn, either. She must have gotten up at some point in the night.

He wrinkled his nose and felt his heart flutter. This seemed like something worth worrying about.

Dudley Chapel tossed and turned. The blame for his sleeplessness laid mostly on his aching back, but his knees and right hip shared the culpability. He'd taken four ibuprofen before bed, but Dudley snapped awake just three hours later with pain biting into his back and side. The older he got, the more everything hurt. He tried to be philosophical about it, but it was now almost two in the morning and he did not much feel like counting his blessings. He just wanted the pain to stop, if only for a little while.

Rose breathed slowly and softly beside him, fast asleep. Unlike Dudley, Rose suffered no such problems in her muscles and joints. She was ten years his junior, and though no spring chicken, she was as fit as a fiddle. He envied her for that, but he also thanked God that his wife of thirty-six years was still so healthy and spry. The way things were going, he expected to be six feet underground before her body began to fail her. It was selfish to be thankful for that, and he knew it, but seeing Rose go to pot just wasn't something he thought he could make it through. Dudley loved her too much for that.

After rolling over for the umpteenth time that night, he finally resolved to just get out of bed. Sleep was going to be elusive, and he was in no mood to chase it. He had half a pitcher of lemonade in the icebox and a recent adventure novel on the table beside his favorite chair downstairs. He figured if he fell asleep while reading, then great. Otherwise, he aimed to read until sunrise and then take the day as it came. Life could be worse.

So Dudley poured himself a lemonade, dunked three ice cubes in the glass and settled into his chair for the long haul.

He was halfway through a riveting sequence in which the American spy is discovered and cornered by KGB henchmen in Soviet-controlled Prague when he heard glass burst and clink apart somewhere inside the house. He dropped the paperback on the table without bothering to bookmark his page and stared, hunching his shoulders and wondering what had happened.

"Rose?"

Dudley exhaled an exasperated breath. The last thing he wanted to do was to get out of his comfortable chair, but he didn't suppose the shattered glass was going to investigate itself. With a frustrated grunt, he heaved himself up and felt the stab of pain in his back as he stood.

"Cripes," he groaned. Then, "Rosie? Is that you, sweetheart?"

Heavy breathing sounded from one of the darkened rooms ahead of him, and shuffling movements, the creak of the floor.

"Rose, honey?"

The sneaking sounds moved across the hall and onto the staircase. Whoever it was—*whatever* it was—it was heading upstairs.

Walt made a sweep of the house, growing increasingly desperate to find Gwyn before something terrible happened. What that meant, he wasn't at all sure. But where Gwyn was involved, terrible things were bound to happen.

He searched the house from the bedrooms to the kitchen cupboard, checked the carport and the front and back yards. She was nowhere to be found. With mounting anxiety, he returned to the hallway between the kitchen and his bedroom.

"Goddamnit," he grunted as he yanked the attic stairs down. The attic was the last logical place to look. And that could not mean anything remotely good.

The ladder clacked loudly to the floor and he scurried up

its steps, his flashlight tightly gripped in one hand. As soon as he poked his head up into the dark, suffocating space, he shone the light in slow sweeps across the area. He saw Sarah asleep on the old mattress he'd laboriously dragged up there for her. She was, for the most part, unharmed. The revolting flaps of tissue where Gwyn's pod once grew continued to rot in the far corner, the raw stink of them overwhelming. There was no sign of Gwyn herself.

She was nowhere in the house. She had simply up and left in the middle of the night while he slept.

There was only one conceivable reason Gwyn would have to leave.

Blood.

Walt had to find her.

Increasingly convinced that a prowler had broken into the house, Dudley crept as quickly and quietly as he could toward the staircase. He'd listened as the intruder made his way up them and now he was giving chase. With each too-slow step he took up the stairs, he tried to figure out how he was going to get to the revolver in the drawer beside the bed without being noticed. By the time he made the landing at the top, he decided it wasn't possible. He was just going to have to confront the son of a gun barehanded and hope to heaven the prowler was not armed himself.

As Dudley pressed himself against the wall and got ready to sneak up on the potential killer, his mind involuntarily flashed back to Mindanao. Cruising downriver in the landing craft with a hundred other guys, waiting with his heart in his throat to charge out of the craft like they did in Normandy. The melting heat and constant rain having taken its toll. He remembered hoping he could take out at least ten Japs before he died that day.

He didn't die, of course. And although he found his brain

dancing over the same steps now as it had back then, he had no intention of dying tonight, either. He crept on, closing in on the bedroom at the end of the long, dark hallway. Then he heard the whine of compressed bedsprings and a low, throaty laugh.

His chest felt tight and his heart leapt, just like that muggy day in the Philippines a lifetime ago.

"Rosie," he whispered.

He came into the pitch-black room, and as he felt along the wall for the light switch, Rose Chapel screamed.

His muscles reflexively jerking and contracting, Walt traversed the backyard, his path lit only by the pale hue of the moon. He had no destination in mind because he had no clue where she might have gone. His new house was in the boonies, the middle of nowhere, and on the outskirts of a nowhere town. There were no shops or housing developments anywhere near the place, no apartment complexes or million-dollar prefab mansions. In fact, there was practically no evidence of human civilization for miles around except for that old guy's farmhouse. Walt struggled to recall his name—*Danny? Dabney?*

Dudley. That was it: Dudley Chapel. The irritatingly friendly old man in the red flannel shirt.

*Through them woods, over the hill,* he'd said. *Right at the bottom, that's my property. Big red house with white shutters. Can't miss it.*

"Christ," Walt said.

He broke into a run for the tree line. Still, somewhere inside he knew he was already too late.

Dudley flipped the switch with a shaky thumb and choked on the scream rising in his throat. The bedroom had been transformed into a grisly abattoir. What had been white bed sheets and a pastel quilt now dripped crimson wherever he looked.

This was no longer his marital bedroom. It was a slaughterhouse.

A terrifying apparition straddled Rose. Like the butchered woman under her, the creature was spattered with blood from top to bottom. All that shone through the gore was its pearly white teeth, straight but overlong, exposed in a rigid, spine-chilling grin. Its right hand was curled tightly around a long shard of broken glass. The shard tapered down to a point at the end. As the creature turned its ghastly smile to Dudley, it jammed the makeshift weapon into Rose's cheek.

Dudley cried out with pain and horror as he watched the jagged glass fragment sink into his dead wife's face, scraping noisily over her teeth before exiting through the other cheek. The creature then gave the shard a sharp yank and it ripped through the flesh, meeting the ends of Rose's mouth. Now it all formed a single gaping gash from one jawbone to the next. Blood gurgled up, flooding her mouth and spilling out on the bed. The creature cackled with mad glee.

Tears squirted from Dudley's eyes as he stumbled forward. His attention leapt between the creature and Rose, the creature and the drawer beside the bed. That inconceivable thing, that devil from Hell, had killed his darling Rose. If he could only reach his revolver in time, he could at least make the monster pay for what it had done.

He sped around the corner of the bed and lunged for the brass handle hanging from the face of the drawer. Before he could reach it, the creature swung a wayward fist in a wide arc, connecting it with Dudley's temple. A bright flash exploded in his eyes, and warm, dull pain spread across his entire skull in a second. He dropped to his knees and heard them crack loudly. The creature smirked.

"Fuck off, old man," it hissed at him. "You must wait your turn. First, I eat this one. *Then*, I eat you."

With that, the thing sank one of its shiny red hands into Rose's bloody torso and pulled out a dripping handful of the corpse's small intestine. It was gray but leaking black, and the horror on the bed made certain to look Dudley in the eyes as it stuffed the guts into its open mouth. It bit down with a sated moan and tore the intestines apart with its hands and teeth.

Dudley moaned, too. He felt his gorge rising but he did nothing to prevent the bilious spray when it erupted out of him like a geyser. The creature merely laughed at his despair as it opened Rose's neck with the glass shard. Her throat came apart like wrapping paper. The thing squealed happily and plunged its face into the freshly cut wound. It lapped up the running, spurting blood like a kid at a water fountain.

Dudley tried to cry out, to vocally demand God explain how this could happen, but the gloom was already creeping in from the corners of his vision. He was blacking out, but he invited it. It was better to be inert when it came. His final thought before the darkness took him was a kind of farewell.

*Goodbye, Rosie. I'll see you very soon.*

Walt cursed at the second tree trunk he slammed into, but he didn't slow his pace. He had never actually been to the old man's house, much less seen it. Finding it in the dead of night was not the easiest task and time was running out, if indeed it hadn't already. He sped on, dodging trunks and naked branches as best he could until finally he emerged from the woods. He sucked the cold air in through his nose and peered out over the low, grassy hill before him.

*Right at the bottom of the hill.* He raced up it.

From the summit, he could make out the shadowed edges of a three-story farmhouse below. Dudley Chapel's house. A single square of yellowish-white glowed on the third story.

"Let me be wrong," he whispered to himself between heaving breaths. "Please God, let me be wrong about this."

He pumped his legs and fanned out his arms for balance as he scrambled down the hill and toward the house. A small pen came into view beside it; three or four hogs lay huddled in a muddy pile. In front of the house, an ancient Chevy pickup was parked, all rounded corners and rusted green paint. Dudley must have been driving that heap for decades. Old folks were always so resistant to change.

*I'll bet they've never seen anything like Gwyn. That's got to be new to them.*

Walt's breath hitched. He hurried to the front door. It was locked. Walt straightened his back and pounded a fist on it hard and fast.

"Dudley? Dudley, it's Walt Blackmore! I live in the house over the hill? Dudley! I need to see you—it's an emergency!"

No lights came on. No footsteps sounded from the other side. He kept pounding, but nothing came of it. He wondered if they were just incredibly heavy sleepers, or if perhaps they were on some sort of medication that knocked them out cold.

Or if Gwyn had already come, and now there was no one left to answer.

Panic swelled in his chest, twisted his stomach. *How could she do this? Does she have no concept of consequences at all? Even if she gets away with it, what if I'm arrested? Who will feed her then?*

He backed away from the front door and began to scan the front of the house in a frantic search for another way in. That was when he finally saw the broken window above a copse of rhododendron bushes. It was not merely cracked, but smashed apart. Someone broke into the place.

Someone.

Gwyn.

Walt shrugged his jacket off and used it as a leather shield as he climbed over the bushes and through the obliterated glass. He tumbled over a plush-top window-seat and rolled onto a dusty carpet beneath it. Holding his breath, he listened. It was a creaky old farmhouse with at least two clocks clicking out of time with one another nearby. But he heard nothing indicative of a struggle, much less terror and death. He let his breath out and got to his feet. He thought he heard skittering in an adjacent room, but he wasn't sure. Probably just a cat, he decided. He moved on.

Halfway across the next room something brushed across the top of Walt's head. He flinched and threw up a hand to wave it off—it was only a jointed cord dangling from an overhead light. He gave it a yank and a frosted globe burned bright above him, flooding the room with much needed illumination. Now he could see that he was in a dining room crowded with faded and nicked antique furniture. To his left was an equally ancient-looking kitchen. To his right was a short, dark hall that ran alongside a staircase. Recalling the sole light he'd seen from outside the house, Walt went for the stairs.

He was only three steps up when a blood-cooling scream filled the air. It was not a scream of terror—that much was immediately evident. Rather, it was a mad howl, the sort of scream Walt would expect to hear in a turn-of-the-century insane asylum.

He froze mid-step. Part of him wanted to get as far away from the source of that horrendous scream as possible. But another part beckoned him forward, toward the heart of the catastrophe he had no doubt he'd find upstairs. He climbed the rest of the steps, rounded the landing and hurried toward the light at the end of the hallway. When his eyes readjusted to the sudden light in the master bedroom, he whimpered and fell against a worn oak bureau.

Gwyn was on the bed, kneeling in a pool of blood and human remains. Beside her lay the eviscerated corpse of a woman, her torso split open like an oversized Bible. Another corpse, headless, was crumpled on the floor at the foot of the bed. Its head was behind Gwyn, resting on a pillow. It was barely recognizable amid all the blood and stringy red waste, but Walt knew to whom it belonged. It was old Dudley Chapel.

He moaned with grief and horror. "Jesus Christ…"

Gwyn's glistening crimson head jerked up as a cruel, evil smile slashed across her gore-spattered face.

"Come," she said. Her voice was abrasive and malicious. "Eat."

She slid her hands into the slippery offal and brought up handfuls of the elderly couple's entrails. "Eat, Walt. *Eat.*"

He spat a single, miserable sob and went spiraling out of the room. As he flew back down the dark hall to the stairs, Gwyn's pitiless laughter filled his ears. He was disgusted and frightened, but most of all he was worried. She'd been easy to contend with when she was rooted to the ceiling, but now that she was free Walt didn't know how much longer he would be able to contain her. As long as she was hungry, Gwyn would stop at nothing to feed. And she was always hungry.

Bursting through the farmhouse's front door Walt ran wildly for the hill, all the while forcing himself to face the fact that if he wanted to keep her at home, he was going to have to bring her meals to her.

# 36

Walt sat naked in the bathtub and ran the shower. He remained there beneath the hot spray until, nearly half an hour later, it turned cold. Even then he let it run for several minutes before he realized just how cold it was. He twisted the knob to shut off the water and hung a fresh towel over his shoulders. It hadn't done much good. He felt no cleaner than he had before.

He emerged from the steamy bathroom and padded into the bedroom, leaving a trail of wet footprints in the hall. The bed was still empty and the clock read 4:45 AM. Pretty soon the sun would come up. It would burn away the darkness

Gwyn needed to sneak back home. He wondered if she'd make it. So too he wondered why he wanted her back so badly. It was her who was dependent upon him, not the other way around. She had nothing to offer him, nothing at all. So why did he pine for her quick return?

Why did he actually *miss* her?

He scrubbed his damp hair with the towel and then tossed it in the corner of the room. From the bedroom window he could see the first hint of gray on the horizon, dawn's prologue. He sighed and stretched out on the bed, letting his head sink into the pillow, and closed his eyes. In a few hours he was going to have to go to work. He was exhausted, even a little ill, but he was also a new teacher and there were impressions being made. There was no getting out of it. A brief power nap would do him good.

Walt was well on his way to sleep when the back door squealed on its rusty hinges. He snapped back into full consciousness but kept his eyes shut. Gwyn had retuned. She was home.

She came into the bedroom. Walt felt the covers pull back as she slid into bed beside him, draping one cool and sticky arm over his side. A sigh of deep satisfaction passed her lips and Walt smiled at it.

He felt strangely content.

## 37

Bored to tears, Walt straightened his back until he was uncomfortable enough to stay awake. His ninth graders were busily filling in bubbles on their exam sheets, at least for the most part. Not Jarod, naturally—the diminutive pale blonde underachiever almost certainly penciled in a straight line of all Cs, like he always did. Clem, his partner in crime, was already asleep on his desk, drooling on the test he undoubtedly just failed. Walt frowned at them. Some kids were just hopeless. In the span of a few short years, these boys would be serving Walt his cheeseburgers from a drive-thru window, and that was if things went well for them. They'd be robbing Walt's house if things went a little less well.

The thought transformed Walt's frown into a knowing smile. He'd like to see those two failures sneak into his house late one night. See how they'd like coming face-to-face with Gwyn. Her ubiquitous grin would be the last thing either of them would ever set eyes on.

A soft titter escaped his mouth. Several kids looked up from their tests, staring at him. Among them was Alice, the portly kid with the jet-black bob. Walt smiled at her. She hoisted a single, well-plucked eyebrow and returned her attention to the exam.

*12. By what method do Romeo and Juliet commit suicide?*

Walt was certain that at least half the class would miss that one. One of the options he gave, a joke, offered "jumping off the Golden Gate Bridge" as a viable option. It was option C, so he knew at least Jarod was bound to have chosen it. *Idiot.*

At the very least the school system might have allowed Walt to teach a more interesting text. Shakespeare was Shakespeare, but he much preferred *King Lear* or *Othello*. Still, after the hubbub his mysterious weeklong absence had caused back in the fall, he was hardly in the position to go about demanding curriculum changes.

So *Romeo and Juliet* it was.

*15. When the Prince asks Benvolio, "Who began this bloody fray?" to what does he refer?*

Who did begin this bloody fray? Walt swallowed hard. It was easy enough to lay every ounce of blame at Gwyn's feet. After all, he hadn't put the stain there. He didn't even know where she came from, much less what she was. Yet there was no denying that he cultivated the monster, even if he hadn't planted the seed. The option was always present to ignore it, to just let it die.

*Was it?*

He smashed her head in with a hammer. Enough to snuff anything living thing out, short of a whale. But not Gwyn.

She probably couldn't be killed. That was the true reason for Walt's actions, as far as he was concerned. Because if she was going to grow and become whole no matter what he did, it was simply logical to make sure she was on his side.

Someone among the students cleared their throat.

Walt snapped out of his reverie and glanced up at Alice, whose arm was stretched taut above her head.

"Yes, Alice?"

"I'm finished, Mr. Blackmore. May I go to the restroom?"

"Sure."

"May I go to the library after? Until the period is over?"

Several students flashed angry looks at her. Jarod grumbled. Clem stirred, but he did not wake up.

"Yes, all right. But just the library."

Alice collected her things, slung her bookbag over her shoulder, and marched to the front of the room with her exam crinkling between her chubby fingers. As she handed it to Walt, he noticed the red box of Marlboro cigarettes stuffed into the netted outer pocket of her bookbag. *Library, indeed,* he thought.

"Thanks," she said flatly before waddling out of the classroom.

"Tons o' fun," Jarod muttered. It was his standard dig at Alice's weight. A few students around him giggled.

"Jarod," Walt barked. The kid shot his ice blue eyes at his teacher.

"Uh?"

"See me after class."

Jarod sneered, and the kids who laughed with him now laughed even more uproariously at him.

They were so quick to turn on one another. Walt thought they were not entirely unlike jackals. Illiterate, unwashed, criminal little jackals. Loathsome creatures, adolescents.

Yet, as he maintained his authoritative glare at Jarod, an epiphany occurred to Walt Blackmore.

Stupid and depraved or not, meat is meat.

*Well*, Walt thought, conjuring Lord Capulet, *we were born to die.*

As she rounded the corner of the gymnasium, Alice spritzed apple-scented body spray all over herself in an effort to disguise the permeating odor of cigarettes. She was no big fan of girly scents, but anything that prevented detention for the high crime of smoking on campus was well and good in her book. And, in her estimation, apple body spray was the best tool for the job. She fanned the moist cloud over her neck and chest as she came around to the front of the ugly red brick building, keeping her eyes and mouth shut.

And ran right into someone.

"Hey, watch out, Chubs!"

Alice's heart dropped. It was Jarod.

"Sorry," she mumbled as she tried to move past the smirking kid.

But Jarod hurried to catch up to her.

"Perfume and smokes," he gibed. "Don't go too well together."

"It's not perfume."

"Yeah? What is it, then?"

"It's none of your business, Jarod."

"Now that's not very nice."

She drew her brows together into a scowl.

"Leave me alone, will you?"

"Hey! I just wanted to thank you is all."

She stopped walking across the quad, halfway between the gym and the cafeteria entrance to the main building. A few minutes ago she'd been famished, but now her appetite was suddenly waning.

Jarod was a bad kid and everybody knew it, teachers included. It was an inexplicable miracle that he'd never gotten himself booted out of school for just a quarter of the crap he pulled, usually with his lackey, Clem, in tow. It began with pulling the girls' gym shorts down in grade school, escalated to routine busts for grass and alcohol in junior high, and just that year rumors started circulating that the nasty little monster raped a girl at a barn party. Naturally, nothing came of it. Jarod pretty much always got away scot-free, no matter what he did.

Now that he was expressing an inane desire to "thank" Alice, she felt anxiety creeping in. Nothing good ever came of encounters with this sociopath.

"All right, I'll bite. Thank me for what?"

"Getting me in trouble."

"I didn't get you in trouble."

"Well, I might have made a little comment when you ditched class for the library. Mr. Blackmore didn't take very kindly to it, so I got in trouble."

"I'll bet I can just guess what you said."

She'd heard it a hundred times before. A thousand. *Tons o' fun.* It never failed to elicit peals of laughter from Clem, who was not so skinny himself. But, of course, it was different for girls. Everything was.

"Never mind that," Jarod said with a serious look. "Turns out, the old prick gave me a choice."

"That so?"

"Yeah. He said I can do a week's detention, seven AM in the cafeteria every day starting Monday. I said I thought that sucked."

"You told him that?"

"Sure I did."

"You're cruising."

"Ah, fuck it. Fuck *him*. Anyway, then I get the second option."

Alice winced, certain she was about to hear about the sort of thing she heard on the news all the time but had never seen in front of her eyes. Was her teacher blackmailing Jarod for sexual favors?

"Said I can drop by his house. Tonight."

"Oh, shit."

"That's what I said. I'm thinking this old faggot wants to ream me. I mean, I was about to knock that queer right out of his fucking chair!"

She shook her head and clicked her tongue. Alice wasn't particularly enthused by Jarod's abundant use of homophobic epithets—the closest girls like her ever got to the opposite sex was by way of gay boys—but a perverted pedophile English teacher was another can of worms altogether.

"Did you go straight to Principal Byrne?"

"Fuck no, I didn't. Blackmore didn't say anything gross, not yet anyways. He said he wants me to know *Romeo and Juliet* like the back of my hand before he makes me retake the goddamn test. You believe that shit?"

Alice said, "Hmm." It still didn't sound right to her. Not in the least. A teacher asking a student to visit his house? Alone? Nothing good could come of that.

"I don't know, Jarod. Sounds...skeevy."

"One, I'm not letting any fudge-packer within a county mile of my shithole."

He was counting off on his fingers. Alice resumed her sneer.

"And two, this is a winning situation for me. And, I think, maybe for you."

"I don't even want to ask," she said. "In fact, all I want to do is eat my lunch. Alone."

"I don't wanna get between a big girl and her lunch," Jarod said snidely. "But why don't you hear me out first."

A long, heavy sigh spilled out of her mouth.

"Can you make it quick?"

"Jesus, you *are* hungry."

She glowered at him as she curled her right hand into a tight fist. One more remark like that was all she needed.

"Okay, here it is. I'm going to rob him."

"What? Who?"

*Why is telling me this? Why can't he just leave me alone?*

"Who do you think, dummy? Blackmore."

"You're going to rob our English teacher."

"Ain't that what I just said?"

Before she could stop herself, she erupted into laughter. In a way, she was glad for the unintended punchline; it made the bad medicine of having to waste time talking to the mean little gnome go down much smoother. They weren't friends, often as he acted like they were.

As for Jarod, he was far less amused. He furrowed his brow at Alice's mirth.

"Knock it off," he growled. "I'm dead serious."

"I know you are," Alice managed between gasps for breath. "That's what makes it so funny."

"You don't think I could pull it off?"

"Of course not. I mean, no offense, but you're what? A straight-D student?"

"What's that got to do with anything?"

"Just that thieves are supposed to be smart. The dumb ones always wind up in jail."

"Ah, I get it. You think I'm dumb? You think I'm going to end up in the slammer?"

"That's about the size of it, yeah."

"Okay, just watch me. I was going to cut you in because I could use a wingman, but fuck that. I'm going in solo."

"Yeah? What about Clem?"

Jarod blew a sharp puff of air through his nose.

"You kidding? He's functionally retarded."

"At least we can agree on one thing."

"I *guess*," Jarod groused.

Alice shook her head again and made for the cafeteria door. Jarod reached out and grabbed her hard by the wrist.

"Hey!"

"Since you're not interested in my offer, you had better keep your fat mouth shut, got it?"

"Let go of my wrist!"

"You hear me?"

"I heard you!"

"Keep it zipped, Chubs. I mean it."

"All right!"

She wrenched her arm free from the little guy's grip. With a snarl and a roll of the eyes, she hustled into the cafeteria.

*Asshole*, she thought.

## 38

Forgoing actually looking at them, Walt stuffed all of the exams from the day in his briefcase. There were seventy-three of them: the total of his first, third and fourth period students. Walt sincerely doubted there would be more than five A-level tests in the lot. He had no intention of finding out tonight, either.

Tonight, he was booked.

As the latches on his briefcase snapped shut, a familiar shape filled the doorway to his left. Short pudgy arms crossed tightly over her enormous breasts and the black Dimmu Borgir T-shirt that was stretched across them.

Alice.

All of her shirts bore screened images of monsters and demons and nude women beneath emblazoned logos of loud metal groups with threatening names. Teenagers were nothing if not predicable.

"Mr. Blackmore?"

He fought back an exasperated sigh.

"Yes, Alice?"

"Can I ask you something?"

Walt clenched his jaw and checked his wristwatch. 3:45. If he left that instant, he might not get home until closer to five. And with that awful Jarod kid coming around at 5:30…

"Can it wait? It's just, I've got this…meeting."

Alice said, "Um."

He forced a smile, trying to make it as genuine looking as possible.

"Tomorrow, okay?"

The girl nodded sadly. Her bob bounced slightly.

Walt grabbed the briefcase, patted Alice gently on the shoulder and then vanished into the hallway.

He pulled into his driveway at 4:40. He smiled at the digital clock built into the dash. Plenty of time. He grabbed his briefcase, locked the car and headed into the house.

She was lounging on the couch, completely naked. Walt had asked her not to constantly remain nude, but she consistently refused. He also requested she lay something down on the couch to keep her seeping scabs from staining the fabric, but that too fell on deaf ears. There was just no arguing with a woman like Gwyn.

But then again, there was no woman like Gwyn.

During the couple of months since she emerged from her place in the ceiling, Gwyn's skin gradually began to grow in. But it was more like healing than growing—by November her entire body was encased in soft, leathery lesions. Now, two weeks to Christmas, the large, octagonal scabs were hard and flaky. And they *leaked.* They leaked everywhere and on everything she touched. Bed sheets could be washed, and he did not mind that much. Walt liked sleeping beside Gwyn at night. But the damn couch…

When she heard the front door creak open, she bolted upright and twisted so that she could face him. Several scabby chunks snapped off of her neck and shoulder with the rapid motion. They drifted down to the couch as the pink, freshly bared areas of raw flesh oozed whitish fluid.

"Walt!" she hungrily called out.

He smiled and set the briefcase down by the door. Her voice was so much nicer now. Feminine. Not scratchy like it had been. Maybe breathy, like Kathleen Turner. He guessed that her vocal cords had healed, too.

"Good news," he said as he approached her on the couch. She arched her neck and lifted her chin. More scabs pulled apart wherever her skin stretched. Walt bent at the waist and pressed his lips firmly to hers. They were dry and scaly, but the kiss lingered for several long seconds before he came back up for air. "We're having a guest tonight."

Gwyn's frosty eyes widened.

"Tonight?"

"That's right."

"Walt! Who?"

"The worst kid in school. A real piece of work."

"What is he, a huge bruiser?" She licked her lips as she considered the possibilities.

He crooked his mouth to one side. "Well, no. He's just a little guy. Looks like he stopped growing around sixth grade."

Gwyn's eyelids slid back down to their normal position, but her eager grin remained.

"That's all right. That's good. I didn't expect…*tonight!*"

Walt checked his watch. "Pretty soon, actually. You might want to make yourself scarce before too long."

Her lips contracted to cover her shiny white teeth.

"Oh, *Walt...*"

"Now don't get like that. You know you can't be seen when he's here."

"You are ashamed of me."

"That's not true, and you know it. But you're my little secret, Gwyn. You're special, beyond that even. You're a miracle."

"I am a monster."

"Not at all. Out there—" He pointed vaguely at the bay window overlooking the porch. "—are where monsters be. Millions of them. But not in here. Never here."

Gwyn's smile gradually stretched back across her face.

"Kiss me, Walt."

He sat down beside her on the couch and wrapped an arm around her coarse, scaly back. Tugging her close to him, Walt then pried Gwyn's lips apart with his own and began exploring her mouth with his tongue. Softly moaning, she pulled back until she was lying down on the couch. She spread her arms out like wings. Then her legs. He ogled at her flaking, scabrous shell, how it completely encased her breasts and disappeared into a fine, dark line between her rusty brown legs.

"*Now,* Walt."

Swallowing a mouthful of saliva, he shook his head.

"Can't. Not just yet."

"Now."

"That kid, he'll be here any minute. Besides, I've got to do the pit."

"There's time."

"There's not."

"NOW!"

Gwyn's mouth twisted into a cruel and threatening sneer. Her eyes bulged, the pale blue of her irises framed by wildly branching bloodshot veins. Walt stiffened.

"Darling, if he sees you as soon as he comes in, you won't get any supper. You'll go hungry, see? Can't we wait, and have it both ways?"

She let out a low, guttural growl. Her old voice, raspy and more than a little unsettling.

"There is meat upstairs," she grumbled.

"No, Gwyn. No. Not her."

"In the attic…"

"She's my *sister*, darling."

"So tender. So succulent."

Gwyn's pink tongue darted out, licked her scab encrusted lips.

"No! The kid will be here. Just a little longer, and then you can feed."

Her eyes narrowed to slits. She bared her teeth like an angry mongrel dog.

"I will have him," she hissed.

He nodded vigorously. She pulled her legs up and dropped them to the floor. Then she hopped up and made for the back of the house, her fingers splayed out like talons.

"And then I will have *you*," she snarled as she vanished from view.

# 39

"It can't be this far," Clem grumbled.

"It's gotta be," Jarod argued. "Directions say ten miles down Highway 5. We haven't gone six, yet."

"Why the hell's he wanna live out here, anyway? This is hillbilly country. Sheepfuckers and shit."

Jarod chortled.

"Sheepfuckers," he mimicked.

"It's true. Knew a guy in eighth grade lived out this way. Swear to God his name was Elvis. Everybody knew him because it got out he boned a sheep on his uncle's farm."

"That's nasty."

"Of course it's nasty. But there it is. This is sheepfucker country."

"Well, we'll just have to wait and see if Blackmore's got any sheep."

"Nah," Clem protested. "Teach's no hucklebuck." He steadied the wheel with his left hand while he fished a joint of his shirt pocket with the other. "But dollars to doughnuts he fucks his sister."

"Hah!"

Jarod burst into phlegmy laughter.

"Bet they got kids together!" Clem went on. "They all got one eye each and no hair. Fuckin' incest babies."

"You're gross, man."

"And they got babies *with* the babies, too."

"Stop it! You're going to make me barf, dude."

"Just calling 'em like I see 'em."

"Gross."

Clem chuckled. He delighted in appalling people, especially Jarod. He was the hardest one to gross out, but he almost never failed. Now he grinned triumphantly as he fired up his jay with the car lighter. Jarod flipped on the dome light and peered at the directions he'd printed out.

"Turn that shit off," Clem grumbled.

"Just a sec. In a few minutes there's a left turn, on Hawthorne. It's not too much farther up there before we hit Blackmore's pad, so we gotta take it slow. I'll get out before we're too close so you can circle around and hang tight."

"Yeah, I know, I know. Jesus, you think I'm stupid?"

"Pretty goddamn stupid, sure."

"Fuck you, man."

"In your dreams, faggot."

Clem slammed down on the brake pad and the car shuddered to a sudden stop. Jarod lurched forward, narrowly missing a collision with the dashboard because, for once, he had his seatbelt on.

"The hell, man?"

"What'd you say to me?"

"Nothing, Clem. Shit—it was a joke. I was *joking*."

"Take it back."

"What do you mean, take it back? I was just ribbing you, man. Fuck's sake, can't you take a joke?"

"I dunno, can you take a mouthful of broken teeth?"

Jarod stared, shaken but not too surprised. Clem *could* take a joke, most of the time, but not when it came to the gay stuff. He drew the line there. Jarod never knew why, and he usually forgot all about it, but at times like these it all came crashing back down on him. *Don't make fag jokes with Clem Lundeen.*

"All right, I'm sorry. Okay?"

Clem glared at him, the dome light creating weirdly long shadows across his face. It made him seem more menacing than usual.

"I said I take it back."

"You'd goddamn better."

"I said I did!"

Clem grunted. Then, after a few awkward seconds of silence, he switched off the dome light and gently tapped the gas. The car rolled on down Highway 5, and neither of the teenage boys inside said another word.

After making sure that the backyard security light was off, Walt quietly slipped outside. He shone the flashlight in his hand around the back of the house until he located the dusty blue tarp. Pulling it down, he exposed the wheelbarrow and shovel he kept hidden underneath. Then he turned and shone the light across the dry, brown lawn where another large blue tarp was laid out. He placed the shovel on top of the dusty white mound in the wheelbarrow and pushed it over to the second tarp. He'd neglected to put on his dust mask, but there was hardly time to go back for it now. He resolved to try not to breathe it in. The last thing he wanted was a lungful of quicklime.

With his lips clenched tight and his breath held in his chest, Walt yanked the tarp to the side and revealed the pit.

The sour, acerbic odor slammed his senses right away. There was nothing like putrid human tissue being slowly dissolved in calcium oxide to wake someone up, and quick.

When he got re-acclimated to the shock of the pit's offensive stench, Walt pointed the flashlight down into it. The lime was doing its job, albeit very gradually. There was little more than porous bone left now, nothing compared to the gruesome horror that once lay in there.

When Amanda passed away, her remains were of little use to Gwyn. The gangrene had spread throughout her right leg, ruining all of it and tainting much of the surrounding flesh. The blood was no good, either. Walt doubted if Gwyn had managed to eat a quarter of Amanda's meat. The rest got tossed into the pit and covered up with the quicklime he bought at the hardware store in town. Then went Margaret's remains, which were reduced to nothing but the bones. Gwyn had a feast for herself with that one.

Margaret elicited no tears from Walt. He barely knew her and never much liked the austere woman. For Amanda, contrarily, he cried at the edge of the pit more often than not. Although lately, that had begun to taper off. He was moving on, getting used to his new situation.

Life without Amanda.

Life with Gwyn.

He did not cry now as he scooped a shovelful of lime over the decaying skeletons in his backyard corpse pit. Not for

Amanda, certainly not for Margaret, and not for the two stray dogs he'd lured into his yard with the promise of fresh red meat. They got crushed skulls for their trouble. Gwyn complained about the flavor and texture. Naturally, she demanded only the best—it had to be human.

When Walt was satisfied that the pit was in good shape, he re-covered it with the tarp, replaced the shovel in the wheelbarrow and pushed it back to the house. He almost groaned knowing he was going to have to repeat the process in a few short hours, but he was thankful that it was all for a good cause. Gwyn could finally—if only temporarily—be sated, and satiation meant comparative sanity. Sarah could live another day without having to worry about Gwyn's ever-growing lust for the hot blood in her veins. And Walt would finally be rid of one of the nastiest thorns in his paw: that bile-inducing rotten apple, Jarod.

That was enough to slow his thudding heart, and even induce a slight upturn at the corners of his mouth, as he wiped his hands on his slacks and went back inside.

Sarah wanted to turn on her side, but she was afraid of reopening the cuts on her back. They were only just beginning to heal up, so she was willing to sacrifice a modicum of comfort in favor of not worsening the wounds. Besides, ever since Walt hauled the twin mattress up to the attic—soiled and smelly though it was—resting was a considerably simpler task for her. It certainly beat stretching out over itchy fiberglass and hard, splintery beams.

Not that this eased the raging hatred she felt for her brother. One stinky mattress for an unwilling captive and blood donor hardly amounted to warm feelings. She doubted she could ever stop loathing him even if the son of a bitch killed that disgusting beast and set her free.

But, of course, all that blood-chilling moaning and growling that filled the otherwise quiet night air did anything but suggest an end to this nightmare. What it *did* suggest was that Walt was having sex with that thing. As far as she could determine, that meant he was lost to her forever. She was on her own going forward.

*Why don't they just kill me and get it over with? Why keep me alive?*

She hated herself for asking that question, mainly because she knew the horrifying answer from the lips of the creature itself. One of the first times it crept up into the attic on its own, while Walt was away, it peeled Sarah's scabs off and split the skin apart. Then, when it was done lapping at the blood that oozed from Sarah's hot, painful wounds, it hissed at her.

"My tasty…little…blooood cowww..."

She shuddered at the memory. It was then that it dawned on her that she was going to be kept as a sanguinary reserve until further notice, or until the monster grew too hungry to wait for the next poor bastard her psychotic brother brought along for it.

So those were her options. Her future. Either she'd be torn asunder by a flesh-eating monstrosity or bled in the attic until her body just gave up.

She forsook her prior decision and rolled over onto her side. Nearly a dozen two- and three-inch scabs ripped apart from the small of her back to the tops of her shoulders. And as they began to bleed anew, Sarah wept.

*Mitch, you lazy son of a bitch,* she thought. *Haven't you even fucking noticed I'm gone?*

## 40

"Out."

Clem didn't look at Jarod when he barked the order. Jarod

sneered, ready to lay into his friend, but thought better of it. Clem was no great fighter, but he had an easy eighty pounds on Jarod. Little guys like him needed to choose their fights carefully, and this one just wasn't worth it.

So, he complied. He gently opened the passenger side door, climbed out the car, and gently shut it again. Almost instantly Clem rolled slowly away, leaving Jarod in the near total darkness of the outlying country road. The only light he could make out apart from the dim sliver of moon and the few stars uncovered by threatening black clouds was the yellow porch light in the distance. Blackmore's house.

He started walking.

At the hesitant knock, Walt turned from the snack he was preparing in the kitchen and went to the front door. He unlocked the deadbolt and opened it to reveal the small fourteen-year-old boy on his porch. Jarod gazed up at him with dead, emotionless eyes. The kid was shivering; his thin tan jacket insufficient protection from the frigid December air.

"Come in, Jarod."

The boy hurried into the warmth of the foyer without a word. Walt locked the door behind him.

"I was just putting a snack together. Do you like crackers and cheese? I'm fairly sure there's a summer sausage around here someplace."

Jarod frowned.

"Not really hungry."

"No? Well, more for me, then. I'm going to put some coffee on, too, but I guess you're probably too young to like that."

"Got any beer?"

Walt snickered.

"Nice try, Jarod."

"What? My dad lets me drink beer all the time."

Walt wanted to say, *I don't doubt that at all*, but he held his tongue. Instead, he silently returned to the kitchen and began preparing the coffee. Once it started to sputter and drip, Walt leaned against the counter and smiled at Jarod. The kid was still frowning.

"Sure you don't want that snack?"

"Said I'm not hungry," Jarod grouchily replied.

"Okay. Then I guess we should get started. When are your folks picking you up? Are they here?"

"I took a cab."

"A cab? What for? That must've cost fifty dollars or more."

"No skin off my ass."

Walt narrowed his eyes with a small laugh.

"All right, then. Do you have any questions before we begin?"

Jarod crooked his head to one side and raised an eyebrow. "About what?"

"The play. *Romeo and Juliet*?"

"Sure—I got a question."

"Shoot."

"Why do I gotta read dumb shit like this anyways? I mean, what good is it? I'm never going to be like you. I'll probably just sign up with the Army or the Marines soon as I'm outta school. Think this faggy Shakespeare crap's gonna get me out of a firefight in Fallujah or some place?"

"No," Walt admitted. "I don't suppose that it would."

"I mean, the world needs ditch diggers too, right?"

"That it does. But that doesn't necessarily mean you have to be one, Jarod."

"What if I want to? Is that a crime?"

"Not in the least. But even ditch diggers can appreciate literature."

"You can feed me all the turds you want, Mr. Blackmore, but that don't mean I gotta like it."

Walt smiled. A quiet and somewhat tense minute passed. Then he went over to the refrigerator, opened it up, and grabbed something from inside.

"Heads up," he said as he tossed a can of Lone Star to Jarod.

The boy caught it with a wet slap against his hand. His eyes widened with disbelief. When Walt closed the fridge, he had a can of beer for himself. He cracked it open and raised it.

"Bottoms up," he said with a mischievous grin.

Jarod's face beamed like he'd just won the lottery and lost his virginity at the same time. He was quick to pop his can open and take a long swig that he finished up with a drawn out sigh.

"Good shit," Jarod said.

Walt laughed. "Glad you like it."

"You're not so bad, Mr. B. For a teacher and shit."

"Thanks, Jarod. That means a lot."

Jarod enjoyed another guzzle and wiped his mouth with the back of his hand. "So, we're done with this Romeo crap? I mean, you get me, right?"

"Sure, Jarod. I get you."

"Solid."

The hardwood floor creaked somewhere on the other side of the house. To Walt it sounded like it came from the dining area. He did his best to ignore it, and Jarod didn't seem to notice it at all. He was too busy snagging cheese-laden crackers from the plate on the kitchen island.

"I thought you weren't hungry," Walt said as he moved his eyes from the dimly lit living room back to Jarod.

"Beer gives me the munchies sometimes."

Another creak. Closer.

Jarod darted his eyes in the direction of the dining area. Walt stiffened.

"I'd better get that summer sausage out, then," he said a little too loudly.

"Nah," the boy said as he returned his dull gaze to Walt.

"This here's fine."

"Whatever you say."

*Creak.*

Clem parked the car a hundred yards down the road from Blackmore's house and killed the engine. The abrupt silence in the wake of his rumbling engine was oddly jarring. He could hear his own pulse thumping in his ears. There weren't even crickets chirping outside. Just the cold, still air of the backwoods night.

The clock in the dash read 5:40 when he stopped the car. That gave Clem plenty of time to get moving. He thought about firing up another jay, but settled for a Kool instead. He wanted to keep his mind as clear as possible for what was coming up.

A robbery. The thought of it alone sent his heart slamming against his ribcage. It also scared him shitless. Clem had gotten himself mixed up with some reasonably wild misadventures, especially since he hooked up with Jarod at the start of the school year, but nothing quite bordering on a felony. Not until now. They'd spray-painted COCKSUCKER on the I-30 overpass by the Pentecostal Church that one night, and there was the time he stood lookout while Jarod bored a hole in the wall between the boys' and girls' locker rooms at school. Clem never thought anything would get better than that, not after seeing a good quarter of the ninth and tenth grade girls' tits in one fell swoop. Yet even though there were no girls concerned this time around, a real, honest-to-Christ home robbery somehow trumped it all.

Particularly since it involved ripping off that shithead Blackmore.

Clem licked his lips and sucked at the menthol cigarette. As soon as he was finished with it, he'd sneak over to the house, case the joint and have a look inside. Then he'd wait for

Jarod to signal him, let him know what to do next. They had to play it by ear, neither of them having been there before. They didn't know Blackmore's routines or even what all he owned. But before too long, that dumb bastard was going to be kicking himself for being so smug and stupid all the damn time.

Clem sniggered between drags on the Kool. Then he flicked it out the window and stepped out of the car.

"Showtime," he said.

# 41

Walt pulled another can of Lone Star from the fridge, cracked it open and handed it to Jarod. The boy gulped a third of it down before belching and then muttering, "Thanks."

"No problem," Walt said. He had not gotten another beer for himself.

Jarod guzzled as another floorboard creaked behind him. He stopped in mid-swallow and his eyes drifted toward the source of the sound.

"What was that?"

"What was what?"

"Is there somebody else here?"

"No. Just me. Well, and you."

"Oh."

*Creak.*

Jarod bunched his eyebrows.

"It's an old house. It makes a lot of little noises, especially at night. Me, I kind of like it that way."

"I think it's creepy as shit."

"Different strokes."

"I guess..."

After he polished off his beer, Jarod squashed the can in his fist and set it down on the island counter. It wobbled for a bit, throwing a tinny echo around the kitchen. When it stopped, it was replaced by an awkward silence. Neither Jarod nor Walt spoke, ate, or drank. They only stared uncomfortably at one another.

"Well, if that's it…"

"Wait, you don't want to talk about anything?"

Walt stepped forward, his eyes a little too wide for Jarod's comfort. The boy winced and stepped back.

"Talk? No. I think I'd best be going…"

"Aren't you maybe a little worried about your grade, Jarod? I mean, let's be honest—you aren't doing so well in English. I'll bet your other subjects are suffering, too. It might not seem like such a big deal right now, but down the road…"

Jarod curled his hands into fists and adopted a defensive stance. His nervous expression gave way to one of rage.

"I knew it!" he bellowed. "I fucking knew it!"

"You knew what?"

"I knew you was a queer, that's what! You don't give a shit about no Shakespeare, you just want to get with young boys!"

"No! That's not…no!"

"Fucking sick, man!"

"You've got this all wrong." Walt apologetically displayed his palms. "It's not like that."

"Yeah? A teacher, who lives by himself, has a fourteen-year-old kid come to his house? At night? And then you're all like, *how about them grades, Jarod?* Well, I ain't letting some nasty old homo touch my dick for an A in his stupid goddamn English class, I'll tell you that!"

*Creak.*

"I ought to kick your ass!" Jarod raged on. "I ought to curb stomp your ass, is what I should do!"

"Okay, calm down…"

"No! Fuck you, man! I'm getting the hell out of here. Then I'm calling the cops!"

*Creak. Creak.*

"The cops! Now, come on..."

"You know what they do to child molesters in prison, *Walter?* They kill 'em! They fucking kill 'em!"

*Creak.*

"What the hell *is* that?!"

His face red and sweaty and his breath coming short and fast, Jarod spun around to face the direction of the creaking. He shrieked.

"Hello, Jarod," Gwyn whispered through clenched teeth.

Jarod sucked in a gasp of air and froze. The reddish-brown creature in front of him grinned broadly and licked its jagged, scab-encrusted lips. The boy wanted to cry out, to ask Blackmore to help him.

But it was Walt Blackmore who slammed two laced fists into Jarod's temple, knocking him to the floor and making the world brown out around him.

The last thing he heard was a low, raspy chortling.

Clem crouched outside the darkened window and rubbed his cold hands together, occasionally exhaling warm, white steam into them. He couldn't remember if it was this cold when he and Jarod set out, but he didn't think it was. It had been chillier than hell, to be sure, but now it was downright frigid. The stagnant air bit at his face. He hoped he wouldn't have to sit out there much longer.

*What's taking him so long?*

He could faintly hear murmuring, voices talking. Jarod and Blackmore, just chatting it up while Clem froze to death outside.

He wondered if he'd been the object of a prank, if the whole robbery thing was bullshit and Jarod would end up laughing his head off that Clem sat out there half the night, waiting to be let in.

But he decided that his buddy wouldn't do that. Not to him, anyway.

So he waited.

If it hadn't been so cold, he might have nodded off.

He nearly did, anyway.

Until he heard an ear-splitting scream, shortly followed by a hollow thump.

*Shit! What was that?*

Clem pulled himself up to the window and tried to look inside. All he could see was pitch blackness. It could have been a curtain, but it was too dark to tell. He sank back down to a crouch.

*Shit! Shit, shit, shit!*

His heart thudding and cold beads of sweat forming on his face, he bounced on his heels while he tried to decide what to do. If it was Blackmore who screamed, then all there was to do was wait. Jarod had it under control. But what if it was Jarod? Or somebody else? Clem didn't know if Blackmore was married, or if he had any kids. He was relatively certain a douchebag like that lived alone, but one could never be sure. The thing of it was, he had no way of knowing *who* screamed in the house.

He had no choice. He had to investigate.

Once again, he pushed himself up to a standing position and then flattened himself against the cold aluminum siding that covered the outside of the house. He listened, but he heard nothing more than his own short breaths. Keeping his body pressed against the side of the house, he began sidestepping toward the front, where the porch light glowed orange in the otherwise black night.

Through the frosted bay window he saw two indistinct figures moving around inside. One of them bobbed up and down, waving its arms. The other seemed to just watch and did not move at all.

Jarod and Blackmore?

Clem crept by the window and continued to peer in, but all he could make out were blurry silhouettes through the dense crystals of frost. The active one was relatively short and thin, not altogether unlike Jarod. But it was impossible to be sure. And Clem couldn't think of a good reason the kid should be flailing around that way.

Staying low and flush with the house, he snuck across the porch to the front door. The globe around the light hung directly above. Dozens of small black spots were backlit inside of it. Summer's dead bugs. He frowned at them, reminded of how he always puzzled at them when he was younger. It never made a lick of sense to him that the stupid insects would continue to climb into the death trap when all their friends and family's fried corpses were so obviously piled up in there.

He reached up and gently grabbed the doorknob. He slowly twisted it, but discovered to his chagrin that it would not give. It was locked.

"Fuck," he whispered.

Something slammed inside, a sharp burst of sound like a belly flop in the pool. His shoulders jerked.

Then a gruff female voice screeched, "Yes! Yes, Walt! *Hurry!*"

Clem screwed up his face.

*Sex?*

*Is Jarod involved?*

Maybe some kind of twisted three-way between Jarod, Mr. Blackmore and some chick. *Mrs. Blackmore?* Clem puffed up his cheeks and slowly let the air out. This was getting too far out for him.

Another loud slamming cracked out.

*More like an old wooden baseball bat hitting a homer*, he thought.

Way too far out.

With a deep breath, he looked out toward the dark country road. Just a hundred yards away, his car sat in the shadows. He had the keys. There would be nothing easier in the world than skittering back to the car and getting the hell out of there. Let Jarod do what he wants. *I'm not getting naked with the goddamn English teacher.*

Slowly Clem rose and checked his front pocket for his keys. They were there, just where he put them.

It was time to go.

"Quick! Cut it off! *Give it to meeee!*"

The skin on Clem's back tingled. He looked back at the hazy forms in the frosted window one last time, and then turned to the porch steps.

He pressed his foot down on the top stair and it creaked. He stepped on the next one more carefully.

A high-pitched squeal erupted from behind him inside the house. He lurched, lost his footing. He shouted out and tumbled down the steps, every impact pounding loudly against the wood.

Crashing footfalls raced toward him from inside, toward the front door.

"*Shit!*"

Clem scrambled away from the steps, anchored his palms on the cold, dead lawn and pushed himself up. He leapt to his feet, but his left ankle burned with pain when his weight fell on it. The ankle gave, and he collapsed to the ground.

Something rattled on the porch and the front door creaked open. Partially obscured by the blinding globe of light above him, Mr. Blackmore loomed in the doorway, looking down at him.

The older man gave a slight gasp. Then he started to chuckle.

"I should have known," Blackmore said.

# 42

The kid was sprawled out on the lawn, his neck twisted so he could look up at Walt.

"Tad chilly out here, don't you think?" Walt asked. "Come on, let's get you inside where it's nice and warm."

Clem reached out and grabbed handfuls of grass, desperately trying to claw his way forward.

"S-s-s'okay, Mr. Blackmore," he stammered. "I wa- was just going home anyways…"

"Don't be an idiot, son," Walt growled as he lunged for the boy's leg.

Clem let out a terrified squeak when Walt seized his twisted ankle and began dragging him back up the steps.

"I've got soup and fixings for cheese sandwiches," the teacher droned on between huffing breaths. "Nice food for dreary weather."

Clem bumped and bounced over the steps. The last one caught him hard on the chin. He moaned in pain.

"It'll be just like a snow day," Walt went on. He was holding the door open with his rump while dragging the kid into the foyer by his foot. "Just like Christmas."

"Please, Mr. Blackmore!" Clem mewled franticly. "*Please!* I don't care what you did to Jarod! I won't tell nobody! *PLEASE!*"

The door slammed shut.

Walt released Clem's leg and secured the deadbolt and guard chain.

The boy rolled on his back, sat up, and saw what he'd been listening to from the other side of the front door.

A slick, glistening pile of chopped up meat and bones and guts. All dark red and pink and black. On one end was Jarod's head, his mouth hanging open and his pale eyes staring at the ceiling. His tongue lolled out lazily, like it was just a prop he'd put there for a laugh. Surrounding the grisly, wet mound were

Jarod's arms and legs. They were bare. Clem did not see his pants, shirt, socks or shoes anywhere. But they'd stripped him. Stripped him and slaughtered him.

Perhaps most upsetting of all was the dead boy's groin, which had been split down the middle, the genitals sliced clean off. All that remained was an inverted chevron of butchered gore.

A low, plaintive bray came from Clem as his eyes darted to Walt. His teacher's pale green polo shirt was splattered with blood. Walt leaned over the butchered body on the floor and came back with a huge cleaver in his hand. It, too, was dripping.

Walt grinned sheepishly and shrugged.

"The lady was hungry," he said, almost apologetically.

Clem didn't bother to wonder what that meant. Instead, he turned away from the reeking, bloody mess, and retched. He vomited for what seemed like a long time, lurching and puking in waves until his insides were completely emptied onto Walt's scuffed wood floor. For a time after that he remained bent over the massive, stinking pool of vomit, spitting out strands of chunky saliva.

"Better be careful," Walt quietly warned. "You'll ruin her appetite."

"Guh," Clem groaned.

"All better now?"

"Guh."

Walt chuckled. He padded over to where Clem kneeled and eased the boy away from his own sick. Clem managed to sit up, his pink, swollen eyes leaking tears, his lips wet and shiny from all the spit and puke. Some of it had splashed back up from the floor and besmirched his faded Pink Floyd T-shirt. He didn't seem to notice.

"Whew!" Walt blurted out. "You're a frightful mess. Let's get you out of those nasty clothes."

He leaned down to take hold of Clem's jacket, but the kid jerked away. He groaned pitifully.

"Ah, yes," Walt knowingly announced. "You share your late buddy's apprehensions. Please, let me set your mind at ease—I have no untoward sexual designs on you. In fact, I am very happily committed to the most incredible woman in the world. Perhaps you'd like to meet her?"

"Nuh," Clem mumbled as he wiped his mouth on his sleeve.

He was beginning to really weep now. His chin trembled as he blubbered and whined. Walt shook his head.

"Come *on*, Clem! You're practically an *adult* now! Stop acting like a fucking baby!"

The boy only cried harder.

The emergence of Gwyn from the kitchen did nothing to assuage his fit.

"*Another one...?*" she said.

"Yes, unfortunately," groaned Walt.

Clem's eyes widened as a nude woman with scabs for skin stepped out of the kitchen and into the light of the foyer.

"Oh, God," he said.

Gwyn gave a throaty laugh. She walked like a model, sashaying her full hips from side to side with every step closer to him. Her motions were so exaggerated that hundreds of dry, brown flakes cascaded down from her scaly skin, leaving a trail of scabs in her wake. Wherever the crusty pieces split away from her, light pink tissue was revealed, piece by piece. It was a slow, repulsive striptease.

"Oh, no. No, no, no, no."

"Who is thissss one?" the scabby woman hissed. She was addressing Walt, but her gaze was firmly fixed on the vomit-spattered boy on the floor.

"Clem Lundeen," Walt ruefully answered. "If that one was the worst of the lot, then this one's a very close second."

Gwyn dropped quickly to a crouch when she reached the kid. She thrust her terrible face close to his and slowly stretched her mouth wide open. Clem shuddered and emitted a quiet whimper.

"Please," he begged.

Her tongue shot out. It was long and it glistened in the light. With a sensual moan, she pressed her tongue to Clem's jaw line and ran it up his face, licking and salivating on his sweaty, pimply skin. When she was done, she licked all the way up the other side. She then retracted the tongue into her mouth, shut her eyes and pursed her lips. She was savoring the flavor of him.

"Mmmm," she hummed. "Delicious."

In spite of himself, Clem felt his crotch squirm.

*Christ*, he thought. *Not now!*

But he had no control over it. No matter how horrifying the bloody tableau before him was, and despite the stomach-churning sight of this abominable woman all covered with crusty, peeling scabs, the fact that she was *licking* him…

Gwyn's tongue slid over his lips, probing them. She shoved it between his lips, and the boy didn't resist. He trembled as she explored the inside of his mouth, licking his tongue, his teeth and the insides of his cheeks. As long as he kept his eyes squeezed shut, it was not totally unpleasant. Even a little nice. To be sure, he'd never done anything like *this* with a girl before. Now her hand slid up his leg, slowing at the thigh and gliding over his swelling groin. Clem softly moaned as Gwyn closed her hand around his crotch and gently squeezed. She pulled her tongue out his mouth, flicking the tip of it against his upper lip. Then the hand went away, too.

Clem took in a sharp breath and waited for the exciting sensations to continue. When they didn't, he held the air in his lungs and cracked one eye open.

Walt loomed over him now. The cleaver in his hand

glinted in the light.

"Sorry, Clem," he said softly. "Wish you'd just stayed home."

With that, the blade shot up high, ready to speed back down into his skull.

Clem gasped. Then he lunged forward and thrust his head into Walt's groin. Walt groaned in pain and dropped the cleaver. The blade sank into the hardwood floor with a dull thud. Clem made a tight fist and pounded it into the side of Walt's head. With a startled mewl, Walt collapsed to the floor as the boy leapt up to his feet.

Lurking just a few feet away, her rough, flaky hands curled into claws, Gwyn growled like a wild animal. She moved swiftly between Clem and the front door. Clem didn't waste a second; he bolted for the back of the house instead.

Walt grumbled something incoherent. Gwyn screamed.

Clem could hear her huffing, her bare feet slapping against the floor as she ran after him. He sank into the darkness of the back of the house. An instant later, he crashed against the back door. His fingers fumbled in the dark for the doorknob, found it and twisted the cold metal knob. It was unlocked. He yanked hard, threw the door open and burst out into the frigid winter night.

The moon cast a gray sliver of dim light across the expanse of the backyard. Clem sprinted into it, his lungs already hot and ready to burst. He had to keep going; that *thing* was still close behind, hissing and scrambling after him. Between rasping breaths, it tittered and mumbled.

Clem pumped his legs harder. Sweat seeped out of every pore in his head, instantly cooling in the freezing air and chilling his skin. He wanted to stop, to catch his breath, but he had to keep on. The dreadful image of poor Jarod, disemboweled and his dick and balls cut off, was burned into his brain. It was enough to drive him on, keep him running, in his desperate fear of meeting the same ghastly fate.

Somehow, the worst part of it all was knowing that the woman ate it. *Give it to me.* That's what they did. They killed people and cut them up and ate them.

A tiny squeak shot out of Clem's mouth when the ground disappeared underneath his feet. He only fell for a fraction of a second, but it seemed like he was drifting through space for a while. When he landed, he sank into softness rather than slamming against hard ground. It felt a bit like sand, but less densely packed.

Clem scurried in the low place, losing his sense of which way was up and which was down. He kicked his legs and thrust his arms out. He felt like he was in the middle of the ocean in the dead of night. One hand rubbed against the slick, muddy wall of the hole he must have fallen into. Another sank deeper into the sandy morass around him, stopping when his fingers pressed against something hard. He felt around for its boundaries, determined that it was round and not too big to pull out. Clem figured it might be good for a weapon.

Above him, pebbles and dirt skittered and rained down into the hole. The scabby woman. She giggled.

"Little man," she cooed, "it's not yet time to be down there. Don't you know that's where the scraps go?"

Clem sniveled. Digging into the powdery mound, he thrust his fingers into it and yanked the object out. It was only then that the hair tumbled down from the thing's top and coiled around his hand and forearm. He was holding a rotting human head by its eye sockets.

He shrieked and dropped the head. It smacked against the grainy surface, kicking up a cloud of the stuff. The grains floated into Clem's face, filling his mouth and nose. At first it was irritating. Then the burning agony set in. It was as if acid had been poured into his eyes and down his throat. He clawed at his face, frantic to rub the smoldering powder away, but he only made it worse. His hands were covered with it. The powder reached his lungs, his chest contracted painfully. He could no longer breathe.

Slowly suffocating while his eyeballs burned, Clem thrashed violently in the hole. He could neither see nor speak, but he could hear the hideous lady at the mouth of the pit laughing wildly at his death throes. His tongue swelled and protruded out of his open mouth. As the asphyxiation reached its crescendo, Clem's skull felt like it was going to burst.

He was dead before he could find out if it would.

## 43

Walt had only expected to butcher one body that night. In fact, he'd prepared for it. Two bodies were something else altogether—twice the work, and it was a school night. He sniffed morosely and stripped naked in his bedroom. There just wasn't any sense in further sullying his wardrobe.

Back in the foyer, he screwed up his mouth and shook his head at the ruin before his eyes.

It was such a nice floor. Now he'd probably have to have it replaced.

"Damn it."

Shoving this to the back of his mind, Walt got down to business. First, he unrolled the dusty blue tarp Gwyn had dragged into the house. There lay Clem, still and well-dusted with quicklime. The chemical had absorbed most of the vomit, a job usually reserved for sawdust. Walt set to undressing the corpse. Once it was naked, he took a damp dishrag and wiped it down, top to bottom and back to front.

A raspy laugh came from behind him when he reached the body's flaccid genitals. He sneered.

"Very funny, Gwyn. Especially when I'm doing this for you."

The laughter died out, but only gradually. Walt dropped the rag beside Clem's corpse and stood up.

"Come to think of it," he said, "I don't see why you can't do it yourself. You're stronger than me." He picked up the cleaver and held it out to her. "Why don't *you* cut it up this time?"

Gwyn's lips spread apart, showing her gleaming white teeth.

"You like it."

"Cutting up bodies? No, I don't. It's disgusting."

"Taking care of me," she said coquettishly.

He dropped his head slightly and smiled. She was right. He was repulsed by the bloody work of dismembering human corpses and stripping the meat from their bones, but in the end he delighted in what it meant to Gwyn. He did relish taking care of her, being her au pair with benefits. And he had no intention of stopping.

Not ever, if that's what it took.

He lifted the cleaver up over his head and brought it down with a resounding *thwack*, dead in the center of Clem's chest.

## 44

In her usual seat in the second to last row, Alice sat alone in the classroom. She was almost always the first to arrive, having no first period to speak of, and she enjoyed the rare moments of calm silence. No one to pick on her. No horny guys to stare at her chest, or to pretend to like her just until they got a chance to actually see them, or touch them. Not that she was ever going to fall for *that* again.

The first time had been at the end of seventh grade; Kyle Casey. A chubby kid himself, Kyle hadn't usually joined in with the others when they chanted *fatty* or *lardo* or *tubby tits*. He did call her Alice Phallus once, having apparently just learned the word and made the rhyming connection, but luckily it never caught on. And even after that incident, she still let her guard down at the Spring Formal when he led her outside to the gravel-strewn playground and started to feel her up. The episode was awkward and vaguely humiliating, but Kyle moaned and grunted so much during the act that she allowed him to continue. Maybe, she thought at the time, he could even wind up her first boyfriend. The rosy-cheeked dork wasn't anyone's first choice of paramour, but she had to start somewhere.

The following Monday, word had spread like wildfire: *Alice Hawkins is easy.*

*She'll let you feel her boobs if you're nice to her.*

*Alice is a slut.*

The legacy of Kyle Casey.

She'd kept her head down for the rest of that school year and most of the next, but the same song played for Alice twice more during eighth grade and once at the beginning of the present year. That last one went further. Much further. "All the way," as Clem Lundeen told everybody in a ten-mile radius after the fact, and with much the same results as her encounter with Kyle.

She thought she'd never stop crying. But she did. And she made up her mind that boys were revolting, no exceptions, and that she was on her own from here on out. Then came Adiel Gallagher. She wasn't a boy. But the mere thought of her made Alice flush hot with shame and confusion.

She opened her composition book up to the midway point, to the page where she'd left off on a blue ballpoint sketch of a dragon exploding out of the roof of a building. The building bore an uncanny resemblance to the school. The charred and flaming bodies splayed all around the building's perimeter could have been anyone, but she knew who they were. Two of them—one impaled on one of the dragon's teeth, the other dangling from the sharp tip of one of the beast's claws—possessed particular identities in Alice's mind. They were Jarod and Clem, neither of the nondescript figures specifically one or the other. Just like they were in real life, the nasty boys were interchangeable.

Now she worked on some of the finer details: the dragon's scales, the building's bricks, the dancing flames and the shadows they formed. All of it in blue, against a backdrop of faint, straight blue lines.

*Maybe it's my blue period*, she thought.

The classroom door jerked open and two of Alice's classmates filed in. Neither of them made eye contact with her, even though she smiled and looked them straight in the faces. She quietly sighed.

*Back to my dragon.*

Soon, more kids started to fill up the room. Mr. Blackmore was not far behind. He was shuffling papers on his desk and half the students were shouting and wandering around the room when the bell rang. Alice kept her eyes on the drawing.

"All right," Mr. Blackmore said. "Let's settle down."

Alice tore her gaze away from the raging beast in her composition book and looked up at the teacher. He looked terrible. His face was drawn and pale, his eyes dark and puffy underneath. Practically the spitting image of her stepdad when he was hungover after a bender in town. All except for the massive bandage wrapped tautly around his right hand.

"I don't know about you," Blackmore droned on, "but I could use a quiet day. For that reason, I've brought two different film versions of *Romeo and Juliet* you can vote on." He rustled in his briefcase, coming back with two clear plastic video cases. "I've got the 1968 Zeffirelli version, and then here's the more recent MTV generation update..."

The class roared except for Alice. Their choice was clear.

Mr. Blackmore smiled thinly.

"As much as I expected. Too bad for some of you lads, though..."

He stuffed one box back into his briefcase as he extracted the tape from the other.

"...the older one's got some naughty bits this one lacks."

A litany of moans filled the air, most of them distinctively male. Alice pursed her lips and looked back down at the dragon in her composition book. She was waiting for the compulsory crass remarks to come spilling out of the resident class clowns, Jarod and Clem. But as the class quieted down, all she could hear was the squealing of the A/V cart's wheels and Mr. Blackmore fumbling with the tape and VCR. It clacked into the machine and began to whir. She looked back up just as Mr. Blackmore switched off the lights. The gray and white static on the television screen gave way to the flickering FBI warning.

A pair of whispers hissed across the room. Mr. Blackmore went, *Shhhh.*

Alice waited for her eyes to adjust to the darkness, eager to get a look around. The bright image of the studio logo on the screen helped. Narrowing her eyes, she glanced over to the corner of the room where the worst kids in class usually holed up, tittering and cutting up.

They weren't there.

*Skipping*, she thought. *They're going to be pissed when they find out they skipped a movie day.*

Shrugging and pushing the thought to the back of her mind, she returned her attention to the drawing on her desk. There was just enough light from the television and the window in the classroom door to work by. Ignoring the film she'd seen ten times already, she continued to flesh out the dragon's many scales.

The boys were nowhere to be seen at lunch, either. Usually Alice caught sight of them bumbling around the courtyard between the gymnasium and cafeteria, harassing some girls or surreptitiously drinking gin from plastic water bottles. Not today. That settled it; Jarod and Clem hadn't come to school at all. Probably they were smoking dope in the woods behind Clem's trailer park or wandering aimlessly around the outlet mall, looking for some trouble to get in. That, or they really did rob Mr. Blackmore and skipped town.

*Bullshit.*

Alice poked a limp, greasy French fry into her mouth and arched an eyebrow. Those boys were doomed.

# 45

There was a lot of work to do after school was out, and Walt was beginning to feel the pressure. For one thing, he needed a chest freezer, one of those big deals folks sometimes kept in the garage for storing excess meat. He'd managed to dig the flyers out of the newspaper in the teacher's lounge, but his many chatty colleagues made it difficult to look it over. He brought the ads with him to his next class—where he also played a videotape in lieu of teaching—and pored over the deals while most of the kids slept or made out.

Jake's Electronics was advertising a sale on appliances that included a seven cubic-foot freezer, which Walt circled in red ink. It was perfectly affordable, only two hundred dollars, but he doubted it had enough space for his needs. The twenty-five cubic-footer at Red's Discount Appliances looked far superior, but that one really jacked the price on him: $687.99. He puffed out his cheeks and ran a cost-benefit analysis in his head.

Jarod couldn't have weighed more than a hundred twenty pounds in his prime; that is, when he was still whole. Minus his entire skeleton and probably half of his internal organs—

and additional water weight—the remaining bounty would probably amount to less than fifty pounds. His good buddy, the late Clem Lundeen, was a bit larger than the impish Jarod, so Walt estimated somewhere in the neighborhood of sixty-five pounds of meat from him.

Beside the Red's Discount Appliances ad for the large chest freezer, Walt wrote: *115 lbs?*

He looked closer at the ad, studying the appliance's features. Lift-out baskets (that he would toss in the garbage), quick-freeze option (whatever that meant), audible and visual temperature alarm system, and easy to read electronic controls. None of this helped Walt's left-brained mind make sense of the problem. The fact that Red's claimed the freezer could hold over eight hundred pounds of frozen food, however, helped immensely.

He grinned and tore the ad away from the circular. This was the one.

And with loads of space to fill up, Walt could butcher four more their size and have room to spare.

In a way, it was a frightening thought. Five were dead already, thanks to Gwyn's sudden appearance in Walt's life. The creepy redneck who trailed his sister to his house was certainly no big loss, and the boys all but sealed their own fates. Amanda, on the other hand, was a painful death to experience. Though the memory was fading, Walt thought of her often, sometimes for days on end, wondering if her horrible demise could have been prevented in some way. She should have stayed away, should have read the signs that the house was not safe. That Walt was not safe. He never really knew if he actually loved her when she was alive and he was no more certain of that niggling question now that she was dead and gone.

Well, not quite gone. Her slowly dissolving bones remained in the corpse pit behind the house. But at least he no longer had to see them, now that they were completely submerged beneath an ever-growing mound of quicklime.

Poor Amanda.

Still, Gwyn *had* to feed. It was every living organism's natural born right. Survival of the fittest and all that. Walt wasn't responsible for her existence, he only took it upon himself to sustain it. He neither knew from whence she came nor did he care. As long as she was happy, his heart was at ease.

And that was love.

There just wasn't any doubt about it: Walt loved Gwyn more dearly, more passionately and savagely, than he'd ever loved before. He would slaughter the whole damn town if she asked him to, no matter how repulsive he found the act of killing and stripping the flesh from a fellow human being.

With that consideration lingering in his brain, he looked up at the dreary, dozing faces in front of him. Only about half of them paid any attention to the film. Others napped, fiddled with handheld electronics or passed notes between them. One of them, Rob Scaife, gazed at the ceiling with glassy eyes while he mindlessly scratched the omnipresent red spots on his forearm. Track marks. Walt had successfully ignored the issue thus far—it was much more than his paltry salary was worth to intercede on some loser junkie's behalf—but he studied the prematurely balding boy more carefully now than ever.

After all, who would miss a junkie?

Floating through the rest of her day in a haze, Alice was more than a little relieved when the last bell finally jangled at three o'clock. It was the weekend's herald, and although she had no particular plans she was glad to be getting away from the school grounds for a couple of days. Maybe pop by In the Reads for another Brite novel, since she enjoyed the one Nora recommended so much. Packing her books up into her black denim book bag, she slung it over her broad shoulder and commenced the labyrinthine journey through the dim and dusty hallways that eventually led its captives to the brightly lit outside world. She crossed the front quad, rounded the rusty flagpole and walked through the teacher's parking lot on her way to her third-hand Subaru hatchback in the student lot.

Along the way, she caught a glimpse of Mr. Blackmore unlocking his car. He stopped and began to stare at her. She only looked back at him for a fraction of a second before quickly whipping her head back to the sea of shitty used cars in front of her. But she knew he was still looking at her, following her with his gaze. It was all at once embarrassing and exhilarating; troubling and flattering.

When she finally reached her own car, she unlocked it and squeezed inside and brought her eyes back up to the teacher's lot at the top of the slight hill. Mr. Blackmore's car was gone. Alice turned the key in the ignition.

She wondered about that look, its subtext, if there was one. The hair on the back of her neck seemed to flutter, as if in a breeze.

Frustrated that Red's couldn't manage a same-day delivery but relieved to have taken care of the freezer's purchase, Walt skipped up the porch steps to the front door. He hadn't forgotten the sheer magnitude of cleanup required inside, but even that didn't piss on his parade. A little bleach, perhaps a little wax and some good old fashioned elbow grease, and he reckoned there would still be a few hours left in the evening for just him and Gwyn. It was only blood. They would dine together—he on braised pork chops and she on the usual, raw human meat. Then, after Walt washed the dishes and poured himself a nice glass of merlot, he'd let her guide him into the bedroom where they'd fuck for hours.

Their often wild lovemaking sessions were at first decidedly awkward; she dealt with the pain of her exposed nerve endings while he had a hard time getting accustomed to all the sticky fluids that seeped out of her from crown to toe. Later, when the scabs began to form, it was as if Walt was screwing an entirely different person. Sticky became bone dry, slippery turned scratchy and coarse. But none of it quelled their heat. Not one night had passed since Gwyn first emerged from her prison in the ceiling that they hadn't fucked like teenagers. Even last night, after she was sated on the raw steaks he sawed from Jarod's thighs, she threw herself at him; right there on the floor between steaming mounds of freshly butchered teenage boys.

Walt set his briefcase down on the floor, shut the door and slipped out of his shoes. He smiled at the déjà vu.

"Honey, I'm *hooooome!*" he called out goofily.

There was no reply. The house was dead silent.

He tiptoed around the yellowing swaths of blood that coated the foyer floor, leaped over the sticky mass that completely blocked ingress to the living room. The couch, he discovered, was unoccupied.

"Gwyn?"

Rounding the couch, he spotted several large sections of brown, flaky scabs littering the living and dining room floors. From the look of them, he decided they must have been ripped off rather than having fallen off naturally. He scowled and followed the scabby trail with his eyes. They cut a path through the various stacks of books and boxes that filled the dining room and vanished around the dark corner.

The hallway.

Walt narrowed his eyes to slits and cautiously proceeded through the maze of cardboard and paper, emerging in the dark hall on the other end. Just as he anticipated, the attic stairs were down. From above, he heard the faint sound of wet, anguished sobbing.

*Sarah!*

His puzzlement rapidly metamorphosing into anger, Walt grit his teeth and raced up the attic steps.

*No, no, no, no, no, no, no!*

He hated himself for having to keep his sister up there; it was no way to live, and certainly no way to treat one's own flesh and blood. But Walt and Gwyn had an arrangement, a clear-cut understanding that Sarah was off limits. Under no circumstances whatsoever was Gwyn to even go near the woman, much less feast on her. Occasionally he took it upon himself to bleed her a little bit, but it was nothing serious and definitely nothing that threatened her overall health.

But there could be no doubt that Gwyn was in the attic now—with Sarah. And not yet twenty-four hours after the frenzied killings of Jarod and Clem.

*There is still meat from those two little shits, goddamn you!* his mind screamed.

He burst upward into a dusty shaft of orange afternoon sun. Beyond the perimeter of the light he could see nothing, but his sister's desperate sobs were loud and clear.

"Sarah?"

The good news was that she was obviously still alive. For how long, he didn't know. He pushed out of the light and into the gray shadows. Getting accustomed to the dimness he found his sister, sitting with her legs crossed on the mattress he'd given her, hunched over and shaking with each heaving sob. Walt quickly looked her over, checking her body and the bed for signs of violence, evidence that Gwyn had finally given in to her bloodlust and attacked the one person she was not allowed to touch.

He saw nothing of the kind.

"Sarah, are you hurt?"

The paper plate beside her had nothing but a bit of bread crust on it; the cup was only half emptied of water. He reckoned she must be starving, and worried that she wasn't drinking anything.

"Fuck off," she mumbled.

"Are you hurt? Did she cut you? Bite you?"

Her head jerked up. Her face was a shiny wet mound of swollen red skin. Her mouth was twisted down into a fierce sneer, her eyes squinty and leaking tears.

"I said FUCK OFF!" she roared. "FUCK OFF AND DIE!"

Walt's breath got caught in his chest. He was startled by her outburst and hurt by her bald-faced hatred for him. Didn't she understand he only did this to protect the women he loved, her and Gwyn both?

Clearly not.

"I hardly think..." he began, trailing off at the realization that he and his sister were not alone.

Across the attic, well out of the available light in the farthest corner away from them, something squished.

And slurped.

And groaned with pleasure.

"Gwyn," he whispered.

"Go to it," Sarah hissed. "Go fuck your monster some more, you demented son of a bitch."

He ignored his sister and started to make his way over the crossbeams and past the insulated portion of the paneled flooring. Halfway across, he saw that Gwyn sat with her back to him, her shoulders jerking and her head slung low. Her back was a marbled pink, like a newborn rat. There were no scabs on it at all.

"What did you do?" Walt asked warily as he slowly drew near. "You've torn them all off..."

"Come here and I will show you."

Walt stepped over onto another beam. He looked up from it and saw Gwyn jerk her arm quickly past her torso. She emitted a high-pitched cry and held up the five-inch scab she'd just peeled away.

"Nearly done now," she purred.

Dancing over the last remaining beams that separated him from Gwyn, he closed in on the bent figure as she spun around to display an awful, ragged visage of torn and bloodied skin. Walt shouted out in fear, stumbling backward while she jutted her tongue through Jarod's mouth and made low groaning sounds that reverberated throughout the attic.

She had separated the dead boy's face from his skull, and she'd done it roughly. The outer edges were tattered, as were the notched holes where Jarod once kept his eyes and lips. Now she pinched the loose pale skin between forefingers and thumbs and held it over her own face, like a Halloween mask. She was cackling hysterically.

Walt's heart jackhammered in his chest.

"Jesus Christ!" he screeched. He was in no way amused by the stunt.

Gwyn wiggled the skin mask over her face. The white, leathery flesh rippled. Red strings dangled from beneath it, dripping tiny droplets of crimson gore. She tittered.

*Tee hee.*

The horrific tableau did not much improve when at last she took the grisly face away to reveal her own. The skin on her face looked just like the skin on her back—irritated, pink and mottled, like scar tissue. All around her on the bare, broken paneling where once her veiny pod grew there were piles of crusty scabs. Walt made a face. She must have been up there for a while, peeling and tearing all those crusty pieces from her entire body.

"Why?" he asked.

She let Jarod's face drop to the ground with a muted slap and ran one palm over the smooth crown of her tender, scraped head.

"It will be so much nicer this way, don't you think?" A sweet smile spread across her face, pushing her round cheeks back. For the first time since the scabbing began, nothing chipped away and sprinkled down with the simple muscle movement. "I am becoming whole. I am becoming beautiful."

"You *are* beautiful," he shakily argued. "To me."

Behind him, Sarah blubbered.

Scooting a foot or so to one side, Gwyn revealed the faceless skull her body had been obscuring. Viscous globs of muscle and tendons and gristle clung tenaciously to the bone. The rest of the head retained its skin, and Jarod's distinctive shock of white-blonde hair still spiked out on top. The eyes were missing, but Walt didn't want to inquire after them. He shuddered at his own imagination as it was; Gwyn digging them out of the sockets with her fingernails, popping them between her teeth and sucking out the juices as though they were grapes…

He gagged and slapped a hand over his mouth. With an admonishing look and a motherly laugh, Gwyn dropped down to her hands and knees and crawled over to him. She thrust her face close to his and licked his trembling lips. Almost instinctively, they parted, allowing her tongue into the warm interior of his mouth. Walt's hands drifted up to her heavy breasts, smooth and dry for the first time. He groaned as his fingertips found the turgid nipples. She moaned girlishly and fingered the buttons on his shirt, popping them open one by one.

Walt did nothing to resist her. He never did.

Across the attic, in the diminishing afternoon light, Sarah moaned.

The mechanism inside the portable CD player whined and ground the new Jesus and Mary Chain album to a halt. Alice snapped out of her reverie, startled by the abrupt silence. She glanced at the drawing on her bed beside her. She hadn't done anything new since she opened the composition book back up. All she'd done since getting home and barricading herself in her room was listen to albums and let her mind free-float.

For the most part, it floated toward Mr. Blackmore.

The way he'd stared at her in the parking lot after school confused and unnerved her. On the one hand, it was creepy as hell. Teachers were not supposed to behave like that, especially male teachers toward female students. He hadn't actually done anything, not really, but the look in his eyes told a story only the most gullible naïf would fail to recognize. There was wanting in those leering eyes. Lust, although not necessarily the sexual variety.

But probably.

Alice pulled the Jesus and Mary Chain CD out of the player, put it back in its proper case, and replaced it with her favorite Fugazi album. As the curt punk sounds punched the air from the speakers, she shut the comp book and fell back against the mountain of pillows at the head of her bed. Any minute now her stepdad was due to start banging on the walls, bellowing at her to turn that goddamn noise off. She wanted to enjoy it as much as possible until then.

*Fucking Harold.*

She pushed him out of her mind. That allowed Mr. Blackmore to creep back in.

He wasn't so bad, not even for a teacher. To most of the kids, he was just one step shy of freakishly weird, but that only served to endear him all the more to Alice. What made him weird to her peers—his passion for old books, the casual way he dressed and the sleepy, almost hypnotized look he usually wore on his bedraggled face—painted the picture of an interesting, even attractive person to her. Still, his role in her life acted as a barrier between them, something not even a perfectly normal friendship could pass through. He was the superior, she the inferior. He taught, she learned, and then they went in their wholly separate directions when that was done for the day.

Anything else, anything *more*, was strictly forbidden.

Maybe that look indicated a disagreement with the rules. Maybe Mr. Blackmore saw something in Alice that no one else did, not even Harold. Maybe he could see the nascent spark of her burgeoning brilliance, hidden deep in her breast from anyone who couldn't be bothered to give her a more detailed analysis. Or even a second look.

Alice made up her mind. She was going to pay more attention to Mr. Blackmore paying more attention to her. See what comes of it. In all likelihood, it would be nothing at all. But maybe...

She closed her eyes, laced her fingers over her stomach and smiled with satisfaction.

Her sweet, comfortable mind trip was cut short by the rapid pounding on the wall just behind her. Startled, she bounced up to a sitting position.

"*Turn that shit OFF!*" Harold yelled from the dingy bedroom next door.

Alice reached over and switched the portable CD player off. Silence once again flooded her head. The inundation of quiet drowned out all thoughts of Mr. Blackmore, leaving only emptiness and loneliness and a queer, unfathomable fear.

*What do I have to be afraid of?* she wondered.

The answer was there before she finished asking herself.

Everything.

## 46

It was Thursday when the freezer arrived in an unmarked white delivery van. The driver and his assistant hauled into the house, set it up in the kitchen, and gave its new owner a very brief tutorial on its most basic functions. Walt signed for it and tipped the driver an extra twenty for the long drive. It was only the work of a moment to get the freezer a third filled up with what was left of the two rowdy boys who had come to the house earlier in the week. To any uninformed observer who might take a peek, it would appear to be nothing more than a ridiculous quantity of frozen meat.

Which, essentially, it was.

## 47

The knock at the door came late Thursday evening. Walt's breath hitched in his throat when he peered out through the window and almost screamed. Two uniformed police officers stood on his porch, shifting their weight from foot to foot, each of their faces bored and impassive.

Walt's sphincter clenched and his chest felt tight. He froze up and his eyes felt wet. The policemen knocked again.

"God," he whispered. "Oh God, oh God."

"Mr. Blackmore? Walter Blackmore—Police Department. Open up."

*They know*, his mind screeched at him. *They know they know they know they know...*

"Mr. Blackmore?"

He was opening the door before he knew what he was doing. It swung in and away, leaving nothing but open air between him and imminent arrest...trial...conviction...surely death. How did they even execute people in this state nowadays? He had no idea, but he knew without a shadow of a doubt it could not be long before he'd find out.

"Hello...Mr. Blackmore?"

This from the shorter cop, his head shiny and bald. Both men wore neatly trimmed moustaches.

"Yes, I'm Walt Blackmore."

"Officer Forsyth," the short cop said. Then, gesturing to his partner, "Officer Klein. We don't want to take up too much of your time, sir, but it seems that a couple of boys have gone missing..."

"Oh?"

"Yes, and these boys were students at your school. In fact, students in your class, I believe."

"Yes, yes of course. Jarod and Clem."

"Well, you would know all about *that*, then."

"Know?" Walt said, his voice a forced calm. "Know what, exactly?"

"That your students are missing, Mr. Blackmore."

"Well, they haven't been in class in several days, if that's what you mean. But I'm only really responsible for reporting their absences."

The taller cop, Officer Klein, stepped forward and sucked a deep breath into his lungs.

He said, "What we'd like to know, Mr. Blackmore, is whether or not you might have any information that could help us find these kids."

"Information? What sort of information? Truth is, I don't know those boys very well, officers. I hate to speak ill..."

"It's all right," Forsyth said. "Go ahead."

"It's just that neither of them are what you might call star students. They skip class quite a lot. Not much drive. I don't know anything about their lives at home, or what sort of trouble they may or may not have gotten into. Heck, I don't even have any of their assignments to show you on account of they almost never did any of them."

"I see," Klein said.

"I'd like nothing more than to be of help to you gentlemen, but like I said..."

"You don't really know the boys."

"That's right. It is my first year at the school and all."

Klein nodded. Forsyth twisted his mouth up to one side and sighed.

Withdrawing a slightly bent card from his shirt pocket, Forsyth faked a smile and handed it over to Walt, who accepted it.

"If you think of anything, anything at all..."

"I'll call you straight away," Walt interrupted, flicking the card with his thumb.

"Thank you for your time, Mr. Blackmore."

The policemen each nodded to him and commenced their way back to the patrol car parked in Walt's driveway.

"You bet. And hey—"

Klein and Forsyth paused, turned to look back up at Walt.

"Stay warm out there, officers. Looks like snow."

Smiles all around.

Walt shut the front door gently, locked it, and leaned against it. He thought for a moment he was going to cry.

Instead, he laughed.

## 48

Friday was a snow day.

The air warmed slightly in the night, allowing the perfect conditions for the flakes to start falling. By sunrise, the ground was covered in a blinding white blanket of snow.

Walt grimaced when he saw it through his bedroom window. He wondered what it meant for the pit.

Alice perked up when she realized that the brilliant light blasting the sheer curtains of her window was due to snow. She wasted no time flinging herself at the CD player beside her bed and switching it to the AM band. The voice on the first clear station she found droned on about the state of the economy, the president's lack of moral fortitude, and the invisible connection that lied therein.

"Come on, damnit…"

The next station played dozy Samba music.

"Come on." She kept searching.

Finally, at the end of the band, she hit upon a news station that promised to repeat a list of school closures momentarily.

And, when they did, hers was among those closed for the day.

"YES!" she cried.

"*Shut the fuck up in there!*" her stepfather bellowed from the next room. "*Try'na fuckin' sleep in here!*"

Alice's heart thrummed. Her joy rapidly melted into a lukewarm puddle of disenchantment.

School would have been better than this. Maybe Jarod and Clem would still be skipping. Hell, maybe they were dead. That would be something.

Most of all, she would have been afforded the opportunity to see Mr. Blackmore afresh in the new light of his leering, lusty gaze in the parking lot the other day. Had it been a week already? She reviewed other glances since, other gestures and expressions, and wondered how much she was reading into them for the sake of hoping they communicated as much as that first ogling stare. Alice's chest tightened at the mental inventory, but she cut off the feed before her imagination had a chance to run wild. But now she wouldn't see him again until Monday, three days away.

It might as well have been three weeks.

Or three months.

Alice sighed. She wondered about how rapidly she'd developed this infatuation. She wondered how mad her stepdad would be if she took the car for non-school-related purposes. And so she wondered what ever happened to her winter snow boots, because it was going to be a long, wet walk to the bus stop.

The morning light shaft to which she'd grown so accustomed was grayish and foreboding. When she actually slept, Sarah always woke up just to see it leaking through the cracks above her. There was nothing else to look forward to. Not anymore. But this one, infinitesimal thing was just barely enough to give her a shred of pleasure. The mere fact that there was anything even remotely enjoyable left to her kept total despair at bay.

Today, however, it was colorless and dull. The freezing cold breeze swept the snow into the attic. It built up gradually into a white bank on the beams underneath the air vent slats, accumulating only a little more quickly than it melted.

Sarah couldn't help but wonder if she would live to see another warm day. Or, if she did, whether or not she would still be chained up in her lunatic brother's attic. Whichever the case, freedom seemed remote to her mind. A wild fantasy, on par with the sort of unicorns-and-rainbows daydreams she entertained as a girl. She would walk away from this charnel house around the same time winged kittens swarmed the sky and blotted out the sun.

Wrapping her bare arms around herself, she shivered. Although she recognized that being this cold was far better than sharing the attic with that horrendous monster her brother called *Gwyn*, she still considered the possibility of asking after warmer clothes. He'd brought her the mattress, and he'd brought her food (such as it was). A damn jacket shouldn't be such a big deal.

Until that eventuality, she rose to her feet and began to move and stretch. She bent at the waist, touched her toes, and twisted back and forth. It kept her loose and warmed the blood in her veins. In lieu of something to read or a television, it was also just about the only thing she could do. So on she went, craning her neck from side to side, stretching her triceps and shoulders and waist.

When she decided to move on to her middle back and twisted her torso as far as the muscles would allow, Sarah screamed. She lost her balance and crashed down to the mattress.

She had forgotten all about the mutilated head that thing left. It still sat there, resting on its side. Its dark, empty sockets weirdly stared at her. A few inches of spinal cord jutted from its butchered, severed neck. The face—the one Gwyn had pried away from the skull and worn like a mask—was gone. Sarah swallowed hard at the thought that the creature probably ate it.

Maneuvering herself on the mattress until the weak winter light was on her face, she closed her eyes and tried to think of something else. She thought of Mitch, but he never made her feel any better when she was at home and in no danger of being killed and eaten by a creature that couldn't possibly exist. *My God, did he even call the goddamned police, the idiot? Or is he just glad I'm not around to bother him anymore?*

She thought of her house, but at this point she really couldn't care less if she ever saw it again. She thought too of her mother, her and Walt's mother, the reason she was out there in the first place. *Jesus, has he gotten to her too?* All she wanted was to live. That, and to get as far away from there as possible.

So instead she squeezed her eyes and thought about killing Walt. The monster, too. Prying their throats apart with a serrated bread knife and chortling as their lives spurted out of their necks.

She continued along these lines for a while, slaughtering her brother and his beast over and over again in a multitude of increasingly grisly ways. Eventually, she permitted the bloody reverie to lull her to sleep. And in her dreams, Sarah killed them some more.

Nora lit another cigarette and glanced at the digital clock on the nightstand. Not long ago, this would have been about the time she'd be getting ready to open the store. She would be shuffling hangers in the closet, looking for the best top to compliment whatever skirt or slacks she'd already chosen. More often than not, she'd also find herself mindlessly whistling whichever song had been playing in her head when she woke up. Something 80s, most likely. Brit pop type stuff. *I'll stop the world and melt with you...*

*Hmm, hmm, hmm hmmmm.*

Not today or any other day since Amanda's disappearance. Today she remained in bed, the sheets bunched up at her feet despite the nasty cold weather. Her cigarette slowly burned down; she only took occasional drags from it. When an inch of gray ash broke away and burst into a dark smudge on the bed, she ignored it. The smudge was surrounded by small, circular burn holes anyway.

Nora stabbed the smoke out in the moldy coffee cup beside the clock—IN THE READS: GET YOUR READ ON!—and lay back down on the dirty bed. She hadn't bothered to wash the sheets for months, and she didn't care. She didn't care about that, or the dishes, or the pile of mail gathering beneath the mail slot in her front door. Nora doubted she could muster much concern if the place caught fire. She'd probably just lay there and burn.

She'd done everything she could. She didn't blame herself for any of that. There were interviews with the police, long nights combing the few crisscrossing streets that constituted "downtown," and even the hundred and fifty photocopied *Have You Seen Me?* posters she stapled to practically every sky-reaching signpost and utility pole in town. Nora broke into Amanda's place, spent the night and drenched her missing friend's pillowcases with her tears. She spent hours at a time on the horn with Amanda's widowed mom, a woman she'd never met face-to-face but in whom she now found a close ally against the forces of desperation and despair. Nora even wasted weeks trying like hell to track down Amanda's weird, elusive boyfriend, the ever-mysterious Walt.

There couldn't have been anyone else in the world with a best friend whose three-year boyfriend remained such an elusive mystery. Only Nora. There were times when Nora was ninety-nine percent certain that Walt didn't actually exist, that he was either a psychotic delusion or the subject of an elaborate joke that never reached its punchline. But Amanda was neither crazy nor cruel, so neither rang true enough to seriously consider. She said the man was just shockingly insular and insecure about meeting new people, especially women. It wasn't just Nora, but practically every other soul in Amanda's life as well. It was one of the sundry eccentricities old Walt displayed that endeared him to her. He was crazy, but good crazy. Unique.

Nora thought maybe he was deformed or something. Then Amanda pinned a photo of them, of her and her beau, on the bulletin board in the shop's office. Walt was not deformed at all. In fact, he was peculiarly handsome. Sort of roguish in the way his brow angled down to the bridge of his nose, even though he was grinning from one ear to the other.

Cameras don't record images of hoaxes and illusions. Walt was real. Just exceptionally strange. Strange enough to have done something awful to Amanda, perhaps? Nora had to know.

What was surprising was the total absence of anything that contained the intangible man's full name in Amanda's apartment. To Nora, that seemed impossible. How could a woman date a guy for three whole years and not have a single letter, sticky note or receipt with his name on it?

What was the fucking deal with this guy?

Giving up was the last thing Nora wanted to do, but she'd hit a brick wall. That was back in November. Since then, she'd been laying around, sucking down cigarettes and subsisting on Chinese delivery and canned beer. She locked up the shop at closing time two and half weeks earlier and never went back. Without Amanda, there wasn't any point. She hadn't left her apartment in that same time. How long before one is officially classified as a shut-in?

She dozed for an hour or so more before finally summoning the strength and courage to rise from the bed. She made a quick survey of her surroundings, all of it dingy and dirty and cluttered beyond belief.

Enough was enough.

With a curled upper lip and a grunting sigh, she threw on some dirty clothes and went hunting for her car keys.

## 49

Despite the relative safety of her boots, Alice treaded warily through the wet snow, careful not to step off into the ditch where all the muddy slush accumulated. The boots only reached mid-calf, and the cold, filthy morass below would undoubtedly splash up and into them. Years ago, when she was little, her mother would collect the plastic bags the newspaper came in throughout the year. Then, when it snowed it wintertime, she'd wrap Alice's little feet in the bags and secure them at the knees with rubber bands. She never got slushed that way. Didn't have to take a hot bath before coming back into the house for grilled cheese sandwiches and tomato soup, if she didn't want to.

Harold didn't know how to make grilled cheese and tomato soup. Even if he did, he wouldn't. Alice was left to fend for herself. But it had been that way for almost half her life now. Gradually, she was getting used to it.

The snow beneath her feet crunched in some places and squished in others. Grackles screeched above her, cawing at one another among the bare treetops. As a kid she would have deemed the landscape around her a winter wonderland. Now it just looked dreary and dead and utterly hopeless, as if spring would never come again.

She trudged on. Eventually she reached the corner where the gravel road on which she lived ended. It formed a T with the oily macadam street that met Highway 5 at the bottom of the hill. At that intersection was the bus stop, although no one would know to look at it. There was no bench or sign or shelter from the threat of rain and sleet. Just another muddy street corner. When Alice got there, she breathed a cloud of warm steam on her ruddy hands and waited.

She waited for the better part of an hour without ever seeing proof of life on Earth apart from herself, a few scattered birds and a mongrel dog snuffling in the woods on the other side of the road. She popped her comp book out of her book bag and got to sketching on the page facing the dragon. In just twenty minutes of drawing while standing in the cold, she had the beginnings of a recognizable portrait. Alice pouted at it. Then she scrawled a quotation beneath the floating head—

*Heaven knows we need never be ashamed of our tears*
*For they are the rain upon the blinding dust of earth*

—and returned the comp book to her bag.

She didn't know the bus schedule, but she was surprised one had not come along by then. Hunching her shoulders and rubbing her hands together, she considered her options. She could go back home, spend the day getting hounded by Howard, but she would rather stand in the cold all day than that.

Otherwise, she could wait some more in hope that a bus might come along, or keep walking in the general direction of town.

With a jerking shiver, she set off down the shoulder of Highway 5.

With no particular destination in mind, Nora just drove. The weather had all but swept the streets clear of competing traffic, affording her a leisurely path to wherever she wanted to go. At first she just wound around the outskirts of town, paying more attention to the classic rock station on her radio than the road in front of her. Before she knew it, her internal autopilot had taken her away from town, speeding west down the interstate. She snapped back to reality then, keeping an eye out for the next exit. She didn't want to end up across the state line and then have to drive all the way back home.

She pulled off onto the exit for Highway 5. She knew she could take its winding trajectory back to town; it only took three times longer than the interstate. But it was scenic, she supposed, although more so in the full bloom of late spring than now, when the forest hunched dead and low beneath the crushing weight of winter.

The world grew darker the instant she took the wooded road. She slowed to accommodate the long neglected pavement. Occasionally she glanced around the interior of the car, looking for color to counteract the outside palate of gray and black. This was a dead time, and with no one else in view—either on the road or anywhere near it—Nora felt like the last woman on a doomed planet. The bright red scarf coiled up on the passenger seat was a warm and welcome sight. At one point, she even smiled at it as though it was an old friend or a treasured child. It was then that the tires skidded and Nora's car went into a spin.

Her breath froze in her windpipe and the spin on the ice patch seemed like it was occurring in slow motion. She simply stared forward, through the windshield at the southbound road, the trees, the northbound road, and the trees on the other side. Over and over again, until at last she skidded off Highway 5 and the car slumped into a snowy ditch. The halt was abrupt and she pitched forward, saved from bashing her face against the steering wheel by her seatbelt. When her head stopped trying to spin in time with the car, she let out the breath and muttered, "Shit."

Alice heard a rush of air and the dull *whumph* that eclipsed into silence. It began and ended in the span of a few seconds. She stopped walking and peered down the hazy road, but she couldn't see anything. The sound must have been deceptive, sounding closer than it actually was. Probably it carried down the corridor that cut through the dense forest, like a gunshot. She continued on.

Around the bend and further down the slope of the road, she finally saw the steam sputtering out of the car's exhaust pipe. Most of the car itself was shrouded in the snow bank it crashed into. Alice knew from experience that the bank concealed a deep reservoir of muddy slush. She wondered if the driver was still in the car, and whether or not they were all right.

As she drew nearer, the passenger side door cracked open a few inches, lingered there, and then slammed shut. A minute later, it cracked open again, only this time someone started to work their way out from inside the car. It was a woman. She looked frazzled, but otherwise uninjured. Alice maintained her languid pace and arrived in front of the car in the amount of time it took the woman to stumble back onto the road.

"Hey, are you all right?"

Puzzled, Nora spun around to identify the source of the voice. She moved too quickly. Disoriented by the accident and the blurry gray haze that enveloped her, she lost her footing on the slick road and fell crashing on her ass. Heavy footsteps clopped wetly toward her and before she knew what was going on, someone was helping her back up to her feet.

She was just a kid, maybe fourteen or fifteen years old. Her pudgy face was expressionless but kind, her ruddy complexion framed by a black bob that curled in toward her round chin.

*Alice?*

"Nora? Jesus! You got a concussion or anything?" Nora just stared. "Nora! Do you need an ambulance?"

She felt idiotic the moment she heard the words come out her mouth. How the hell was she going to get an ambulance out there? The car looked pretty well screwed and it wasn't as if Alice had a magic phone in her pocket. But if Nora *did* need medical help, something was going to have to be done.

Eventually, Nora's eyes cleared and she looked down at Alice.

"No," she said weakly. "No, I think I'm fine. Just a little... shaken."

"Nothing broken?"

"No, I don't think so."

Nora released herself from Alice's steadying hold and shuffled forward a few steps. She appeared to be testing herself out, making sure everything was working the way it was supposed to work. Apparently satisfied, she turned back toward Alice and smiled weakly.

"Yeah, I think I'm okay. Thanks."

"Don't mention it," Alice said. "Do you remember me? Alice...I come in for horror books sometimes?"

"Yes, of course," Nora said, crinkling her nose. "Of course, sweetie."

For a moment thereafter, the two of them stood in the middle of Highway 5, puffing intermittent clouds of steam from their mouths and not saying a word. Once or twice a bird cried somewhere in the middle distance, but apart from that the world was quiet and still. Finally, Alice spoke up.

"Suppose we should try to get your car out of that ditch?"

Nora nodded.

It was hard work, wet and cold and sweaty. Alice pushed from the ditch, the slush rising almost to the tops of her boots, while Nora pushed from the passenger side. They were eventually successful, steering the car back up onto the road. It even started up with no problems.

"Thank God!" Nora exclaimed upon hearing and feeling the roar of the engine coming to life.

Even Alice grinned. She stood nothing to gain from a vague acquaintance's good fortune, but having been integral to the process made her feel warm and pleasant.

"The least I can do," Nora said to her, "is offer you a ride."

Alice stared off in the distance, down the road she'd planned to keep walking down until a reason to stop surfaced in her mind.

"Not really going anyplace," she mumbled.

"Yeah? Me neither."

They looked at one another's faces. They both found sadness there.

Alice climbed into Nora's car.

They chatted idly but amiably.

After a short while, Alice grew comfortable enough to slide her cold feet out of her boots and prop them up on the dash. She then extracted her composition book, opened it up to her last work-in-progress, and got to sketching while she and Nora chatted about the weather and the town and the futility of it all.

"Who's that?" Nora asked, pointing at the developing portrait on the open page.

Alice flushed even pinker than before.

"Him? He's...well, fuck it. He's my English teacher."

Nora chuckled.

"Oh? Well, I'll be."

"Mr. Blackmore. He's kind of weird."

"Handsome, though."

"Yeah, I guess."

"You guess? You're the one drawing him. Pretty damn good, too."

"Thanks."

Nora fiddled with the heater, adjusting the knob to make it blast a little hotter. She didn't recognize the comp book as any of the fancier variety she'd sold at In the Reads, and almost felt stung by it.

"What's all that underneath?" she asked.

"What, this? Just a quote."

"What's it say? Can't read it while I'm driving."

"*Heaven knows we need never be ashamed of our tears...for they are the rain upon the blinding dust of earth.* It's from *Great Expectations*."

"You don't say."

"We read it in his class. Everybody hated it, and I mean *everybody.*"

"But not you."

"Nope. Not me."

"That's cool. I like people who read. Not that I really still run a bookstore or anything..."

"Oh yeah?"

"Well, I still do, technically. It's just, well...it's more or less in limbo right now, I suppose."

"That's too bad," Alice said, keeping her eyes on the page.

"Can't say we see a lot of sales by way of Mr. Dickens, but..."

Nora suddenly gasped, her eyes wide and glossy.

"Holy fucking shit," she said.

Alice jumped, looking at Nora and the road in front of them, trying to determine the cause of the woman's glossed over glare.

"What is it?"

"Fucking Dickens!!"

*Oh no*, Alice thought. She's nuts. *I've gotten into a car with someone I hardly know and she's a crazy loon. What the hell was I thinking?*

Nora began to breathe more loudly, harshly. She then turned her bulging eyes on Alice, who slightly cringed at the wild expression.

"You mind if we run a little errand?" Nora asked expectantly.

"I...I...I guess not," Alice weakly stammered.

Nora would never have guessed in a million years that Charles Dickens and a fourteen-year-old kid would give her the key to get to the bottom of this mess.

Yet there it was.

*Martin Chuzzlewit*, she repeated over and over again in her mind. *Special friggin' order.*

*I've got you, Walt.*

## 50

The book was right where she'd left it, on the cluttered old oak desk in the back office. A sheet of paper, folded in half, was wrapped around it with a rubber band. Nora seized the paperback as soon as she burst through the office door and tore the band off. In a frenzy, she unfolded the paper so hurriedly it tore. Quickly, she read the receipt's pertinent contents.

IN THE READS
7856 Front Street, Suite C
ORDER FORM SUMMARY
Dickens, Charles. *Martin Chuzzlewit.*
Penguin Classics.
FOR Blackmore, Walter
$6.99 + tax PAID IN FULL

She stuffed the receipt in her front pants pocket like it was a soiled tissue and stretched across the desk for the newest telephone directory.

"Walter Blackmore," she requested and began flipping through the thin, yellow pages.

From the doorway, a puzzled Alice asked, "You *know* him?"

Nora paused in her frantic page-turning and turned to look at the confused girl. Alice's hands were stuffed in her pockets and her head was cocked to one side. She raised her eyebrows.

"Mr. Blackmore," Nora whispered.

## 51

Walt stood at the end of a long and narrow hallway. There were no windows and no doors. There were no lights, either, but somehow the hallway was dimly lit. Enough to see clear down to the other end, at any rate.

Walls, floor, and ceiling were constructed of freshly cut pine. Walt could smell it. It was like sticky sweet smelling needles on the forest floor in summertime. When he took a step forward, the beams comprising the floor creaked and groaned. Light spilled up from the cracks beneath and melted away when he stepped off the plank. He screwed up his face and shoved his lower lip out. He could not remember where he was or how he got there. Judging from the structure of the place, he would have been boarded up in there. There was no way out, so there could not have been any other way in.

It was not a hallway at all. It was a coffin.

Walt crept forward as the light began to die out, leaving the space shrouded in increasingly darkening shadows. Each time the wood creaked and buckled beneath his weight, the ceiling planks mirrored them. Clumps and clods of dirt rained down from above. Walt gasped. He was being buried.

He opened his mouth to scream, but it was instantly filled with earth. He could taste the loamy dirt, feel the worms and insects burrowing out of it and slithering down his throat. Walt clutched at his neck and shot his head forward, but the dirt only packed more deeply in.

The giant coffin shook. The light was almost completely gone now. From the darkness at the far end a figure emerged. It was Walt's sister. It was Sarah. She looked incredibly sad, like something dreadful had happened.

She had no skin.

"*WAAAAAAAAAAALT!*" she shrieked.

*Odd*, Walt thought. *She didn't even open her mouth.*

"*WALT! WAAAAALT! HELP MEEEEEE!*"

The light snuffed out. So did the air.

Walt snapped awake gasping for air.

"*WAAAAAALT!*"

He blinked dumbly and sat upright, not entirely certain if he was still dreaming or not. When he heard Sarah squeal and cry he decided he was awake. It came from the attic, not his head. And Gwyn wasn't in bed.

"Oh, hell."

She wasn't blacking out, but Sarah's mind was in the process of switching off. It was instinctual; her psyche was simply protecting her from the horror that had come.

Like Walt, she too had been dreaming. In her fantasy, contrarily, Sarah maintained total control. She was free of her shackle and armed with the two sharpest and longest knives ever made. When she sliced into Walt and his beast, they came apart like overcooked meat. Wet slivers of them sloughed off with each swipe of the blades and slapped the gore-soaked floor below. Never before had Sarah entertained anything so gruesome, much less enjoyed it. She couldn't even stomach the most innocuous horror film. But this was catharsis. This was her new and only dream.

The last image in her mind's eye before she was startled awake was the monster's terrified face. The first thing she saw after the dream faded away was its awful grin and leering, hungry eyes. That was the first time Sarah screamed.

Naked as always, it loomed over her on the mattress, smiling like a hyena and licking its lips. The last time Sarah had seen the thing, it was mostly covered in scabs. Now it was pink and veiny. Its breasts swung pendulously as it crawled over her, snapping at her with its teeth and clawing at her tattered clothes and skin. She cried out, alternately screaming her brother's name and whimpering from the repulsive terror of it all.

It laughed and hissed before sticking out its dripping tongue and licking Sarah's lips. She clamped them tightly together and tried to move her head away, but the creature dug its fingers into her hair and forced it back.

"Lovely," it rasped. "Lovely girl."

"Don't," Sarah murmured.

"Lovely and divine. *Scrumptious.*"

"Please."

Its face plunged at her and the thing pressed its lips to hers in a hard kiss. It moaned with pleasure as it forced its tongue into her mouth. Sarah struggled but she couldn't overpower the creature. Her eyes squirted tears, blurring her vision. The thing seized the front of her blouse and clawed at her chest, digging furrows in Sarah's skin with its sharp fingernails. Sarah gasped in pain and screamed again.

"*WAAAAALT!!*"

She expected no assistance from the sociopath who locked her up in the first place, but it was Walt's law that his pet demon leave her be. If there was any consistency in his madness, the fact that his nightmare creature was doing this would upset the bastard. Yet despite the immense racket the struggle created, there were no indications that he was coming to her rescue. In all likelihood, he'd abandoned her to this fate. Whatever was left of his humanity, the revolting monster on top of her had destroyed it.

Despair sank into her brain. No one was ever going to save her. Sarah was completely on her own. She let out a wet sob.

*This thing, this fucking thing...if it kills me, I'm taking this goddamned fucking thing with me.*

And then she thrust her hands up and clutched the creature's head. Fine, tiny hairs had sprouted from its scalp, almost too blonde to see in the dark attic. Sarah pressed hard on the temples and the thing grunted. She pressed harder yet and it shrieked. It relinquished its hold on her and seized her wrists. Sarah shot up and drove a knee into its stomach. It groaned angrily and bore its teeth.

"Get off!" Sarah growled. She kneed it again and then jammed the crown of her head into its throat. The humanoid thing wheezed and rolled off of Sarah and off the mattress. It gurgled and gasped.

Sarah scurried away from it, off the soiled mattress and up to her feet. The steel line that secured her to the post went taut. There was only so far she could go.

The creature was already recovering.

It was now on its hands and knees, spitting blood on the insulation. It snapped its face toward Sarah and snarled. Its teeth were stained red. Its eyes gleamed with rage.

Sarah trembled.

The monster sprang at her, screaming and opening its maw wide.

Alice switched the radio on, but it was nothing but static, probably as much the wreck's fault as the twisted fender in front. Nora immediately reached over and turned it back off again.

"I need to explain," she told the sullen girl.

"I just want to listen to some music," Alice griped. "And you should take me back home now, too."

"I will, I'll do that. But this is an emergency. Really. My best friend is missing, maybe dead. I don't know. I've been trying to figure out who this weird sack of shit is for *months*, and I swear God himself must have sent you my way because now I've got him. I've finally got him!"

Nora's babbling did little to assuage Alice's apprehension of her. The more she tried to explain herself, the crazier she sounded. Alice just wanted to get away from her, almost enough to jump out of the car while it was still moving. Maybe at the next stop sign or red light…

"Look, this is my last chance. My last lead. I've tried everything else and everybody else. Maybe this Blackmore guy is as innocent as the driven snow, but there's a chance he's not. I've got to find out, Alice."

"He's just a nerd!" Alice protested. "I mean, he's a high school English teacher! How many guys you ever met get their jollies off friggin' Shakespeare, and then go home and kidnap or kill some chick?"

"I might be about to meet one."

"I don't think so, lady. Not Mr. Blackmore. He's hardly going to snatch somebody everyone would miss and…" Alice trailed off with an audible pop of her lips. Nora took notice of the young girl's unsettled expression from the corner of her eye. Something was amiss.

The boys. The troublemakers. The supposed skippers, Jarod and Clem. Jarod went to see him, after school. At his *house.* He never came back…

Alice shook her head. This was bullshit. Mr. Blackmore didn't kill the nasty little fucker, he just ran off someplace to smoke grass with his chucklehead buddy rather than come to school on Thursday. Hell, they did that all the time. There was absolutely nothing to it worth giving a second thought. No matter how strange it was for a teacher to insist one of his students come to his home at night.

"Alice? What is it?"

"What's *what?* It's nothing. This is crazy, Nora."

"What's crazy is a close friend's boyfriend you've never laid eyes on. What's up with this guy? What's he hiding?"

"Nothing!" Alice shouted. "He's not hiding anything! You're paranoid!"

Nora winced at the outburst. Adolescent girls were prone to them, she guessed—she remembered her own unstable teenage years all too well—but Alice's blind, too amorous defense of the man seemed peculiar.

"Alice," Nora began gently, "how much do you really know about the guy? He's got his teacher hat on at school, but he's not like that all the time. Not at home, or when he's just out with friends. Teachers are people, too. And sometimes people are really, terribly messed up."

Alice scowled.

"*I'm* the one between us who actually knows him," she said in a low voice. "Let's not forget that."

Nora sighed. The kid was getting to her. Nora didn't remember ever having had a crush on a teacher herself at that age—they were all women or trolls to her memory—but even so, she found it difficult to comprehend the bizarre lengths to which this girl was willing to go in a grown man's defense. It begged the question: what had Walt Blackmore done to her? *With* her? Was he a pedophile on top of a kidnapper and murderer?

But no, she did not know that for a fact. Any of it. That was why she was driving somewhat recklessly toward a complete stranger's far-flung country house.

"I guess we'll just have to find out," Nora responded at length.

"*We?*" Alice blurted. "What do you mean, *we?* You're taking me home, right?"

"I hate to break this to you, kid, but I'm going to need you for this."

Alice blanched.

"Fuck that!" she cried. "I'm not helping you get all up in Mr. Blackmore's face about this whacked out crap! He's—he's my friend."

"He's your *teacher.*"

"He's not like other teachers," Alice pouted. "He...sees me."

Nora pursed her lips but refrained from saying anything. Kids were so predictable; it was no wonder they tended to be such easy targets for predators. Predators like Walt Blackmore.

After a stretch of strained silence, Nora said, "Look—maybe I am wrong about this. Hell, I haven't got a shred of evidence against the guy. Otherwise I'd just let the cops deal with it, wouldn't I? All I want to do is talk to him, ask him a couple of questions. If nothing's fishy, fine. If something seems off, we book it and I *will* call the police. Either way, I'm not planning on getting all up in his face or making any kind of scene. I just think it'll help smooth things out if you're there with me. A common acquaintance, you know?"

"What if she's there?" Alice asked nonchalantly.

"Who?"

"Your friend. Mr. Blackmore's *girlfriend.*"

"We'll cross that bridge when we come to it."

Alice sniffed. "He probably just dumped her ass," she said.

Nora surreptitiously rolled her eyes. She drove on, ignoring the speed limit entirely, and neither she nor Alice said another word until Walt's house came into view.

# 52

Sarah crab-walked to the support beam, leaving as much slack on the cable as possible. Gwyn launched herself into the air like a panther, her fingers curled like claws, her mouth open and snarling. Gathering the cable in her hands, Sarah held it up and drove it into Gwyn's neck when she fell upon her. The cable smashed against Gwyn's throat. The momentum made the impact hard; her neck burned red in a deep furrow all the way across. Gwyn coughed and dropped to her side.

"*Kuuuuh,*" Gwyn moaned.

"Yeah, whatever," Sarah growled as she scrambled to her feet, in agonizing pain but energized with a surge of adrenaline, and delivered a solid kick to the monster's ribs. Gwyn grunted and flashed a furious gaze at Sarah.

"*Kuh-kuh-KILL YOU!*"

"I very much doubt it."

Sarah seized Gwyn by the neck and dragged her closer. Gwyn burbled and grumbled, her breath strained. Sarah then made a tight fist and punched her directly in the trachea. She could feel the airway crumple like paper against her knuckles. Gwyn spit blood and wheezed. Sarah punched her again.

"What was that?" Sarah shouted. "You were going to kill me? *Is that fucking right?*"

Sarah got back to her feet and recommenced kicking

the struggling creature at her feet, again and again. Her foot crashed against bone and cartilage, collapsing ribs and obliterating Gwyn's nose. After a while, Gwyn stopped moving at all. As far as Sarah could tell, she wasn't even breathing.

Feet pounded against the steps leading up to the attic, but Sarah ignored it. As Walt surfaced from the opening, she drove her heel into Gwyn's temple. She heard a dull, damp thud and then did it again. This time she felt the skull give a little. The third attempt made a shallow crater in the side of Gwyn's head.

Sarah laughed triumphantly.

"No!" Walt cried as he scrambled toward them. "Sarah, no! What have you done?"

"Not much. I just killed your fucking monster, that's all."

"Killed? Oh God! Gwyn!"

His face twisting with sorrow, his dropped to Gwyn's side and pulled her limp, bloody body into his arms. Tears spilled down his cheeks and he peppered her pink, fuzzy head with gentle kisses. There was no doubt about it; Sarah really had killed her.

"How could you, Sarah? How *could* you?"

Sarah blew a laugh through her nose and groaned.

"You really have lost it, haven't you? You've always been kind of a sociopath, Walter, but now you've really gone over the edge."

"You didn't have to kill her!"

"Yeah, Walt, I did. That thing came up here to kill me. Tear me apart like all the others. What am I supposed to do, lay down and just fucking take it?"

Walt wrapped his arms around Gwyn, pulling her tight to his chest, and shuddered as he wept over her.

"Disgusting," Sarah scoffed under her breath.

She crouched and then sat down on the paneling. The adrenaline was receding and she was beginning to realize how sore she was. Her palms burned from the steel cable scraping against them. And though the monster was dead, she remained tethered to the support beam—with Walt so far gone he was unlikely to ever let her go.

"Damn it," she whispered and she dropped her chin to her knees.

Walt just wept, clutching at the nude corpse in his arms. For a moment, Sarah considered giving him some of the same, but that wouldn't set her free. It would only result in two corpses rotting beside her until her own death eventually came to pass. At least by letting him live he would probably take the revolting dead thing away.

*The sick son of a bitch will probably eat it.*

*How long until he decides to kill and eat me, too?*

Her imagination turning dark and beginning to run wild, Sarah felt a shiver work its way up her spine. She swallowed hard and her ears popped as though she were at a high altitude. Then she heard the pop again and realized it wasn't in her ears. It was outside, just below the vents.

It was the sound of car doors slamming shut.

"I'm staying in the car."

Alice folded her arms and pouted. Nora pursed her lips at her.

"Fine," she said. "Do what you like. But I'm not leaving the engine running just to keep you warm."

Nora got out of the car, shut the door and headed for the house. She was at the front porch when she heard Alice's door slam shut and her small feet scrape the walkway toward the porch.

"I'm not going to freeze my butt off," said Alice. Nora gave the girl a reassuring pat on the shoulder. Then she knocked on the door.

After several minutes dragged by and no one answered,

she knocked again.

Alice said, "He's not here."

"Maybe not," Nora said. But she waited anyway.

There was still no answer.

"Hey, I've got an idea," Alice said after a protracted and uncomfortable silence. "Why don't you take me home now?"

Nora furrowed her brow. The kid really wanted to get home, but that put a kink in her plans. She was not particularly interested in getting slapped with a kidnapping charge, but if Walt *was* home then he was going to be prepared when she came back, and she didn't want him to be prepared. She wanted him off-guard and red-handed. Balling up her fist she pounded hard.

The latch clicked and the door swung open several inches.

"I guess it wasn't quite closed all the way," Alice theorized.

She took in a sharp breath as Nora waltzed boldly inside. "What are you doing?"

"Getting to the bottom of this," Nora responded at a normal conversational volume. She vanished into the house.

Alice bounced on the balls of her feet, afraid to follow but just as nervous about waiting on the porch. Mr. Blackmore could come back home at any time, find her standing there. What would he think? Probably nothing quite as bad as he'd think if he found her breaking and entering. Either way seemed bad. But it was cold outside, so she made up her mind and went into the house.

It was dark inside, but there was enough light filtering in through the windows to see where they were going. Alice gently and quietly shut the door as Nora advanced through the foyer and into the living room. Everywhere there was clutter, like the occupant of the house had only just moved in and hadn't finished unpacking. It smelled musky and dank. Nora wrinkled her nose and crossed over to the dining room. It was even darker in there, due to all the boxes that were stacked up against the room's only window. It was also stuffier than the other rooms. There was a sickly sweet odor in the air, almost metallic. It was like rust and mildew. Nora made a face and continued through the room and into the hallway beyond.

Alice went the other way, into the kitchen. She jumped a little when Nora appeared in the adjacent hallway.

"Just me," Nora said.

"*Shhh!*"

Nora narrowed her eyes and cupped a hand to the side of her mouth.

"Walt? Walt Blackmore? Are you home?"

Alice's eyes bulged.

"Jesus, Nora!" she hissed. "Be quiet!"

"I'm not here to rob the place, kid. I have to talk to this guy." She resumed her booming shout. "Walt Blackmore! My name is Nora, I'm a friend of Amanda's! I need to talk with you!"

"Great," Alice groaned. "He's obviously not here. Can we go before he comes home and finds us, please?"

Nora wagged a finger at Alice without looking at her. "Just a minute," she said.

Alice rolled her eyes.

Nora checked the bedroom next. She found a light switch and flipped it. The room was strewn with dirty clothes. The sheets on the unmade bed were filthy and mottled with brown stains. She sneered at the repulsive mess and went back to the hall.

"There's no one here," she said quietly, mostly to herself.

"I told you that already," Alice grumbled.

"You were guessing."

"I was right."

Nora gritted her teeth. The kid had a hell of an attitude problem, and it was getting to her, but she knew practically all kids that age were pretty much the same way. Besides, she'd all but forced Alice to join her on this adventure, so she couldn't really blame the girl for getting so grouchy. She unclenched her jaw and went over to the kid in the kitchen.

"Okay, maybe next time. How about we go get some burgers and shakes? My treat. You know, for ruining your snow day."

A faint smile played at the corners of the chubby girl's lips. "Yeah," she said. "All right."

Nora placed a hand on the middle of Alice's back and gently guided her back to the front door. It had been a wash, but she was far from done with the elusive Walt Blackmore. He had to come back home sometime, and when he did, she would be waiting. And even if she never got him on his own turf, she now knew what he did for a living. He was Alice's English teacher, which meant he would be back at school as soon as the weather cleared up. One way or another, a confrontation was coming. She was going to get some answers about what happened to her best friend.

Alice finally let herself smile, and she looked a little guilty doing it. She reached for the doorknob and gave it a twist. The hinges squealed slightly as she stepped to the side, opening the door for Nora, who let out a stilted gasp.

The man on the front porch hefted an axe over his head and quickly sent the blade crashing down into the middle of her skull. Nora's head split open as the heavy blade sank down to the handle. Her arms jutted out, her hands and fingers dancing spasmodically for a minute before she drooped and collapsed onto the floor. The man jammed a booted foot against Nora's sternum for leverage to extract the axe from her face. Blood and chunky gray globs of brain bubbled out of the wound when the axe came free.

Alice stumbled backward, her thick lips working rapidly but unable to make a sound. Mr. Blackmore stepped into the foyer and gave the axe a hard shake. Blood and flecks of bone flew from the blade, splattering the facing wall. He turned his cold gaze on Alice and brought his eyebrows together in a sharp V.

"Alice?"

A wet sob exploded from deep in the girl's chest. Spittle and snot sprayed out of her face and she began to tremble all over.

"You shouldn't be here, Alice," Mr. Blackmore said as he nudged Nora's body out of the way of the door with the axe. "You shouldn't be here at all."

He kicked the front door and it slammed shut.

## 53

His back and ankles aching from the drop out the attic vent, Walt stumbled awkwardly toward the terrified teenage girl. The bloody axe hung limply from his three-fingered hand, the nubs of the former two shone red from all the exertion. Up in the attic, he'd only heard the one woman's voice. Walt was not prepared for Alice's unexpected presence in the house. He did not know what to do with her.

She trembled as she backed up to the wall. Once she was flat against it, she began moving sideways toward the kitchen. Walt watched her slow movements, careful to keep her in view while his addled mind searched for an answer to the predicament he faced.

Tiny whimpers spilled out of the girl's wobbling lips. Her knees faltered as if any moment they would buckle and send her crashing to the floor. His crippled hand growing tired, Walt switched the axe to his other. Alice cried out and bolted through the kitchen.

"Alice!" he screamed.

He gave chase, and by the time he made it into the kitchen,

the back door was already slamming shut.

"Shit!"

Walt's feet pounded the linoleum as he strained to maintain enough energy and momentum to pursue her. His ankles throbbed and his lungs were already burning before he even made it to the backyard. But he could see her now, pumping her arms and legs like a cartoon runner in her mad dash for the field between Walt's yard and the tree line in the distance. He tightened his grip on the axe handle and ran after her.

The snow crunched under his feet and slowed his progress. Somehow Alice kept right on running, unimpeded by the four-inch deep hindrance. He got it in his boots, soaking his socks and freezing his feet. This was the stuff he and Sarah would scoop up in plastic cups when they were children, pour vanilla or maple syrup on it and eat it quickly before it melted. Now it was preventing him from killing that interfering little cunt as quickly as he'd like.

A fox skittered over the surface of the snow at the edge of the woods as Alice disappeared into its thick growth. To Walt she seemed miles away. His chest ached and his breath came in shallower and shallower bursts. Still, he forced himself to keep moving. To let her get away would be nothing short of suicide.

He had no choice in the matter. Alice had to die, even if he had a heart attack in the process. He was not particularly delighted by the prospect of killing an adolescent girl—much less another one of his own students—but as far as he was concerned she'd brought it upon herself by walking into his house.

He made it across the snowy field and ducked into the dense copse of trees at its edge. Between the icy snow and the dead leaves and the broken branches that littered the ground, he could hear nothing over the seemingly deafening crunches of his own steps. Nevertheless, he had a fairly good notion of where she would end up heading. There really wasn't anyplace else for her to go.

The faded red farmhouse exploded into view the moment Alice cleared the woods. Her face was chilled with cold sweat and every muscle in her body screamed at her to stop running, but she pounded on toward the house. Mr. Blackmore might have looked fitter than her, but he was still floundering somewhere back in the trees. She raced down the hill and across the unkempt grass in the front yard.

She was already screaming before she got to the door.

"Help! Help me! *Somebody!*"

The heavyset girl barreled toward the front door only to find it standing wide open upon her arrival. She skidded to a halt and paused to catch her breath. Off to her left, a ragged pigpen was hidden in the knee-high grass, its railings rotting and broken. One pig rooted around in the mud, snorting and snuffling. Alice dismissed the animal and turned back to the house. The last time she'd just walked into somebody's house hadn't turned out well for her. She didn't even know who lived in this one. Still, the chances that the only two houses in the area were both owned by psycho murderers seemed too remote to seriously consider. Alice screwed up her face and looked over her shoulder.

Mr. Blackmore had emerged from the woods and was huffing down the hill, his arms pinwheeling and his face crimson with rage. She yelped and rushed into the old place.

All at once the repulsive miasma of rot and decay slammed her in the face. The house smelled like a slaughterhouse, or at least what she imagined one would be like. Blood and shit and decomposition lingered in the air like a nauseating fog, but she didn't see anything that might have caused it. The carpets were caked with mud, picture frames knocked over and china broken on the floor, but apart from that the house seemed relatively normal. She clamped a hand over her face. It was almost too much to bear.

"Alice!" Walt screamed from the front yard.

She shrieked, rushing for the adjacent staircase. The stench only worsened as she ascended to the upper floor, but there was no turning back now. Blackmore was already in the house.

"Goddamnit, stop!" he roared from the bottom of the stairs. "Come down here *right now!*"

She almost wanted to laugh at him using his teacher voice at a time like this. It might have been funny if the man wasn't carrying an axe he'd just used to split a woman's face in two. She turned into the dusky hallway, away from the stairs. Blackmore growled like an animal and started stomping up after her.

"I'm coming, Alice!"

He was snarling his words now, grating them out his throat harshly and powerfully. Alice sniveled as she hurried down the hall and into an ink-dark room. She quickly found the edge of the door and pushed it shut. She locked it. Then she began searching the wall for a light switch. She found one and flipped it, but nothing came on. The house must have been abandoned, she reasoned. *But what in hell is that awful smell?* It was so strong now her eyes stung and watered. As she gradually adjusted to the lack of light, she noticed dim yellow hazes on either side of the room. Windows.

Alice tumbled across to the nearest one, tripping over something that squished against her foot and rolled away. Ignoring it, she reached out and grabbed handfuls of the window curtains and yanked them open. The dying afternoon sunlight leaked in through the dusty glass panes, illuminating what she could now see was a bedroom.

A loud crack echoed. Blackmore laughed on the other side of the door. He sounded insane. Another crack and the wood of the door began to splinter.

Tears silently ran in steady rivulets down Alice's face as she scanned the room for something—anything—to use for defense.

The first thing her eyes settled upon was a rotting human head on the floor. It was what Alice tripped over, what squished warm and soft against her shoes. She drew in a sharp breath as she hurried away from the hideous thing. When the axe finally broke through the door, she lost her footing and fell backward on the bed.

Alice planted her hands on either side of her to heft herself up, but she slid on the slippery ooze that coated the comforter. She had been so focused on Blackmore and his axe that she failed to realize what she was lying in. The entire bed was covered with malodorous, rotting gore. Alice clamped her mouth shut and frantically looked all around her. At the head of the bed lay a human body, its flesh greenish brown and dripping off splintered bones. The torso had been ripped open as though it exploded from within. The jaw yawned open with no tendons to support it, and the sunken, ghostly face stared without eyes.

She screamed and rolled off on the other side, under the other window. When she crashed against the floor she found herself face to face with a filth covered pig. Its entire head was awash in mud and shit and rot. The animal bucked and squealed at her. It was gnawing on the few tattered chunks of flesh that still clung to the brown, broken skeleton on the floor. Alice leapt over the pig and hurried back to the first window. She unlocked the latch. It heaved open as Blackmore's axe burst through the door again.

"I hardly ever wanted this, Alice," Walt shouted as he hacked the door apart. "It's anathema to me, I swear it. Damn bloody work, but I've got to. I've got to do it for Gwyn, don't you fucking see that?"

The door finally came apart when he delivered a sound

kick to it, dividing the hollow wood right down the middle. Alice wasted no time. She climbed up onto the window ledge and leapt out.

She felt no pain or discomfort when she landed on the slushy ground, two stories beneath the bedroom window. Only when she started into a sprint did her ankles throb and complain, sending white hot messages of radiating pain to her spinning head. She disregarded it. The dilapidated barn a hundred yards ahead commanded her attention for the moment.

Like the house, the barn had once been painted red. Now what little paint remained was a faded pink. The rest of the decrepit structure was gray and brown—black where the wood was rotted completely through. The barn's roof was half caved in at one corner and the crater formed there was filled with forest detritus and debris.

The wide doors slowly opened at the pressure of her shoulder and she pumped her tired, aching legs as hard as she could in a mad dash for the barn's relative safety. She was fairly sure Blackmore didn't follow her through the window, but that only meant he would race back down to the front door and come running after her any second. She was right about that—as soon as she plunged into the cold darkness of the abandoned barn, she saw her insane teacher round the house. He was screaming like a Viking berserker and holding the axe over his head as he crossed the yard with astonishing speed. Alice whimpered and pushed deeper into the stuffy shadows.

Almost immediately she tripped over something long and metal, some farming instrument. She slammed into it with her knees and pitched forward, tumbling over and smacking against a spiny post with a thud. The accident kicked up a cloud of dust that filled the air and got in her nose and mouth. She hacked and sneezed. The silhouette between the open barn doors laughed and readjusted the axe.

"Bless you, child," Blackmore said.

Something in Alice's subconscious suggested that she plead for her life, but her reason argued that such a pathetic display would do her no good. A man like this felt no sympathy. He was too far gone. Instead, she heaved herself back up and scrambled into the corner, her hands thrust out in front of her. She felt blindly in the darkness for something to save her, a weapon or a means of escape. She found dry, frayed ropes and slippery piles of rotten hay. A plastic broom handle and a burlap sack half filled with dirt or seed. Then the corner, which was solid and offered no exit. No matter how much she fought it, despair was beginning to set in. Alice pounded her fist against the wall. She might as well have tried to push over a skyscraper.

She sank to her knees and let herself drop back. A tiny, quiet sob erupted from her throat. When something smacked hard like metal against wood, she knew Mr. Blackmore was only a few yards away. A thin, dry chuckle trickled out of his mouth like sand.

*This is it*, Alice told herself. *This is how I die.*

She covered her face with her trembling hands and waited for the axe to fall.

## 54

Stupid girl.

Walt could hear her sniveling back there. Undoubtedly she believed she was hiding well, masked by the total darkness of the barn, but he could hear her sobbing. Giving up.

A smile cut across his stiff, winter-beaten face.

Gwyn would have been so pleased with him, happy as a newlywed when he brought home *this* bacon.

"Here, piggy, piggy, piggy," he sang. "It's time to come out now. Farmer Walt's got something nice for you." He laughed.

"Nice and *sharp.*"

"No," the girl whispered.

Walt shook his head.

"No? *No?* You don't tell me *no*, you little shit. *You* don't tell me *anything!*"

He was surprised by his own sudden switch from mirth to rage, but he embraced it. And he charged toward the corner of the barn, lifting the axe high over his head, screaming with frenzied anger.

When he was sure that he was close enough to reach her, he brought the axe down hard.

*So pleased.*

*Bacon for Gwyn.*

*Piggy piggy piggy.*

Abruptly he felt a sharp pull and he was yanked backward and up. The axe fell out of his hands and made two thudding sounds as it hit whatever was beneath him. Not Alice. Just dirt and useless farming supplies. He squealed and clawed at his neck. He felt rope, scratchy and frayed but strong enough to hold his weight. His face flooded with blood and the fusty air was difficult to gulp. His temples throbbed painfully.

Someone had roped him like a steer and he was beginning to black out.

*Who?*

Alice heard the impact, the drop of the axe, but she felt no pain. She supposed it was the same thing as her ankles when she dropped out of the second story window—it didn't come right away then, either. In just a second or two, though, she knew the agony would finally reach her fear-addled mind and then she would know she was cut and bleeding and dying. So she squeezed her eyes and waited for it.

But it never came.

Instead, her senses only registered the cold, the stifling,

decayed air, and the muted gagging sound that seemed to emanate from above. Alice opened her eyes, half expecting to see Blackmore leering over her, waiting to strike. But only the dark remained. The muffled retching continued. That, and the creak of an old rope pulled taut and slowly swinging back and forth.

All she wanted to do was curl up into a ball and disappear. She was still alive and relatively unharmed, but the panic had not subdued. She swallowed hard. Her throat was dry and sore.

"Hello?" she whispered.

"Hurry," a feminine voice called back. It sounded like it came from the rafters.

"Hello? Who's there?"

"I cannot hold him forever. Come and help."

"What—" The words got caught in her gullet. She swallowed again and cleared her throat. "What do you want me to do?"

"Come here. Find him with your hands."

"Find who? Mr. Blackmore?"

"Who else?" The voice *tsked.*

"Who…who are you?"

"I can drop him if you want. Let him get his axe and hack you to bits."

"No!"

"Then come here, girl."

Alice rose slowly to her feet. Her weight seemed to crush her throbbing ankles. She winced and took a step forward.

"What do you want me to do?" she asked hesitantly of the disembodied voice.

"I have him strung up by a rope. But he must have gotten his fingers between the loop and his neck. He is struggling, but he is not dying."

Alice felt the blood drain out of her face. "God," she said softly.

"This is kill or be killed, child," the voice continued. "When

I let go of the rope, if Walt is still alive he will chop you apart. Do you understand?"

Her breath came in short, shuddery bursts.

"I asked you if you understand me, child."

"Y—Yes, I understand."

"Excellent. Find the axe."

"What?"

"*The axe!*" the voice bellowed.

"Okay! But—what for?"

"Surely you would not have lived through this ordeal so long if you are as stupid as you sound."

"I'm *not* stupid."

"No?"

"No! I'm not!"

Despite her terror and befuddlement, the accusation rankled her. She knew that she was fat and that she was awkward, but the charge of stupidity would not stand. If she had anything going for her at all, it was her smarts. Her neck flashed hot and she sneered in the dark, wishing the stranger could see it. Wishing she could see the stranger.

"Then do as I tell you. Find the axe."

"All right, fine."

Falling into a crouch, Alice fanned her arms out and commenced the search. Everything she touched was cold and rough against her palms. Layers of grime and dust coated everything inside the barn. She didn't like it at all.

After groping at clods of earth and pebbles and what felt like a greasy engine part, she came at last upon the handle of the axe. Brushing her fingers up the shaft she then felt the cool, sticky head of the thing. She picked it up with both hands and stood back up again.

"I've got it," she said.

"Can you hear him struggling?" the voice asked with macabre glee.

Alice listened. She could.

"Yes."

"Musical, isn't it?"

Blackmore wheezed and croaked. Something in his throat clicked wetly. Alice did not find it musical at all. To her, it sounded horrific.

"If you say so," she said, wondering how the person with that weird voice could even see in there.

The voice laughed softly. "Follow the sound, girl. Find him. Find him, and I'll give him to you. You will have him and kill him."

Alice gasped. Some naïve part of her wanted to believe that the stranger in the rafters only wanted her to get the axe for defense, for protection. Her more reasonable faculties knew that this was not true from the start, but she sometimes chose to ignore that voice. She'd ignored it now, but the heavy truth of the matter ended up smashing into her like a sixteen-wheeler.

"No!" she cried. "I can't!"

"You must. You don't want to die, do you?"

"I'll call the cops. I'll go back into the house and call them..."

"There's no phone there. The line is dead."

"Then I'll call from *his* house."

"I can't hold him that long."

*Can't or won't?* Alice wondered.

"Use the axe," she offered.

"That's your job."

"I meant to keep him here. Until the police arrive."

"Kill him!" the voice roared.

Alice jumped. She was starting to feel as afraid of the owner of that deceptively feminine voice as she was of Walt Blackmore.

"*KILL HIM!*" it screamed again, louder this time.

"But I can't!" Alice sobbed. "I won't!"

A loud sigh drifted down from above.

"Then I will let him go," the exasperated voice said. "Good luck, Alice."

She heard the whine of the rope skidding over wood, followed by a thump. Blackmore coughed and hacked. He moved around, adjusting this and scraping that. Then he said, "Bitch."

Alice shook and gripped the axe handle more tightly.

"Bitch!" Walt rasped wrathfully.

Dirt and rocks scratched and kicked up. Blackmore groaned, and the groan turned into a mad wail. His feet pounded the ground as he blindly lunged in Alice's direction.

"NOW, ALICE!" the voice shouted.

Alice swung the axe as hard as she could. It halted abruptly in mid-swing, blade meeting flesh. Blackmore moaned. Then his grubby fingers found Alice's face and neck.

"Fuck…ing…kill…you," he gasped.

She shrieked, half from fear and half from the adrenaline rush of her fury. She kicked Blackmore with the flat of her foot, separating him from the axe. He dropped to the ground like dead weight. She bolted for the barn doors, for the light.

Blackmore gurgled and grunted. And then he lifted himself up again and came at her. He emerged from the darkness covered in dirt. Foamy blood flecked his lips and face. He held one hand firmly against his midsection. Blood bubbled up between his fingers.

His grimy face was twisted from pain and anger, but he forced a strained grin.

"O there are days…in this life," he croaked, "worth life… and worth *death*." Scarlet saliva sprayed out of his mouth with every word. His teeth were stained red.

Alice gave a wild scream and ran at him with the axe hefted over one shoulder. Blackmore had no time to react; in a second the glistening blade tore into his face and cut clean through to the other side. A wet, red slab of flesh curled off the front of his skull and dropped to the snow with a dull splat. Blackmore wobbled for a moment, and then fell backward. He landed hard without so much as bending his knees.

Alice hyperventilated and stared with shiny, bulging eyes at the ghastly fruit of her bloody labor. Walt Blackmore's face was almost completely sheared off, leaving a cross-section of his head that exposed brain and bone before quickly filling up with red-black blood. Half an eyeball bobbed at the surface of the steaming fluid, tethered to a stringy red stalk. When the blood spilled over, a ruby red puddle blotted out on the white snow around the body.

Alice emitted a wet sob and let the dripping axe fall. Mr. Blackmore, her ninth grade English teacher in whom she had found a kind of kindred spirit only hours earlier, was dead by her hand.

"I killed him," she said, too quietly to hear. "Oh God...oh my God."

A series of sharp slaps erupted from the shadows inside the barn. She lifted her head to see what it was. Her head felt as though it was filled with concrete.

From the darkness emerged a completely nude woman. Her hair was shaved down to a buzz cut, her flawless skin nearly as white as the snow into which she walked, barefoot.

She didn't seem cold at all; her skin was not pink and she didn't shiver. She merely applauded and smiled like a proud parent at a spelling bee. When she reached the gruesome remains of Walt Blackmore, she gave him nothing more than a brief glance before spreading her arms out like wings and looking adoringly into Alice's eyes.

She stared. There was puzzlement and wonder in the gaze, but she was too exhausted to speak. After the sensory overload of fear and rage, and the grisly killing of the dead madman in the snow, she had nothing left to say.

The naked woman wrapped her arms around her and squeezed her into a tight embrace. Alice did not resist.

"What a day," the woman whispered into her ear. She delivered a quick, cold kiss on Alice's neck. "But everything is going to be all right now. Everything is going to be just fine."

# SPRING

# OPHELIA

## 55

Her side of the bed was warm from her own body heat, but when Alice rolled over she found the sheets to be cool, as if they hadn't been slept in. Shrinking away from the sudden chill, she quickly returned to the familiar comfort of her own warmth. That was when she felt the dampness underneath her, soaking against her thigh. She switched sides once more and threw back the blankets to investigate.

The late morning sun shone through the cracks in the blinds, delivering a hazy saffron glow to the dinner plate-sized bloodstain on the fitted sheet. Alice exhaled noisily.

"Goddamnit," she grumbled.

The boy's boxers she wore to bed—white with a yellow smiley face on the ass—were soaked through as well. The formerly white cotton was now bright red and glistening from the crotch of the underwear all the way down to her thighs. Her period had come a week early, just as it had the month before and the month before that. Ever since she moved in with Ophelia.

Alice had never actually observed any signs that Ophelia suffered from the monthly visitor herself, but she was young and healthy and surely did. Alice supposed her cycle was just adjusting to more closely match that of Ophelia's. A hundred women's magazines had insisted to her that such things were common, that it happened all the time. She was just going to have to get used to the new routine.

She threw her prickly legs over the edge of the mattress and sucked in a sharp breath when her bare toes touched the cold hardwood floor. Winter was gone, but the mornings were still too chilly for her liking. Once there had been a large Oriental rug on the floor in this room, but it got ruined by all the blood and dirt and human waste. There just wasn't anything for a mess like that. The rug had to go.

Now she quickly tiptoed across the room to where her fuzzy bunny slippers rested, right beside the bedroom door where she left them. She shoved her pudgy feet into them and wiggled her toes. It felt good. Then she grabbed a fresh pair of boxers out of the wardrobe at the foot of the bed and padded down the hallway to the bathroom.

Sliding the soiled drawers down, Alice felt the sting of the stubble and decided to shave her legs before stepping into the shower. She felt like a royal mess, like she woke up a substantially less attractive girl than the one she'd been when she went to bed. Standing in the middle of the bathroom in nothing but the white tank top she'd woken up in, she turned to get a look at herself in the mirror. She didn't particularly like what she saw. Cheeks too round and ruddy; breasts already beginning to sag despite her scant fifteen years; nipples enormous and too puffy, which she could see through the shirt, along with the push of her belly rolls. Her hair was greasy and needed cutting. If she squinted she was sure she could make out the faintest trace of a moustache coming in on her upper lip.

*I'm a fucking hag*, she told herself, pouting.

Behind her, from the hallway, Ophelia said, "Beautiful girl."

Alice flashed her a look of incredulity.

"Angelic," Ophelia added.

Alice cocked her head to one side and pursed her lips. Per usual, Ophelia was not wearing a stitch of clothing. Her shoulder-length, blood-red hair was shiny and perfect, even though she never brushed it. The triangle of equally red hair between her legs jutted out in wild spirals. Alice thought it complemented her faultless alabaster skin. Ophelia's eyes met hers, then slowly worked their way down the length of Alice's body. When Alice realized that Ophelia was seeing the bloodied place between her stubbly legs, she threw her hands over her groin and flushed pink.

"I started my period. While I was sleeping. It got all over the fucking bed."

Ophelia smiled, although it didn't show in her icy blue eyes. It rarely ever did.

"Out, damned spot," she said.

"That was Lady Macbeth," Alice said mock-pedantically, "not Ophelia."

Ophelia only grinned in lieu of response.

Pulling the top over her head, Alice bent naked over the bathtub faucet and started the water. Over the crashing din of the tub, she looked over her shoulder at the stunning red-haired beauty in the doorway.

"Where were you, by the way? When I woke up you were gone. The bed was cold."

Ophelia answered, "Breakfast."

Alice nodded soberly. The water was hot enough to her liking now, so she pulled the plunger that shut off the faucet and turned on the shower head.

"Oh," she said.

"All gone now, our Walt."

A brief tremor rocked Alice's stomach. So much blood. So much awful violence. Necessary, yes. But so repugnant to her.

First, Ophelia ate the woman—Blackmore's sister, she said.

That bounty lasted her three weeks, and that was really parceling it out. She'd explained to Alice that the dead woman was her brother's partner-in-crime, as it were, that together they were responsible for the deaths of those two nasty boys from school. There were others, too—the bones in the lime pit and the putrefied corpses in the bedroom Alice and Ophelia now called their own. But Ophelia's hands were not sullied by the blood of murder. She *had* to eat, but she was no killer. It took plenty of time for Alice to process the fantastic, singularly grotesque nature of the thing, and even now it turned her stomach to think about so much death and rot, and to remember what she had done to Mr. Blackmore. It was all for the best, however—this she knew and at least vaguely understood. Alice loved Ophelia, truly and deeply loved her in a way she had never loved anybody before. The strange and incredible woman came into her life in a burst of terror and bloodshed, but ever since that dreadful winter day, Ophelia had done nothing but take care of her. She was Alice's only friend; her mother, big sister and lover all rolled into one.

And, had it not been for Ophelia, that monster Blackmore would surely have chopped poor, young Alice to bits of flesh and bone.

Of course he was the next to slide down the ravishing redhead's gullet, piece by raw, bloody piece. And as of that morning, according to the elder woman's report, nothing edible was left of the late lunatic killer.

"He is dead and gone, lady," Ophelia recited with dramatic flourish. "He is dead and gone; at his head a grass-green turf, at his heels a stone."

Alice smiled in spite of her troubling thoughts; she even gave a little laugh.

"Now *that's* Ophelia," she said as she stepped under the hot spray.

The afternoon was spent doing chores around and outside the farmhouse. Alice cut the grass and painted the front door and fed their one remaining pig. Soon she would slaughter it just as she had the other one. Like Ophelia, she too had to eat.

For her part, Ophelia changed the linens on the bed and flipped the mattress, since the blood had leaked through to stain it. After that, when a tired and sweaty Alice came back into the house, she prepared a sumptuous hot lunch of pork loin with garlic for Alice and pan-seared flank of Walt Blackmore for herself. It was what remained of her breakfast and, indeed, of Walt.

Alice dug into her lunch with gusto; the yard work had built up a mighty appetite in her. Only twice did she glance up at her companion as the tall, buxom woman poked a sliver of pink, rare meat into her mouth with her fork. Once, not long after Alice first began to accept Ophelia for who and what she was, Alice gave in and sampled a bite of the anthropophagus' meal. In that instance, it was the woman from the attic, Walt's sister Sarah, from whom the meat was cut. A thick slice of what Ophelia dubbed "back bacon," it was sweet and not at all unpleasant to Alice's palate. Which was precisely why she never dined on human meat again—the last thing she wanted was to turn herself into a cannibal, craving the succulent taste of her fellow man.

Ophelia swallowed the sliver and dabbed at her mouth with the cloth napkin from her naked lap.

"Empty now," she said matter-of-factly, gesturing toward the icebox in the corner of the kitchen.

Alice gazed at the large, humming box. It was the last item they had taken from Walt's house before Alice lit the match that ignited the blaze. All that night and into the following morning, the old Gablefront cottage burned tangerine orange and schoolhouse red until at last it was finally reduced to ashes. Alice even had a pretty good story ready for when the fire marshal and investigating police came knocking on the farmhouse door asking questions. But they never came. It was the last they ever had anything to do with the legacy of Walt Blackmore. Except, of course, for his meat.

Alice sped up her chewing and swallowed a mouthful of pork, trying like hell not to think about the sight of that very pig feasting on the remains of the house's prior occupants.

"What do you suppose we should do?" she asked.

"I think you know," Ophelia answered gravely.

Even though her mouth was now empty, Alice swallowed again. Her throat bobbed and gurgled. She was not happy about where this was going.

"Not that, Ophelia," she said glumly. "Not yet. I—I can't."

"You've said *that* before."

"It's too awful. I don't even want to think about it."

"All you have to do is make a phone call. I will deal with everything after that."

"Where? In the barn?"

"It is as good a place as any."

Alice heaved a weighty sigh. She looked down at her plate and her stomach did a flip. Her appetite was dead and gone.

"And what then? After that, I mean. Who will be next? And then after that?"

"We'll find out."

"Before it was all…circumstantial. Now you want us to start…"

She could not make herself pronounce the word. *Killing.*

Ophelia dropped her eyelids halfway down over her pale, glinting eyes and rose from her chair. She rounded the kitchen table to where Alice sat, squatted beside her and placed a cool, gentle hand on the girl's bare knee. An involuntary tremble worked its way throughout Alice's body. It was the same every time. Ophelia's touch thrilled her.

"I watched you slaughter the pig. That one right there." She pointed at the half-eaten pork loin on Alice's plate. "You swung the axe, severed the jugular. You never even flinched at all the blood."

Alice sulked childishly. "I'd had practice," she said ominously.

"You have to when you're self-sufficient like we are. We have no one upon whom to depend but each other. And we have to eat, both of us. I never asked to be this way, darling..."

*Darling.* Ophelia was bringing out the big guns.

"I know you didn't."

"I was dead. I was nothing. Then I came back. And I came back...like this."

Alice knew all of this. Ophelia told her the whole sordid story after the fire, how she was cut to ribbons by her own kin and left to bleed to death in that very same Gablefront cottage, long ago. A horrible time and a horrible life. Why she returned she could not tell because she did not know herself. She simply did, gradually, and she would have died a second time had it not been for a steady diet of the very stuff she was made of. It kept her together, she said. It made her whole. Alice couldn't argue with that. Not when it meant life or death for the other half of her own heart.

"I know," she whispered. "I know."

Tears formed in her eyes, blurring her vision before spilling over her eyelids and dribbling down her round, pink cheeks. Ophelia wiped them away with her thumb on one side and kissed them away on the other. That only made Alice cry harder.

"Shh, darling," Ophelia cooed. "Shhhh."

## 56

After she hung up the phone, Alice realized she was holding her breath. She let it out slowly, like a balloon leaking out of a pinprick. Then she waited.

A little more than an hour later, as the horizon turned a

bruised purple and the sun disappeared behind the woods, the rumble of an oil-deprived engine grew steadily louder outside the house. He was coming, and her knowledge of that fact made Alice's chest feel tight.

She had to let her breath out again when she heard the knocking at the door. Ophelia slipped into the satin robe slung over the back of the kitchen chair, a sacrifice Alice insisted upon. As Ophelia tied the belt around her ample waist, Alice crept cautiously toward the door.

The deadbolt clacked noisily as she turned the knob. The door squealed on its hinges when she opened it.

The tall, gangly man at the door glowered at her with steely eyes and said, "So here you are, you goddamned stupid little bitch."

The words assaulted her as though she'd been punched in the nose. She flinched and stepped aside.

"Come in, Harold."

He sauntered into the house like he had been there a dozen times before.

"Whose fucking place is this, anyway?"

"It's mine."

Harold snorted derisively as he noticed Ophelia for the first time. He raised his eyebrows at the beautiful woman and made an O with his mouth.

"Mine and hers," Alice corrected herself.

"That so?"

His face melted back into a scowl.

"You know this bitch is a minor, don't you?" he growled at Ophelia.

The redhead smiled thinly.

"The only bitch I see here is a pathetic old man," she seethed.

"I could call the police, you know. I could press fucking charges."

"Go right ahead," Ophelia said. "The telephone is on the

counter."

Harold erupted into a peal of laughter.

"I'd bet you'd like that, you goddamn dyke. Here you only got one broad to play finger-fuck with, but in prison? Hoo boy, that'd be a fucking buffet for a cunt like you."

Alice lunged forward. "Don't talk to her like that, *Harold*," she snarled.

Harold spun around to face her. His mirth having gone as quickly as it came, he resumed his furious gaze.

"First off, don't you ever tell me what to do. Get that? And second, you call me Dad, or Father, or Sir. You've disrespected your elders long enough, you dumb little bit—"

The raging man fell silent the moment he felt the sharp, ripping pain in his abdomen. Without moving his head, he turned his glistening eyes downward to see his stepdaughter's fist up against his belly. Jutting from the back of the fist was a rounded wooden handle. Harold could see nothing of the blade, but he knew it was buried deep in his guts.

"I'll call you whatever I want," Alice said. "Now Ophelia—that gorgeous redhead over there—I reckon she'll just call you *meat*."

Harold mouthed the word meat, but no sound passed his lips.

"And for the life of me," Alice continued, "I don't see why I won't, too."

In her mind she flashed on every terrible, hateful thing the man had ever said and ever done. His appalling physical abuse of her mother that lasted until her death at forty-six. The times he'd get stewed and make passes at the few friends she ever made in all her years at school. The morning she woke up with him in her bed, naked as Adam and snoring drunk.

Tightening her fist even more, Alice jerked the knife up, dragging the blade through soft innards until it jammed against Harold's sternum.

She also thought back to every indignity she had ever suffered at the hands of others. The busy hands and bragging mouth of Kyle Casey. The terrible, dirty roll in the sheets with Clem Lundeen, and his buddy Jarod's never ceasing smirk, denoting his familiarity with her most private intimacies. Every classmate who called her names, and every boy or girl to whom she'd given her misplaced trust. All of them monsters, none of them human at all. Not like her. Not like Ophelia. No, indeed—the ones like them, they were just flesh and blood and bone with no soul to speak of. They were nothing more than meat.

Out came the blade, and with it, a spouting fountain of blood. Harold squealed as he staggered to one side and clutched at his abdomen with desperate, useless hands. He could do nothing to prevent the agony burning up his open torso, nor the pulsing spray of his lifeblood pumping out of him, spurt by viscous spurt. Then, with only the quickest of swipes, Alice slashed the gleaming blade across her stepfather's neck, carving the flesh apart in the blink of an eye. Three rapid bursts of blood flew out of the severed arteries on either side of Harold's neck, then slowed to a steady dribble. He faltered, lost control of his ankles and knees and everything all at once. Finally, he crumpled like a pile of dirty laundry. The floor was awash in the dead man's draining fluids; the white and tan design of the tiles vanished in the sticky red deluge.

Alice's chest heaved with every massive breath. She gulped at the air, dragging it into her lungs. Her mouth hung open in an animalistic snarl, and her eyes looked hooded and far away.

Ophelia untied the silk belt and shrugged out of the robe. She walked around the widening wine-colored pool on the floor and stepped close to Alice.

"My darling," she said softly, seductively. "Are you all right?"

"Yeah," Alice said between guzzling breaths. "I'm just fine."

They hung him by his feet in the barn, Alice and Ophelia, with the same rope with which the latter had tried to hang Walt Blackmore. By that point there was precious little blood left to drain from the corpse, so Alice tended to the stripping and washing of the body. Once that was done, she made a long incision down the middle of the back, from nape to crack. She then set to sawing the flesh from the bone and cartilage, flaying the meat and exposing the glistening vertebrae. These she expected to be excellent cuts. The first of many for at least two weeks of very fine eating.

Ophelia had done well reminding Alice of all those grim hunting experiences she'd had with her real dad in years long gone by. She'd hated it then—the killing, the evisceration—but this…

This was different.

Of course, two weeks was not a particularly long time. It would be over before either of them knew it. Then they would be hungry again.

But the world was their abattoir. Their sex would be the snare. Blood would flow and flesh would be rent from the bones of those they butchered. They would feed then, and it would begin again.

Alice was never happier. She was in love.

And that love was the most beautiful thing on earth.

## 1923

*Papa was mine, Agnes shrieks, he was mine and you took him away. Mine, mine, mine.*

*The girl cannot comprehend the ghastly insinuations or at the very least she must not; it is too horrendous, too sinful to ponder. She clambers to her feet and scrambles to escape but Agnes stands between her and the square hole in the floor where the ladder is. Agnes rumbles and roars like a mad-dog and breaks into a clawing dash after the girl, who runs screaming for the open edge, the end of the never completed addition—a dead end into open air and a drop twelve feet down. She can make it, she knows she can and anyway it has to be better than what crazy Agnes has in store for her.*

*She bends at the knees, ready to leap, but Agnes has her again, tight in her grasp. The child flies back as though she is being sucked into a whirlpool, and in an instant Agnes is on top of her, slapping her face raw with one hand. The other holds up Papa's hand plane. Little more than a brown block with a strap for the carpenter's hand but it's got teeth; nasty, serrated metal teeth that bite and tear and flay.*

*Another sound slap rattles her brains as Agnes lifts up the girl's nightdress and slaps the plane down on her thigh. She screams for leniency, for mercy and sanity and peace. For it all to go away and to start over afresh like it always was between them when Papa was gone for days and it was just they two. Sisters and soulmates and the best friends in the world. But nothing comes out of her.*

*The planer's jagged blade bites down into the flesh of the child's thigh and Agnes drags it along the bare, trembling leg.*

*Flaying her sister alive.*

*Now she screams. All the world can hear it. Even the moon that does nothing but perversely leer at the bloody goings-on can hear the agonized shrieks of the tortured young girl it passively watches.*

*Agnes strips her flesh away and grunts with rage and mania, and all the child can do is flail her one free arm against the sawdusty boards, making the loose nails dance and the steel square bounce closer to her pain-curled fingers. She feels the cold metal at her fingertips and the sharp right angle of its cruel corner. Then the square is in her fist.*

*When the corner pushes into Agnes' eye, the girl can only vaguely understand what she is doing. Agnes roars and the child drives the steel square into her face and neck again and again and again. Like chopping down a tree, she hacks at the stalk, the trunk Agnes' neck, until the skin has been all but sheared off and Agnes is reduced to a pulpy, gurgling parody of a person. But not really a person at all. From where the girl stands, her sister looks more like slaughtered game.*

*She continues to hack until the gurgling is no more and the eyes stop looking at her.*

*And then she hacks some more.*

*Eventually, after the helpless moon has gone to its hiding place and the sun is peeking over the treetops, she even manages to get Agnes' head off and with just the steel square and nothing else. She is hot and sweaty, and the salty perspiration pours into the open meat of her freshly skinned leg and it burns worse than Mama's stove. But instead of crying out, she laughs.*

*The girl laughs for all she is worth at the red stump between Agnes' shoulders and at Papa's pudding mushed head downstairs—she laughs and laughs and does not believe for a second that she will ever stop laughing because Agnes was a bad girl, the worst, but now she is dead. And the dead don't come back. They just can't; everybody knows that.*

*The dead never come back.*

Ed Kurtz is the author of *Bleed*, *The Rib From Which I Remake the World*, *Nausea*, *The Forty-Two*, and other novels. His short fiction has appeared in numerous magazines and anthologies, including *Best American Mystery Stories* and *Best Gay Stories*. Ed resides in Minneapolis.

CPSIA information can be obtained
at www.ICGtesting.com
Printed in the USA
LVOW08s0431210517
535300LV00001B/1/P